Also by Beth Merlin

The Campfire Series

One S'more Summer
S'more to Lose
Love You S'more

S'more to Lose

Beth Merlin

fhp

FIREFLY HILL PRESS

Published by Firefly Hill Press, LLC
Firefly Hill Press
4387 W. Swamp Road #565
Doylestown, PA 18902
www.fireflyhillpress.com

ISBN 9781945495052

For M & H

Chapter One

I flipped through the channels for the umpteenth time. How was it possible that in one of the nicest hotels in London, the TV only had a dozen channels and two of them were currently showing reruns of my season of *Top Designer*? I threw the remote on the bed and picked up the phone to order room service when there was a knock on the door. I rushed over to answer it. I'd been counting down the hours 'til Jamie's arrival. There was no way I was getting through these next few days without my partner.

"Whoa, look at you. Did you change in the car?" I asked as Jamie gave me his usual European kiss on each cheek.

He rolled his carry-on into my room. "No? Why?"

"You flew wearing that Burberry three-piece suit and those studded Louboutin loafers?" I shook my head in amazement. Only Jamie.

"Let's talk about your outfit, darling. It's almost noon—why are you still in your bathrobe?"

"I tried going out for some coffee earlier, but there are paparazzi everywhere. How do they even know we're here?"

"The London tabloids are the worst. Your hotel phone is probably hacked. I hope you haven't been talking to anyone about the dress."

I looked over at the phone on the nightstand. "Are you serious?"

"It's supposedly illegal now, but to get the inside scoop on the wedding of the century, I wouldn't put it past any of the papers."

The wedding of the century. That phrase had been echoing in my brain from the moment we got the call letting us know our design house, G. Malone, was among Victoria Ellicott's top choices to design her wedding gown. Jamie and I were in London to present her with our sketches and, if selected, start the collaboration process.

"Okay, now I *really* need that coffee. Can you pass me my sunglasses from the nightstand? I'm gonna have to take my chances outside."

"What has you so stressed out?" Jamie handed over the frames. "We got through all the awards shows this year, didn't we? We survived New York Fashion week. This is just another job."

"We were asked to design a dress for the future queen of England. This isn't just another job! You thought the dress we did for the Oscars got a lot of media coverage? This dress will get about a million times that. This dress will be part of history. *We* will become part of history."

Jamie rummaged around in the mini bar. "Here," he said, handing me a small bottle of Kahlúa. "Slip this into your coffee later. Liquid courage. This isn't about the dress, is it?"

I shrugged.

"Does Perry know you're in town?"

"According to you, *everyone* knows we're in town. But if you're asking whether I told him I was coming to London, then no, I didn't."

He tilted his head to the side and his eyes softened. "Why not?"

I shot him a look. "You know why not."

Jamie put his arm around me for a quick, supportive squeeze, then left to check into his room. We met up a few hours later for a snack and debrief session on how we were going to approach our meeting with Victoria Ellicott.

Victoria was not only marrying the very handsome and sought-after Prince of England but was, in her own right, an established fashion icon. Born into a well-respected, wealthy British family with all the right connections, Victoria had spent most of her life in the spotlight and had been an "it" girl long before she caught the prince's eye. From the reports, Prince Alexander had been pursuing her for years before she finally decided to give him a chance. He'd even been given the nickname "Love 'em and leave 'em Lex" by the press, who liked to comment on how fast he blew through girlfriends and relationships. Once he started seeing Victoria, though, all that changed, and it didn't take long for the world to see he was head over heels in love with her.

Jamie's original ideas for the wedding gown were pretty over the top. He wanted something elaborate and ornate. A one-of-a-kind creation that could only be worn for a wedding of this magnitude. I wanted to keep it simpler, focusing on Victoria's beauty and the traditions of the day. After some heated arguments in our New York design studio, we finally agreed on four sketches that incorporated elements of both our styles. Per her publicist's orders, we'd come to London prepared to present our top options.

Over afternoon tea at The Wolseley, Jamie and I carefully examined each sketch, making sure we could address any concerns or questions. We looked over our fabrics and discussed potential alternatives in case Victoria was unhappy with our choices. Around four, we left to meet Victoria at her parents' home in Kensington, one of the most exclusive neighborhoods in London. The paparazzi was already camped outside the house gate when we arrived.

I cracked open the taxi door. "The wedding isn't for months—what are they hoping to get a picture of?"

"Us, I guess. She's been meeting with a few designers. I heard Vegas is even taking bets on which one she's going to pick." Jamie pushed his phone back into his pocket and slid toward the door.

I still couldn't believe G. Malone was in the running. To say our first two years in business had been a struggle would be putting it mildly. We used every last cent of my second-place winnings from *Top Designer* to get the company off the ground. We started small, running a website out of my studio apartment and selling specialty evening pieces and wedding gowns. The first year, we barely broke even. Perry played piano at a nearby jazz club just to help cover rent. By year two, things started improving and some high-end boutiques and retail stores began carrying our line.

Things really took a turn when last year's Best Actress winner wore G. Malone to the Oscars. Suddenly, the world knew our brand, and investors came calling. We had enough financial backing to put together a show for Fall Fashion Week. The show was highly praised and enthusiastically covered by the press, even landing us on the cover of *W Magazine*. The company, more or less, exploded after that and we were finally able to move our company out of my apartment and into a proper design studio.

While I knew we were on the fast track to an IPO, I never in a million years expected we'd be considered for a dress of this level of importance and magnitude. I'd been pinching myself since we got the call from Victoria's team and now that we were actually in London for the presentations, the enormity of the opportunity was taking hold.

I pushed my hair behind my ears and tried to swallow down the large lump in my throat. "This is insanity. You know that, right?"

Jamie was grinning from ear to ear. He loved this kind of attention. Really, he loved any kind of attention, but limelight of this degree was once in a lifetime.

We ran to the gate and were quickly ushered inside the property by a security guard. The house was incredible. Set back from the street, behind its own landscaped front garden, the Victorian façade was both elegant and contemporary.

"She moves from here to Buckingham Palace?" Jamie said. "Rough life."

"I don't think they'll live in Buckingham Palace, but point taken."

Before I could ring the bell, a petite blonde woman opened the door and introduced herself as Gemma Landry, Victoria's publicist. She led us down several hallways to a beautiful glass-enclosed sunroom, where Victoria was waiting to greet us. She was even more stunning in person than in any of the photographs I'd ever seen of her. Standing at about five-foot-eight or nine she had a model's figure and gorgeous light brown hair that fell in waves to her shoulders, perfectly complementing her big hazel eyes. She was dressed effortlessly in a YSL white blouse I'd seen go down the runway during Fall Fashion Week and impeccably tailored black pants I guessed were from Zara. Victoria was famous for her ability to mix high-end and low-end pieces, and it wasn't uncommon for the items she was photographed wearing to sell out at stores within minutes of the picture going viral.

Victoria gave us each the obligatory double kiss on the cheek and invited us to sit. She told us her mother would be joining us in a few minutes to look at the sketches and asked if we wanted any tea. Gemma jumped up and handed each of us a huge leather-bound book with the word *Wedding* embossed in gold on the cover.

"This is your dossier for every event being held in celebration of the wedding," Gemma said. "In it, you'll find brief descriptions of the venue, the theme, the guest lists, and the general attire. This should help you get a sense of the different pieces we'll need."

"Different pieces? I thought we were just in consideration for the wedding dress?" I said.

"We told the press we were speaking to several designers to throw them off track," Victoria said, "but I've known I wanted a G. Malone dress from the first time I saw you show at New York Fashion Week two years ago."

Gemma continued, "Victoria will need several different gowns for all the dinners and parties that week, as well as some less formal day pieces for the teas and other receptions."

"And you want us to design all of them?"

"I may mix in a few other designers, but I want there to be a continuity to my looks that week, almost like each one is building toward the finale."

"I see," Jamie said, his eyes sparkling with possibilities. He loved that kind of theatricality.

"We didn't come prepared to show you much more than the wedding gown sketches." I reached for our portfolio cases and passed them to Jamie.

"That's fine. When you're back in town next time you can bring the rest," Gemma said.

Jamie unzipped the case and pulled out our four sketches.

"Perfect timing." Victoria stood and greeted a woman I assumed was her mother as she entered the sunroom.

"Hello, I'm Margaret Ellicott," an elegant, older woman, wearing a navy and cream Chanel pantsuit said through a warm smile. She shook my hand and then Jamie's before taking a seat next to her daughter on the couch. They looked very much alike, and there was no question Margaret had been every bit as beautiful as Victoria at that age, if not more so.

Jamie handed the stack of sketches to Victoria, explaining that we attached swatches of the fabric choices we felt would best serve the designs, but any of it could be changed to suit her taste.

I watched as the two of them carefully studied each option, whispering to one another as they flipped through the deck.

Victoria shook her head and smiled broadly. "You guys are it. I love everything about your aesthetic."

"I agree," Margaret said. "Simply breathtaking."

"Like Jamie said earlier, if you don't love any of the fabric choices, those can be changed"

"I'm not sure my gown is in this specific grouping of sketches, but I've seen enough to know you guys can create my dream dress," Victoria said with tears in her eyes.

"Wow, that's really incredible to hear, right, Jamie?" I looked over at him. His mouth was hanging open, but no sounds were coming out. He was in shock. "So, what happens next?" I asked, turning to Gemma.

"When you get back to the hotel, there'll be a nondisclosure and confidentiality agreement waiting. A copy was also emailed to you. Have your attorneys read it, sign it, and get it back to us. I don't know what you know about the London tabloids, but they are unscrupulous and will go to any length to get the scoop, especially when it comes to the royal family. It's very important to Victoria that she maintains the element of surprise. Nobody can know you're designing the wedding dress. From now on, you and Jamie should take different flights to London and stay in different hotels. My team's going to leak to the press that we're considering having Valentino design the gown, and that should buy us some time."

"We'll all have to meet for feedback and fittings, though," I said.

"We'll find secret locations to do that. You and Jamie will have to arrive separately, of course."

"Of course," Jamie chimed in like we participated in these type of covert fashion operations every day.

I started making a mental list of all the moving pieces involved in creating what was essentially an entire collection for Victoria Ellicott. For an event of this size and scale, we'd need to source unique fabric and textiles from all over the world. We'd have to partner with the best ateliers across Europe for one-of-a-kind embellishments and accessories. My head *and* the room were spinning.

"It's going to take some time to get the textiles created and beaded, but we can be back in a few weeks with some options," I said.

"That sounds wonderful," Margaret said.

"And what about the rest of the looks?" Victoria asked.

"Right. The rest of the looks. Are we allowed to take the dossiers with us?" I asked.

"Yes. They're mentioned in the confidentiality agreement. It goes without saying that we expect you to guard them with your lives," Gemma said.

"Of course," Jamie chimed in again.

Victoria jumped off the couch and pulled me in for a hug. "I am so excited! I just know the two of you are going to wow the world with what you create."

Her exuberance caught me off guard, but I squeezed her back before pulling away, trying not to let her see the panic I was sure had registered firmly on my face. Never in a million years had I expected us to get the gig. I thought for certain she'd thank us politely for our time and decide to go with a more experienced label. I looked over to Jamie. He was calmly packing away our sketches like we'd just finished up a meeting in our studio.

We said our goodbyes, and Gemma escorted us out to the front. She handed Jamie a card and told us to call with any questions and that she'd be in touch regarding the next location where we'd be rendez-vousing. Then, a security guard picked up a phone to call for a car before escorting us out of the iron gates.

"Did she just say rendez-vousing?" I asked, sliding into the black cab.

"She most certainly did," Jamie answered.

I lowered my voice so the driver wouldn't hear. "Jamie, I don't know how we'd say no to this kind of opportunity, but this just seems, well…huge. Too huge, maybe. I mean, the confidentiality agreements and staying in different places. Having to *rendez-vous?*"

"Are you crazy? Four years ago we were standing at Camp Chinooka, deciding if we should take the leap and start our own label. We took the leap. Now look around at where we are. We *have* to do this."

"It'll be all-consuming. We might end up having to move here for a few months."

"Would that be the worst thing? We could do a few months in London. Design the wedding pieces, maybe get new inspiration for the fall line."

"Not the worst thing, no."

He put his arm around me and pulled me into his chest. "It's a big country, Gigi. You can avoid Perry if you want to."

"London's a small town, and he's the toast of it. You don't think our paths will cross?"

"Only if you want them to. Do you want them to?"

I pressed my face against the car window and muttered, "I don't know what I want."

"Well, I want this. The chance to design the wedding gown of the century and play James Bond while we're doing it—sign me up. I just need my partner. What do you say, partner?"

I squeezed my eyes shut. "Okay, I guess I'm in."

Chapter Two

ater that night, I curled up in the hotel bed with a glass of pinot noir and the wedding dossier. I flipped through the first few pages of events—mostly teas and luncheons for the out-of-town guests and close family—and jotted down some ideas for daytime dresses and suits. Then, I turned to the pages dedicated to the five-hundred-guest reception at Buckingham Palace and read through the lengthy descriptions of each wedding event. Cocktail hour would be held in the candlelit palace courtyard, where bagpipers would welcome guests. Following cocktail hour, the guests would be escorted into the palace ballroom for dinner and toasts. After that, they'd be ushered through to the throne room, which would be transformed into a nightclub complete with a stage, dance floor, and cocktail bar.

I picked up my notebook and made some notes about the three outfit changes just for the reception alone. No question Jamie would be chomping at the bit to get his hands on designing the dress for the club. I flipped the page and ran my finger down the list of artists set to perform. Madonna, Elton John, and Adele were among the confirmed acts. I skimmed down farther and stopped at his name.

There he was. Perry Gillman listed next to the cast of his hit West End show, *Elizabeth. Of course* he'd be asked to perform a song from *Elizabeth.* It was the hottest show in the world right now.

Perry's idea to tell the story of Queen Elizabeth I using not just period music but also rap, hip-hop, and R&B ballads had turned the theater world on its head. So had his push for diverse casting. There were rumors Beyoncé was taking over the lead role of Elizabeth I when the show transferred to Broadway in a few months. When he first told me his idea to marry all of these styles of music in one show, I'd thought he was crazy. But then I remembered his brilliant Color War songs where he mixed different genres to create something new and completely original. He was a musical genius, and it didn't take long for the theater world to notice. Now, getting a ticket to *Elizabeth* was nearly impossible, and scalpers were charging thousands of dollars to people desperate enough to see the show. It was nominated for almost every Olivier Award it was eligible for, and in just the last few weeks, Perry'd graced the cover of most major magazines and newspapers.

I skimmed through a few more pages of the dossier to the guest lists and saw Perry was also invited to several of the wedding events. Either his celebrity was just that stratospheric, or he was a close personal friend of Victoria or Prince Alexander. Maybe both of them? My head was swimming.

I laid back down on the pillow and stared up at the popcorn ceiling before looking over at the nightstand clock. It was almost two a.m. I wasn't sure if it was jet lag or knowing Perry was only a few blocks away, but I was wide awake. I turned on the TV and flipped through some channels before landing on the *Top Designer* finale episode, where I lost to Kharen Chen. I picked up my phone. It was only eleven in the States. I knew Alicia'd still be awake.

"You'll never guess what I'm watching," I said as soon as Alicia picked up the phone.

"*Doctor Who?*"

"The final episode of my season of *Top Designer.*"

"Why are you torturing yourself like that? Did you lose to Kharen yet?"

"I'm about to. Charlotte Cross is just going to tell me what a promising designing career she's sure I'll have and give me the double kiss goodbye."

"Well, she wasn't wrong. You *are* in consideration to design the wedding gown for the future Queen of England."

"Shhhhh," I hissed.

"What's wrong?"

"Jamie told me our phones could be bugged."

"He's crazy, and you're even crazier for believing him."

I stood up and poured myself another glass of wine. "Is he? Victoria's camp is making us sign a confidentiality and nondisclosure agreement around the wedding dress details."

Alicia laughed. "Did you just breach it by telling me that it exists?"

"We didn't sign yet. It's with our attorney for review."

"Ahhh, so you're having your father look it over?" she said.

"He's the best. Not to mention free. We're still building a business."

"I know. I'm just giving you a hard time. How's London? Perry's face must be plastered everywhere. He was on the cover of the Arts and Leisure section of the *New York Times* this weekend. I left a large coffee ring around it just for you."

"Billboards and ads for the show are all over London as if it needs any more hype. I stepped off the sidewalk and almost got taken out by a red double-decker bus with an *Elizabeth* banner across the side of it."

"Are you going to see it while you're there?"

"Like I could even get a ticket if I wanted one."

"All you'd have to do is call him."

I opened the window curtain and looked out onto the quiet street. "He doesn't want to hear from me."

"You don't know that."

"I do know." I closed the curtain and sat back down on the bed. "I should let you go. I shouldn't have called this late."

"I was up. Sloane will be wanting a midnight snack soon."

"I still can't believe you have a daughter and she's almost four months old already."

"Is it normal I can't stop staring at her? I just sit in her room and stare at her."

"Very normal. Especially when a baby's that beautiful. She's your twin."

"Really? When I look at her, I see Asher."

"She's you. The green eyes and wisps of blonde hair. How can you not see it?"

"I don't know, I just don't. When are you back?"

"A couple of days. I wanted to do a little sightseeing before coming home."

"Let's do dinner or a mani when you're back. Baby's crying, I should go. I'll see you next week. Night."

"Night, Alicia."

I hit the off button with my thumb, placed the phone on the nightstand, and settled back into bed. The *Top Designer* finale was over, but worse, the reunion show was playing. Naomi Campbell had just introduced a montage of our first challenge, episode "Code Wed," where the designers were asked to create wedding gowns using nothing but toilet paper. Poor Jamie—almost six years later and it was still tough to watch him struggle through this challenge. I fell asleep right before Naomi started questioning him about what it felt like to get booted off first and woke up to him knocking on my hotel door.

"One sec," I mumbled.

"It's eleven, Gigi. You promised me we'd be at Harrods by noon," Jamie shouted through the door.

I unlocked the deadbolt and let him in. "Sorry. I had trouble falling asleep last night."

I couldn't help but look him up and down. He looked impeccable in an ombré mohair Gucci sweater, Dsquared2 jeans, and a different pair of studded Louboutin loafers than he'd worn the day before.

I shook my head. "How do you do that?"

"Do what?"

I motioned toward him. "Look like that?"

He kissed me on the cheek and whispered, "It's called a shower."

I tilted my head to the side. "Nice, Malone. You sure you don't want to do some real sightseeing, like the Tower of London or Hampton Court Palace, today? Get some more inspiration for the royal wedding?"

"I agreed to go on that downtown abbey tour with you tomorrow, didn't I?"

"It's *Downton Abbey*, not down*town* abbey."

"Aren't we saying the exact same thing?"

I shook my head. "No, we're not, but fine, we can do whatever you want today."

"Harrods, then Harvey Nics. If there's time, the rest of Bond Street."

"Let me just take a quick shower. I can be ready in five. If Camp Chinooka taught me anything, it's the art of the quick shower," I said with a smile.

When I got out, I threw on jeans, a white button-down, and my newly acquired Burberry trench. The coat had been a bit of a splurge but now seemed like a good investment piece if we were going to be spending so much time in London. I grabbed my purse from the floor and phone from my nightstand. I quickly scrolled through my emails.

"My father responded about the contract," I yelled to Jamie from the changing room.

"And?" he called back.

I walked back into the main room. "He says it's all pretty standard, and we should sign if we want the job."

"So, let's make this official." He yanked the contract out of the large manila envelope and handed it to me.

"Are you sure you want to do this? You realize what a huge commitment it is—it's going to take time away from our other collections and clients."

"Gigi, this is the finish line. This is the type of opportunity designers spend their whole careers dreaming of. This will change everything for us."

I inhaled deeply and looked him square in the eye. "I know."

He took the contract from my hand and scribbled out his signature. "Your turn," he said, handing it back to me.

I closed my eyes, and before I could change my mind, signed on the dotted line.

We went down to the front desk to ask for a courier service that could return the agreement to Gemma Landry's PR firm. The concierge picked up the phone to call the messenger and handed Jamie another envelope that had been delivered to our attention that morning.

I stood up on my tiptoes and peered over his shoulder. "What's that?"

"No idea," he said, slitting it open with the letter opener from the desk. He pulled out the beautiful cream and gold-leafed stationary.

Ms. Goldstein and Mr. Malone:
Please take these two tickets to tonight's performance of Elizabeth *as a token of my appreciation. Thank you for making Victoria's dreams for our wedding day come true. I very much look forward to meeting you both.*
Yours,
Alexander

Jamie held up two tickets. "Box seats."

"No." I ripped them from his fingers and stuffed them into my bag.

"You know how hard these are to get. Gigi. The Prince of England personally invited us. We have to go."

"It was a gesture. We don't have to accept it."

Jamie held the letter up to my face. "Alexander said he looks forward to meeting us both."

"I don't think he means tonight. He probably just means at some point in the next few months."

"Give me your phone," Jamie said, motioning for me to take it out of my bag.

"What for?"

Jamie put one hand on his hip and reached out his other one. "Just give it to me, Gigi."

I reluctantly pulled it out and handed it to him. He scrolled to Gemma's name in my contacts and stepped a few feet away. Although I couldn't hear her end of the conversation, when Jamie said, "I look forward to seeing them later this evening," I assumed Gemma had confirmed Victoria and Alexander would be in attendance.

Jamie walked back over to where I was standing and slipped the phone back into my bag.

"They'll be there, although they aren't sitting in the same box as us," he said. "Victoria doesn't want to bring any more attention to the fact we're in consideration for the gown."

"We better get going, then. I guess I'm gonna need an outfit for tonight." I turned to Jamie. "So tell me. What does a girl wear to meet up with the former fiancé she may still be in love with *and* the future King and Queen of England?"

He put his arm around me. "I'm not sure, but we'll find it on Bond Street. I promise."

Chapter Three

Several hours and tried-on outfits later, I found myself in the most incredible open-backed black and nude vintage Givenchy lace dress. As I examined myself from every angle, I couldn't find one thing I didn't like about it until I caught a glimpse of the price tag.

"Gigi, I'm dying out here," Jamie said from outside the changing room door.

I came out of the dressing room and did a twirl. "What do you think?"

He set his glass of champagne down. "I think it's perfect. Tasteful yet sexy. Just the right amount of skin."

I held up the tag. "It's eleven hundred pounds."

"Considering all the things this dress has to accomplish, it's a bargain. Pay for it, and let's go. We don't have much time to get ready."

I sat down next to Jamie. "What am I doing? Perry won't want to see me. We haven't talked in months. Not since I sent back the ring."

"You should've kept the ring. I know a jeweler in Sheepshead Bay who could've turned it into a killer pair of earrings."

I threw back the rest of my champagne. "No, no, that ring was in exchange for a promise that never came to be."

Jamie squeezed my shoulder.

"So, this dress?" I said, trying to change the subject. "What do you really think?"

Jamie moved away to take in the full look. "I don't think we could have designed anything better. You look ravishing."

I took a step toward him and placed my hand on his forearm. "Thank you, friend."

As soon as we got back to the hotel I made a beeline to one of the blowout bars around the corner and begged them to slot me in. An hour later I had the most perfect beachy waves as the cab dropped us off in front of Her Majesty's Theatre and the large marquee for *Elizabeth*. We fought through the huge crowd hoping to win the nightly ticket lottery and got in line to go inside.

Jamie pulled out his phone. "Let's take a selfie."

"Seriously?"

"I promised Thom we'd document tonight. He's beyond jealous that we're seeing *Elizabeth*."

After six years of their on-again, off-again relationship, Jamie and Thom finally got married last summer. It was a beautiful and intimate wedding right on the beach in Montauk. I'd never seen Jamie happier than he'd been this last year, and he'd recently confided that he and Thom were looking into surrogates to try having a baby.

"Hey, have you seen any of these?" Jamie asked, pointing to the posters of scenes from the show that lined the walls outside the theater. "I hate to say it, but Perry Gillman sure looks good in a pair of breeches."

I turned to examine the picture more closely. He looked better than good—he looked right off the cover of a Harlequin. Perry'd cast himself in the role of Robert Dudley, Queen Elizabeth's rumored lover and closest confidant. He'd played the part during all the workshops and the investors had loved his portrayal so much, they encouraged him to take it on when the show hit the

West End. In its short run, he'd already established himself as a bona fide star.

We made our way inside the theater, and an usher directed us to our box. I peeked over the railing. There wasn't one empty seat in the house. Prince Alexander, Victoria, and Victoria's arguably even more beautiful and fashionable sister, Annabelle Ellicott, were seated several boxes over from us, with security posted on both sides. I settled into my chair and flipped through the program. The first few pages told the story of *Elizabeth's* inception, starting with Perry's writer's block through his major breakthrough and the completion of the show's original concept album.

I closed my eyes and was transported back to our small apartment in Hell's Kitchen. The Gordy award sitting on our fake mantle, Perry at his keyboard holding his tape recorder, asking me to step away from my drafting table to listen to a new song or lyric for the show. I couldn't have predicted what a phenomenon *Elizabeth* was going to become, but as the show continued to develop, we both knew he was doing something completely brilliant. I remembered how we'd acted out every part—Elizabeth I, Mary Queen of Scots, William Cecil, The Archbishop of Canterbury, Robert Dudley. Admittedly, I wasn't up on my British history, but it didn't matter. His interpretations and music were so captivating, he not only made the past come to life but made it relevant to our own times.

I flipped through a few more pages to the cast bios and acknowledgments. Perry's was peppered with academic qualifications, composition awards and recognitions, regional and local theater credits, and in bold, the one acting triumph I'd never expected to see: **Fiddler, *Fiddler on the Roof*, Milbank, PA**. I sucked in a quick breath and sank down into my seat. The lights of the theater dimmed, and I looked up from the program. Jamie grabbed my hand, squeezed it, and gave me a reassuring smile. As the familiar first notes of the opening number floated up from the pit and the white spotlight hit Perry, dressed in period costume, his wavy hair pulled off his beautiful face, my heart burst in two.

The first act went by in a flash, ending with Elizabeth I's coronation and the imprisonment of Mary Queen of Scotts. Perry's complex lyrics and modern melodies had the audience on its feet half a dozen times. His performance as the lovelorn Robert Dudley was so layered and heart-wrenching, I was sure at least half the women in the theater were in love with him by the time the curtain fell indicating the end of Act I.

When the house lights came up for intermission, I barely noticed. Jamie called my name at least four times before I heard him.

"Gigi, do you want anything to drink or not?"

"I'm good," I muttered.

"I'll be right back then."

I reached into my bag to pull out my compact mirror and felt a tap on the back.

"I'm really fine, Jamie, just get whatever you want," I said without turning around.

"It's Gemma Landry," she answered.

I stood up to greet her. "Oh, I'm sorry. I thought you were Jamie. He just walked out to get something to drink."

"Are you enjoying the show?" she asked.

"Very much. Please thank Victoria and Prince Alexander again for the tickets."

"You'll be able to do that yourself. They sent me to invite you to join them backstage after the show."

"Oh, um…that's very kind of them. I'll see what Jamie wants to do. We have an early day tomorrow. We're doing the *Downton Abbey* tour of Highclere Castle."

"Victoria really wants to introduce you to her sister, Annabelle, and also Perry Gillman."

I blinked hard. "Victoria knows Perry Gillman?"

Gemma placed her finger over her lips. "Annabelle's been seeing him for a few months, but you didn't hear it from me."

"Annabelle Ellicott is dating Perry Gillman?" I asked, my voice going up to an octave I didn't know I was capable of reaching.

"I know. Isn't it amazing they've managed to keep it from the press?"

I sank down into my seat. "Truly, I had no idea."

"I don't know which sister is luckier in love—both of them snagged princes." She laughed at her own joke. "Anyway, when the show's over, just come to the backstage door. Your names are on the list."

The house lights flickered and a voice came over the intercom, letting the audience know it was almost the end of intermission.

Gemma looked up at the ceiling. "I should get back to my seat."

I waved her out, and a minute or so later Jamie came back to our box holding two champagnes.

He passed a champagne flute over to me. "I thought you might change your mind."

I downed the champagne before he even took his seat.

"Did I miss something?" He looked around our box.

"Gemma Landry came by to invite us backstage after the show," I said.

"I see," he said as he passed me his own full glass.

I clutched the stem my hands visibly shaking. "It gets worse. Perry's been dating Annabelle Ellicott. Gemma isn't sure how the press hasn't gotten wind of it, but they've been an item for a while now."

Jamie's mouth fell open. "He's dating Annabelle Ellicott?"

I nodded as my eyes welled with tears.

"Bottoms up," he said.

I threw back the second glass and set it down on the ground. "I can't go backstage. I can't see him."

He leaned toward me and put his hand on my knee. "Of course, you can't. I'll go. I'll make your excuses. It'll be fine."

"I really do feel sick. I think I have to go back to the hotel."

Jamie jumped up and grabbed my coat from the back of my seat. "I'll go back with you?"

"No, no, finish the show," I said, motioning for him to sit back down. "Make our excuses. I'll meet you in the lobby at eight for the tour tomorrow."

Jamie shook his head. "Annabelle Ellicott? She really doesn't seem like his type at all."

"Of course, she does. Sophisticated, beautiful, cultured, and well-mannered. I'm the one who wasn't his type." I slipped my coat on. "The show's wonderful. Make sure you let Perry know."

"You sure you don't want to see how it ends?"

"No. I know how it ends," I said, softly.

Chapter Four

Jamie was already waiting for me in the lobby when I came down to meet our *Downton Abbey* tour group the next morning.

He passed me a familiar green and white cup. "Here. A triple Venti, caramel, soy, no-foam latte."

I opened the lid to inspect the contents. "Caramel? Soy? Are we even friends?"

"It was simpler to ask for two of the same thing."

I popped the lid back on and swirled the cup around in my hand. "Simpler than just asking for a black coffee?"

"Jeez, someone's crabby. How 'bout a thank you?"

I kissed him on the cheek. "Thank you, and I'm sorry. I didn't sleep well."

He raised his eyebrows. "Up late Googling Annabelle Ellicott?"

Jamie knew me too well. As soon as I left the theater, I'd pulled up every UK tabloid website I could think of to get the dirt on Ms. Ellicott. Unfortunately, what I quickly surmised was there wasn't all that much dirt. She'd supposedly dated Harry Styles (but really, who hadn't?) for a few months last year. There was also some chatter about her and a Jonas brother, but I couldn't find it corroborated on more than one site. The majority of press on her was pretty flattering. I learned she worked in Investor Relations at one of the largest investment banks in London, loved horseback riding, and was involved in several important charities. She kept a lower profile than her sister, and unlike Victoria, there were very few pictures of her at any nightclubs or parties. Most of the images were from exclusive society events. Her style was also different than Victoria's—still impeccable, but simpler, with a little bit of a bohemian edge. I couldn't identify most of the designers so assumed she did a lot of high-end vintage shopping. Gemma was right, though. In all my research, I didn't find one mention of her name with Perry's. They'd done a brilliant job of keeping their relationship under the radar. So brilliant, in fact, I couldn't help but wonder if maybe Gemma was wrong about them?

"Just some mild cyberstalking," I answered.

Jamie cocked his head to the side. "I'm sure. So, what do you want to know about last night? Fire away."

"What did Perry say when he saw you?"

"He didn't. He was dealing with press and never came to the receiving area."

"Well, that's a relief. What about Annabelle?"

"I thanked Victoria and Alexander for the tickets, they introduced us, and we chatted about the show a bit."

"That's it?"

He unwrapped the scarf around his neck, knelt down, and tucked it into his bag. "What do you want me to say, Gigi?"

"What's she like?"

"She's lovely. Just like you guessed—sophisticated, beautiful, well-mannered. But she isn't you, and anyone who ever saw you and Perry together could see you brought out the best in each other."

"The best and worst. Are you sure they're really dating? I couldn't find one story linking them."

"She didn't come out and tell me they were, but it was apparent in the way she talked about him. They're obviously keeping it under wraps though. Mostly, we just talked about her bridesmaid dress for the wedding."

"Her what?" I said, practically spewing out my coffee.

"The bridesmaid dress we are apparently designing for her. You must not have gotten to that page of the dossier. She wants something vintage inspired. Ethereal, but not too whimsical. Bohemian, but not too avant-garde." He stood up and swung his bag over his shoulder. "Here's the strange thing though. I couldn't get a read on whether she knows about you and Perry."

"How could she not know? We were together for over three years. You don't just erase that kind of history."

"I'm just telling you the vibe I got. Look at how curious you are about her. Don't you think if she knew you were Perry's former fiancé she would've been grilling me for intel?"

I suppose it was possible she didn't know. It wasn't like Perry ever expected we'd cross paths. Up until two days ago, the closest I'd come to being in the vicinity of the British aristocracy was binge-watching *Downton Abbey*. Still, if Annabelle really didn't know about our history, then neither did Victoria. How would she feel knowing the woman designing her wedding gown was once engaged to her sister's boyfriend?

"Hey, kiddo, let's go enjoy our day at this monastery you're so excited about," Jamie said, handing me my bag and snapping me out of my thoughts.

"It's a castle, not a monastery."

"Isn't the show called downtown abbey?"

"Again, it's Down*ton*, not down*town* abbey. It's filmed at Highclere Castle."

"I still feel like we're saying the same thing," he said with a playful smile as we went outside to meet the tour van.

Almost two hours later we pulled onto the grounds of Highclere Castle. I nudged Jamie, who'd been snoring on my shoulder the better part of the last hour.

"Hey, sleepyhead, we're here," I said.

He slowly sat up and looked around. "Where's here?" he said through a yawn.

I pulled out our printed itinerary. "First, we'll check out the castle, then we'll head over to the coach house for high tea, do a walking tour of the grounds and gardens, and end our day at the Blue Hen."

"What's that?"

I read straight from the itinerary. "The Blue Hen is a proper village pub serving local and regional ales and authentic British fare. Steeped in history from bygone eras, you can almost hear the Downton servants conversing over a pint."

Jamie closed his eyes and pretended to fall asleep. "Sounds thrilling."

"I've been looking forward to this for weeks. Can you at least try to feign a modicum of enthusiasm?"

He handed me my backpack from under the seat and smiled. "Okay. Feigning. Feigning."

We got off the van and were ushered over to a ticket booth, where our tour packets were waiting. Out of the corner of my eye, I noticed a guy wearing a Highclere Castle T-shirt struggling to sort them. I bent down to stuff my umbrella into my bag, and a few seconds later felt a tap on the shoulder.

"Excuse me, what tour company are you all with?" the guy with Highclere shirt asked.

"Oh, umm, I can't remember. We booked through The Dorchester Hotel. Let me look for my confirmation." I dug through my backpack, found the itinerary, and handed it to him.

He looked it over and thrust it back at me.

"Problem?" I asked.

"The wrong tickets were sent over from the main office. These," he said, holding up the packets, "are for tomorrow's groups. Yours are still in London."

"So, what does that mean?"

He handed me back the folder. "That for today, you and your boyfriend over there are Mr. and Mrs. Codswild from Vancouver,

Canada. Maps for the castle, gardens, and woodlands are enclosed. So are your tickets for tea at the carriage house and your drink vouchers for the Blue Hen. Enjoy."

I thrust it back at him. "We paid for the special *Downton Abbey* tour, so I'm not sure if this is going to work."

"I have news for you, everyone's here for the *Downton Abbey* tour. Don't worry, you'll get to take a swing at Mr. Carson's gong. So, which one are you?"

"What do you mean?"

"Who do you fancy yourself? A Mary, an Edith, or a Sybil?"

"You know, I'm not sure."

He stood back to study me. "You're a Mary who's convinced herself she's an Edith."

His comment hung in the air for a moment. Jamie came over to see what was taking so long.

"Are we gonna go see some old stuff or what?" he asked.

I handed him his entry tickets. "We sure are, Mr. Codswild."

Jamie put his name tag on. "Do I even want to know?"

"Just say thank you to our new friend over here. Sorry, I didn't catch your name?"

"Gideon," he answered.

"Say thank you to our new friend Gideon," I repeated.

"Thank you, Gideon. Now which way to the house?" Jamie asked.

"Follow that path there," Gideon said, pointing to a brick paved trail. "It'll lead you to the entrance, and there'll be signs there for different tours."

Jamie and I set off for the castle and decided to start with a tour of the staterooms. Our guide was amazing, taking us through the smoking room, library, state dining room, and drawing room. She provided colorful commentary on the art, the family who occupied the castle, the architecture, and the ways the different rooms had been utilized on *Downton Abbey*. Jamie pulled a pad out of his pocket and began sketching away.

I nudged his side. "I thought this wasn't your thing?"

"Opulence, grandeur, and luxury—totally my thing."

I rolled my eyes and followed the group into the music room.

We finished touring the upstairs and joined the group going down to view the kitchen and the servants' hall and quarters. Jamie was far less impressed, but I thought it was fascinating that two entirely different worlds could exist under one roof, side by side. In the last few days I'd gotten a crash course on the inner workings of the British aristocracy, and from the little I'd already observed, there was still a huge class divide.

After finishing our tour of the downstairs, we had afternoon tea at the coach house and walked the huge gardens, public parks, and footpaths on the property. Even Jamie had to admit the rustic beauty of the grounds was inspiring. Eventually, both of us headed in different directions to do some sketching. He was so engrossed, he jumped about two feet in the air when I finally tapped him on the shoulder to remind him we should be setting off for the Blue Hen.

Tucked away down a dingy, cobbled alley, the Blue Hen was everything the description promised. The inside was dark with oak beams and wood paneling, creating the kind of gloomy charm I loved about England. I grabbed a space on the couch by the roaring fire, and Jamie took our drink tickets up to the bar. I leaned back into the limp cushions, pulled out Jamie's sketch pad, and flipped through the pages to examine the drawings.

"Those are quite good. Are you a student?"

I looked up and saw Gideon standing over me. Was he this handsome earlier, or had I just not been paying close attention in the ticket kerfuffle? He had neatly cut auburn hair with slightly longer sideburns, giving him an edgier look than he may have intended. The light copper stubble across his face became visible in the glow of the crackling fireplace. His gray-green eyes were on the smaller side but, as a result, more piercing. He was wearing a light blue button-down, dark-washed jeans, and a gray tweed newsboy cap that made him look sophisticated and boyish all at the same time. He caught me staring at him as he walked around the couch to sit beside me, and I quickly shifted my eyes to the ground.

"Umm, no, I work as a designer. That guy up there," I said, pointing to Jamie at the bar, "the one you thought was my boyfriend, is actually my design partner. These are his sketches."

"So, he's not your boyfriend?"

"He's married and gay, so no." I chuckled.

"I see. What'd you think of the estate?"

I tucked Jamie's sketchbook back into his tote. "It's hard to believe people used to live like that."

"Some people still live like that," he said. "Maybe not quite at that scale, but the aristocracy is alive and well in England."

I shifted in my seat. "Oh, I'm aware."

Gideon narrowed his eyes. "Where are you from, Mrs. Codswild?"

I took off my name tag. "It's Georgica actually, and New York City."

"Georgica? That's pretty. What brings you to this side of the pond, Georgica?"

"Work."

"Wanna give me a hand?" Jamie said, coming over to join us. He was balancing two pints and a basket of fish 'n' chips and trying to navigate through the groups of people congregating by the fire. "Sorry, mate, I didn't see you, or I would've bought you a beer."

"No worries. I'm kind of a regular here." Gideon motioned to the bartender to bring over one more pint.

"You work at Highclere Castle year-round?" Jamie asked, settling down next to us in a tattered dark green velvet armchair.

"I'm in charge of their tourism and I handle most of their special events."

"Must be an interesting job," Jamie said.

"Pays the bills." Gideon shrugged nonchalantly. "Georgica's been telling me you two are design partners?"

Jamie took a sip from his mug and nodded.

"Dress anyone famous?" Gideon asked.

With the nondisclosure agreement fresh in my mind, I quickly chimed in, "Just some B-list celebrities in the States."

"Was this the last stop on the hit parade, or are you both staying in town for a few more days?"

"Gigi's staying a couple more days, but I'm heading back home tomorrow."

I added, "I've been to London a few times, but it's been a while since I played tourist. I had a little time, so figured I'd get in a few more sights."

The bartender sent over the beer and a few starters for us. Gideon reached over for a deviled egg and asked me what was on my to-do list.

"The Victoria and Albert Museum, the Tate Modern, Westminster Abbey, the Tower of London, and St. Paul's Cathedral," I answered.

"If you're going to St. Paul's Cathedral, you definitely need to check out the Whispering Gallery. Did you know anything you whisper against one side of the dome can be—"

"Heard anywhere in the room," I said, finishing his sentence with enthusiasm. "Yeah, it's supposed to be pretty incredible." My mind drifted back to the time we'd played the Dating Game at Camp Chinooka and Perry described his perfect first date at the Whispering Gallery. That summer felt like a million years ago now.

The three of us chatted a bit more before the tour driver came into the pub to announce the van going back to The Dorchester would be leaving in ten minutes. Jamie stood up to collect our coats and shopping bags of *Downton* souvenirs.

"I hope you got the Crawley commemorative tea mug," Gideon teased.

I held up my Highclere Castle gift shop bag. "I got two, actually, one for me and one for my friend Alicia—also a huge fan."

We stepped outside and walked to the main road, where half a dozen vans were waiting to pick up other tour groups.

"This one's your ride," Gideon said, pointing to the first van in line. "Before you head out, I need to know. Did we make a *Downton* fan out of you?" he asked, turning to Jamie.

Jamie held up a DVD set of all six seasons. "What do you think?"

Gideon laughed and Jamie hopped on the van.

"Thank you for all your help," I said, extending my hand.

"It was my pleasure, Mrs. Codswild." He took off his cap and leaned down into a half bow. "Enjoy the rest of your time in London," he said and turned to walk away.

I climbed on and grabbed a seat across from Jamie. Using my backpack as an improvised pillow, I was just closing my eyes when I heard a tap at the window. I pushed it open.

"I just wanted to tell you, now that I know you a bit better, you're definitely a Mary. Definitely," Gideon said.

I pulled the window closed, and as the van slowly pulled away, I found myself feeling actual butterflies for the first time in a very long time.

Chapter Five

amie left for home the next morning, and I spent the day at the Victoria and Albert Museum, wandering the vast exhibits and getting lost in the Fashion collection. Housing one of the largest collections of European fashion, fabrics, and accessories from 1750 to the present day, the fashion gallery had every source of inspiration a designer could wish for. In fact, the last time I was in this gallery was for the elimination challenge before the finale of *Top Designer*.

The other two final contestants and I were flown to London and given £350 to create a modern-day look inspired by a seventeenth-century gown on display in the exhibition. Ironically, I'd been immediately drawn to a portrait of Elizabeth I in a black and gold brocade gown and the adjacent replica of the dress on display in the same gallery. Without any second-guessing or hesitation, I had sat down and sketched a sleek woman's tuxedo with ornately patterned shoulders and pressed velvet lapels. It was the type of outfit I could imagine the powerful and commanding Elizabeth wearing had she been born in the twentieth century instead of the sixteenth.

The judges called the ensemble an unexpected breath of fresh air, and the piece had won me the coveted spot in the *Top Designer* finale and the chance to show a complete collection at fashion week. After the show, I framed a copy of the sketch and hung it in my apartment as a reminder of my achievement. In a weird twist of fate, the rendering ended up serving as the inspiration for Perry's contemporary retelling of *Elizabeth*.

While we were sitting together on the couch, enjoying some takeout and jazz, Perry had honed in on the picture hanging on the wall to our bedroom. He stood up and studied it, asking at least a half-dozen questions about my modern interpretation of the Tudor queen. He rushed back to his keyboard, picked up his composition book and began furiously jotting down the ideas that eventually became the foundation for the entire show.

Hoping to draw some inspiration of my own for Victoria's wedding looks, I'd brought along my sketch pad and colored pencils, planning to spend some time finding ideas for either outfits or textiles. Almost two hours later, the pages were mostly blank except for a few sketches of Renaissance gowns I thought might prove inspirational later. I flipped back to look at some preliminary mark-ups I'd done of Annabelle's bridesmaid dress at Highclere Castle and found myself imagining how she'd look on the royal wedding day. Perfect. She'd look perfect, so much so that she might even outshine the bride. I closed the notepad and my eyes, picturing Perry standing beside her, the photographers going crazy snapping shots of London's newest "it" couple.

I felt a light tap on my shoulder. "Miss, the museum's going to be closing in a half hour."

"Thank you," I replied, getting off the cold marble bench. "Which way is the gift shop?"

The guard pointed it out on my museum map and continued her patrol down the gallery halls.

I stopped into the shop and asked the clerk where the books on fashion were located. He directed me to a large row of shelves stacked floor to ceiling with books on every imaginable topic. After skimming through a few, I found what I was looking for, a complete anthology on the costumes and fashions of Elizabethan England.

"I think this might weigh more than you do," the clerk said as he rang me up. "Do you want the book gift wrapped?"

"No, that's okay. It's for me."

"A fan?"

"Of fashion?"

"Of *Elizabeth*. We've had a hard time keeping books on her in the shop since the show opened in the West End. I wish you'd said that's what you were looking for—we made an entire Elizabeth I section with books, postcards, even CDs from the show. The composer, Perry Gillman, did a lot of research right here in the museum. Nice guy. He came back and signed some items as a thank you to the docents he worked with. We have a few things left on sale. I can show you some if you want."

"I'm okay, thanks. How much do I owe you for the book?"

"It's £50 even."

I handed him my credit card.

"Sure I can't interest you in an *Elizabeth* CD? For those of us who'll never get tickets to see the show in this lifetime, it's really the next best thing." He handed back my card and the receipt to sign.

"I saw *Elizabeth*, actually."

His eyes got huge. "Who do you know? The Queen of England?"

No, just the crown prince and soon-to-be princess, I almost said out loud. Instead, I simply answered, "Just got lucky with the ticket lottery."

He nodded in astonishment and passed me my shopping bag. He reminded me the museum was closing in a few minutes and directed me down the hall to the nearest exit.

Outside, it was dark and raining hard. Since the clerk was right and the book really did weigh almost as much as me (or so it seemed), I decided to take a taxi to the hotel. Unfortunately, it was rush hour, so finding one took forever. By the time I got back, I was wet, cold, and looking forward to a hot bath and curling up with some room service.

I got up to the room and struggled with the key card, almost missing the envelope slipped under the door. I grabbed it off the floor and tossed it onto the bed, along with all the packages and my coat. I was heading into the bathroom to run the bath when my phone rang. I grabbed it off the pillow and laid down horizontally across the thick duvet.

"Hi. How was the flight home?" I asked.

"Great," Jamie said. "A Xanax, glass of bubbly, and the *Elizabeth* soundtrack. It was a delightful six hours. How was your day? Lots of sightseeing?"

"I lost track of time at the Victoria and Albert Museum, so I have some ground to make up these next two days." I sat up. "Really, Jamie, the *Elizabeth* soundtrack?"

"Have you listened to it? It's amazing. Anyway, what's on the agenda tonight? Dinner plans? Hitting the town?"

I picked the envelope up off the bedspread and pulled out the card inside. "I'm pretty tired, so I think just a bath and some room service."

"Too bad you didn't exchange info with Gideon. He might've been a fun distraction."

"Funny you should mention him." I quickly scanned the card "He left a message for me at the hotel."

"What's it say?"

"It's just a note with his name and a number to call him back on. How'd he know where to find me?"

"He knew which hotel we were staying at. How many Georgica's could there be? Are you gonna call him?"

"No, I mean, what's the point, right? I'm only in town a couple more days."

"That's *exactly* the point. You're only in town a couple more days—have an adventure."

I leaned back into the headboard. "I don't know."

"Call him, Gigi. Live a little. What do you have to lose?"

Jamie hung up, and I turned on the water for my bath. I poured a glass of wine and looked down again at the card. Before I could overthink my decision, I dialed Gideon's number. He picked up after the second ring.

"Gideon Cooper," he said formally.

"This is Georgica Goldstein," I responded.

His voice softened immediately. "Good, you got my message. I know it's last minute, but I'm going to be in town tonight and wanted to see if you were free to meet up for a drink later?"

I looked over at the tub and room service menu and thought about Jamie's advice to live a little. I squeezed my eyes closed and said, "I'm free."

"Want to meet at the Red Coat Club at nine? Do you know it?" he asked.

"No, but I can find it."

"Great, your name will be at the door. See you tonight."

Two hours later, I found myself back in the black and nude backless Givenchy dress. I jumped into a taxi and gave the driver the name of the club.

"Your name on a list there, Miss?" he asked.

"I think so, why?"

"That's the hottest club in South Kensington. Maybe in all of London right now."

I pulled out my phone and searched the Red Coat Club. A few dozen articles pulled up, all of them linking the club to A-list celebrities or royalty. Victoria and Alexander were apparently regulars. The car pulled down a long alley and stopped about halfway.

"I can't go any farther, or I won't be able to turn the car around," the driver said.

I rolled down the window. "Are all these people lined up to go inside?"

"All these people and those," he said, pointing the where the line snaked around to the other side.

"What's the big deal? It's just a nightclub, right?" I said.

"Most of 'em won't get in. They're just hoping to catch a glimpse of Prince Alexander or Emma Watson going inside."

I paid for the taxi and headed to the front of the velvet ropes. I gave my name to the bouncer, who stamped my hand with the letters RCC and let me right inside. I hated places like this in New York, the club was almost half empty, but the managers liked to have people waiting outside to make it seem that much more elite. I did a quick scan of the room for Gideon and spotted him sitting at the smallest bar in the VIP area. He turned around and our eyes met. He motioned for me to join him. Security checked my hand for the stamp and let me down the stairs to the lounge.

The blood red walls, black lacquer bars, and dim lighting made the room seem more intimate than it was. The servers, most of whom I guessed were aspiring models, were dressed uniformly in short red military-style double-breasted blazers paired with even shorter black leather pleated skirts. The DJ booth was up on the second floor, so it was far quieter in this section of the club. I was glad Gideon and I wouldn't have to shout to get to know each other.

"A VIP lounge seems a bit like overkill in this place, don't you think?" I asked looking around.

He laughed and passed me the drink menu. "What can I get for you? Glass of champagne?"

I nodded and Gideon motioned to the bartender to get two. "You look beautiful—is the dress yours?"

I looked down. "I bought it a few days ago."

"Oh, I thought you'd designed it?"

"No, I wish I had, but I have to give Givenchy all the credit," I said.

The bartender handed us our flutes of champagne, and Gideon clinked his to mine and took a sip.

"Get to all the sights you wanted?" he asked.

"I spent way too much time in the Victoria and Albert Museum, so I'm not sure I'm going to have enough time to get to see much more this trip. Looks like I'll be back in London for work a few more times this year, though, so hopefully I'll make it through my list."

He nodded. "And now you can check off the Red Coat Club."

I peered around. "I guess this really is the new hot spot? The line to get in stretches around the block," I said. "Do you know someone who works here?"

There was really no polite way to ask how he'd managed to gain VIP entrance at a club that seemed harder to get into than Fort Knox.

He put his hand on the small of my back. "Excuse me for one minute. I need to say a quick hello to someone." He leaned over the bar, "Hey, Craig, two more," he said, pointing to our glasses and tossing down his credit card.

It wasn't just a credit card. It was an Amex black card, with the name Viscount Satterley on it. The room was starting to fill up with some familiar faces, most of which I couldn't name, but recognized from all the cyber-sleuthing I'd been doing on paparazzi sites these last few days. I looked over to the corner of the room where Gideon was chatting with a small group of well-dressed women. He had his arm around a gorgeous redhead, who was laughing at something he'd just said. Who was Viscount Satterley? And who was the redhead? Suddenly this decision to "have an adventure" seemed like a very bad idea.

I quickly turned back to the bar so Gideon wouldn't see me spying on him. A few minutes later he returned, apologizing for having stepped away.

"It's no problem. I actually think I'm gonna get going, though."

"You just got here. What are you talking about?"

"I'm not sure this is really my scene, but you seem to know a lot of people, so stay and have a good time," I said, picking my clutch from off the bar and pushing into the crowd that'd gathered by the stairs.

"Georgica, wait a second. Let me explain. Let's go somewhere a little quieter." He took my hand and led me to a small room off the bar.

"What's this place, the VIP room within the VIP room?" I asked, looking around.

"It's the coat closet. Look, I'm sorry you don't like the club. Let's go somewhere else."

"The club is fine. I'm just a little confused as to what we're doing here, and why your credit card has the name Viscount Satterley on it. Who is that?"

"I'm Viscount Satterley, heir apparent to my father, the Earl of Harronsby."

I put my hand up. "This is a little too *Game of Thrones* for me. What does all that even mean?"

"That when my father dies, I'll be the Earl of Harronsby and owner of Badgley Hall, our family home."

"So, why are you working at Highclere Castle?"

"It's one of the most successful houses in England. I have to learn the business of running an estate if it's going to be mine one day."

I rubbed the back of my neck. "When you said the aristocracy was still alive and well, you really meant it."

"I'm not that guy, I promise. I took you here tonight to impress you. After you left Highclere, I googled you and read all about your fashion house and the celebrities you've dressed. I thought you'd like this sort of scene."

"You googled me?"

His green-gray eyes stared into my own. "It felt like we had a connection that day at the Blue Hen. I wanted to know more about you." He took my hands into his. "You wanna get out of here?"

"The coat closet? Definitely," I said, smiling.

"I meant the club. Do you want to go grab a coffee or nightcap?"

"Sure, yeah, that'd be nice."

"Go wait by the front door. Let me close out the tab and say goodbye to my sister and her friends, and I'll be right there."

It all made sense. The redhead he was chatting it up with a few minutes earlier was his sister. I felt foolish for assuming the worst. I made my way to the front of the club, which was now packed wall to wall with people. Most of them were clamoring to get to the corner bar. I tapped the guy next to me on the shoulder.

"Who's over there? Emma Watson? Daniel Craig?" I asked.

"Victoria Ellicott and Prince Alexander," he said.

"Exciting," I muttered. I turned back around to push my way closer to the door and felt a hard tap on my own shoulder.

"It's Victoria Ellicott and Prince Alexander," I shouted behind me.

"Gigi," said a voice I would recognize anywhere.

I closed my eyes and slowly turned around. When I opened them, Perry Gillman was standing right in front of me.

Chapter Six

Perry motioned for me to follow him out of the crowd to another VIP area of the room. He found us a small table, and we took seats across from one another. He looked even better up close than on stage the other night. His dark, curly hair was longer than I was used to, and I figured he'd grown it out for his role as Robert Dudley. He'd also grown back the same neat beard he had when he played the Fiddler. I started to reach across the table to touch his face but stopped myself, slipping my hands underneath me so I wouldn't be tempted again.

We sat in silence for what felt like forever, neither one of us knowing how or where to begin. Finally, when I couldn't stand the silence a second longer, I spoke.

"This place is a far cry from Rosie's," I said, looking around. "Unless there are cigarette machines by the bathroom? I haven't been down that way yet."

I looked up at Perry. He was staring at me but saying nothing. My heartbeat pulsed in the center of my throat. It was echoing in my head so loudly, I was sure my eardrums would explode from the sheer force of it. I kept talking just to reassure myself I hadn't gone completely deaf. "Do you think Rosie's is still open? It has to be, right? It's a Milbank institution."

"I knew we'd eventually run into each other," he said, interrupting my prattle.

There was an edge in his voice. I couldn't tell if I was making him uncomfortable or just irritated. It was the same fine line I remembered straddling when we first met.

The pounding in my chest was slowing down, and my voice wasn't quivering as noticeably. "Well, London's a smaller town than I ever realized."

"In some circles it can be, I suppose," he replied coolly. Perry called over a waitress and ordered us both a drink.

"The ones you seem to be traveling in these days, anyway," I said, more harshly than I intended.

He leaned back into his chair and crossed his legs. "That's rich, coming from you. Wasn't it your name I saw next to Alexander and Victoria's on the list of people coming backstage after the show Saturday night?"

"I'm sure your girlfriend told you I'm not allowed to talk about what I'm doing in town."

He uncrossed his legs and sat upright. He looked straight into my eyes. "I wanted to tell you about Annabelle in person. I'd hoped we'd have a few minutes to talk Saturday night."

I broke from his gaze and looked down. "It's fine. Your publicist filled me in on all the details."

"Gemma works for Victoria and Annabelle, not for me."

"It doesn't matter how I found out. I'm happy for you. I'm happy for all your success. You're the toast of the town," I said, lifting up my glass.

He lifted up his own to meet it. "Sounds like G. Malone will be soon."

"Maybe we both got what we wanted, then."

"There you are, darling." Annabelle Ellicott approached our table. She was even more beautiful than I remembered. Taller than her sister and less curvy, she easily could be a model. She was wearing the most perfect little silver sequined Jenny Packham dress. Jamie'd begged me to try it on when we were shopping the other day, but I wasn't sure I could pull it off. Annabelle more than pulled it off. She looked stunning. She put one hand on Perry's shoulder and waited for introductions.

He put his hand over hers and guided her to the seat next to him.

I extended my hand. "I'm Georgica Goldstein, Perry and I—"

"Just had the pleasure of meeting," Perry said, speaking over me. "Georgica came over to introduce herself and apologize for not making it backstage the other night."

I did a double take. I'd just assumed Perry told Annabelle we were engaged or at the very least that we knew one another. Why keep our past a secret? I had two choices. I could speak up, hurling myself into one of the most awkward conversations of all time or play along until Perry had a chance to explain himself to me. I chose the latter.

"Unfortunately, I wasn't feeling well and left after the first act," I said, my eyes on Perry the whole time.

"I'm glad I got a chance to meet your partner, Jamie. We got on so well I feel like I've known him for years. Shame you didn't get to see the second act of the show, though. Perry, maybe we can arrange another ticket for Georgica before she leaves town?"

"Whatever you want, darling," he said.

I moistened my lips and leaned back in my chair. There was always something sensual about the way Perry pronounced the word "darling." His posh accent almost eliminated the letter *r* from the world altogether so it came out more like *dahling*. A familiar ache filled my chest and suddenly, the club felt ten times more crowded than it had mere seconds before.

"Have you been here before? It's not really our scene, but Victoria's been raving about this place so much, we finally said we'd nip in for a peek," Annabelle said, snapping me back into reality.

"No. A friend invited me here for a drink. I had no idea I'd agreed to meet him in the social epicenter of London." I placed my hands in my lap and adjusted my posture to match hers.

"These places always feel that way until the next one opens up," she said, smiling warmly. "I'm sure it's the same way in New York."

I rose from my seat. "I should actually go look for my friend."

"Annabelle! I never would have expected to see you here in a million years," Gideon said, approaching our table.

Annabelle stood up and leaned over to give Gideon a kiss hello. "You either."

"Perry, this is my old friend Gideon Cooper," she said, introducing them. "And this is Georgica—"

Gideon put his hand on the back of my chair. "Goldstein. I know, I've been looking everywhere for her."

Perry's posture stiffened as he shot a glance at Gideon. "You two know each other?"

"We met the other day at Highclere. Georgica was taking the *Downton Abbey* tour."

Annabelle turned to Perry. "What a small world. I went to boarding school with Gideon's sister, Linney."

"Linney's here. She's over in the VIP area," Gideon said.

"I'll have to say hello before we leave, then," she said.

"We should get going," Gideon told me, handing me my coat. "I promised Georgica a nightcap somewhere a little less outrageous."

I stood up from my chair and locked eyes with Perry.

"It was so lovely to meet you," Annabelle said. "Darling, we should get back to Victoria and Alex." She slipped her hand into Perry's back pocket.

Gideon extended his hand toward Perry. "Sorry we didn't get a chance to chat more. Perry, was it?"

"Didn't you know, this is *the* Perry Gillman, writer, creator, and star of *Elizabeth*." The words spilled out of my mouth before I could stop them. All three of them looked a bit taken aback by my eruption.

"Just Perry is fine," he said, taking Gideon's offered hand. "Nice to meet you, mate. Have a good night." He looked over in my direction. "You too, Gigi."

Gideon took my hand and led me out the club. When we got outside, Gideon called over a taxi for us. We slid inside, and he gave the driver directions to a nearby restaurant. I leaned against the window and gazed out onto the busy streets.

"You okay?" Gideon asked.

"I'm fine."

"You don't seem fine."

"That guy you just met, Perry Gillman...we used to be a little bit engaged."

"A little bit? Oh, that's a relief. A lot engaged is a harder thing to overcome on a first date."

I turned to face him. "We were a lot engaged, but it's been quite a while since we've seen each other."

"I see," Gideon said. "Would you like me to have the driver take you back to your hotel?"

"Actually. I'd love that nightcap if you're still offering?" I said.

"Offer still stands. Although, if you're game for an adventure, I have another thought."

I raised my eyebrows. "I could be game."

Gideon tapped the driver and gave him a different address. Fifteen minutes later the car pulled up to St. Paul's Cathedral. Gideon paid and we got out.

"St Paul's on your list, right?" he asked.

I looked down at my watch. "It's almost midnight. Isn't it closed?"

"Churches never really close. Wanna go check it out?" He held the car door open for me.

I nodded, and he took my hand and led me inside. He was right. The doors were unlocked, but a security guard stopped us as soon as we walked in. Gideon pulled him to the side. I couldn't hear their conversation, but the guard smiled and motioned to me that I could come farther into the chapel. Gideon walked back over to where I was standing.

I took two tenuous steps forward. "What did you say to him?"

"I told him I impromptu decided to propose to you tonight, and it had to be in the Whispering Gallery since that was where

47

we had our first date. I also slipped him £100. So sightsee away. He won't bother us," he said, handing me a map of the cathedral.

We slowly walked down the large aisle separating the church taking in its magnificence. He took hold of my hand again, and I felt a small flutter of excitement in my stomach.

Gideon pointed up at the ceiling. "What's this architecture style called? I've spent my life in estates and old churches and don't have a clue."

"Baroque, I think?" I looked down at the guide and read aloud, "The present church, dating from the late seventeenth century, was designed in the English Baroque style by Sir Christopher Wren. The cathedral is one of the most famous and most recognizable sights of London. Its dome, framed by the spires of Wren's City churches, dominated the skyline for three hundred years."

I peeked up at Gideon to see if he was still interested. He nodded for me to keep reading.

"St. Paul's Cathedral occupies a significant place in the national identity. Services held at St. Paul's have included royal weddings, the funerals of Sir Winston Churchill and Margaret Thatcher, and jubilee celebrations for Queen Victoria."

"Think Victoria and Prince Alexander are getting married here?" Gideon asked.

"No, Westminster Abbey," I answered, before realizing I'd just blown my cover.

He narrowed his eyes. "How would you know that?"

He rubbed the soft stubble on his face and sat down in a pew. I sat down beside him.

"I signed a confidentiality agreement. I can't talk about this."

"You realize my interest *only* piqued just now when you told me you signed a confidentiality agreement?" he said.

"You can't say anything," I said.

"Cross my heart," he promised, making the motion over his chest.

"You might as well pinky swear for all that's worth," I teased.

"No," he said, "the crossed heart is much more binding than the pinky swear, especially when you do it in a church."

Maybe it was the sacred setting or the sweet look on his face, but for some reason, I trusted Gideon.

"I'm designing Victoria's wedding gown. Jamie and I are. It's really important to her that the press doesn't get wind of it."

He crossed his heart again. "I won't say anything. "Does that mean you'll be in London more?"

I nodded, and a smile tiptoed across his face. We continued to explore the cathedral floor, slowly making our way to the entrance of the Whispering Gallery. When we got to the doorway, Gideon took the guide from my hand, shook it open, and started reading.

"Climb two hundred fifty-nine steps up the dome and you will find The Whispering Gallery, which runs around the interior of the Dome. It gets its name from a charming quirk in its construction, which makes a whisper against its walls audible on the opposite side." He finished, glanced down at my stilettos, and looked at his watch. "It's almost one a.m. You sure?"

I kicked off my shoes and stood barefoot on the cold stone floor. I extended my arm up the staircase. "Lead the way."

Gideon chuckled and started climbing. I followed closely behind him. We made it to the halfway point and sat down on the stairs for a break. He took off his blazer and tied it around his waist. He was wearing a fitted tee underneath, and I could see the faint outline of his well-defined chest. I pulled my hair off my neck and into a tight bun.

He used his pocket square to wipe some sweat off his forehead. "Since I'm about to propose to you," he said, eyebrow raised, "can I ask you some questions about your last fiancé?"

I'd just begun to cool down from the climb, but his question caused all the heat to rush back to my face.

"Um…sure," I answered.

"If it's too personal, that's okay. We don't have to talk about it."

"No, it's fine, ask away," I said.

"Back at the club, things still seemed pretty unsettled between the two of you. What's the story there?"

Considering my outburst, it was a fair question. It was only our first date, but I could understand Gideon was worried that getting involved with me might mean walking straight onto an emotional minefield.

"Perry and I met as camp counselors a little over four years ago. After the summer ended, we did the long-distance thing for a while, and then he decided to move to New York to be with me. Jamie and I were trying to get our line going, and Perry had just started writing *Elizabeth*. It was wonderful." I closed my eyes and continued.

"We shared this tiny apartment that barely had room for a bed, let alone my drafting table and his piano, but we made it work and soon after got engaged."

I thought back to the beautiful warm summer night when he asked me to marry him. We'd been in the apartment, working for hours, neither of us stopping long enough to eat a proper meal or have a conversation of more than a few words. Around eleven, Perry convinced me we needed to leave for dinner and some air. We went to our favorite hole-in-the-wall Vietnamese restaurant a few blocks away and shared spring rolls, glass noodles, and a cheap bottle of Merlot. Afterward, we wandered over to Lincoln Center, taking seats at our spot across from the fountain, where we loved to people-watch. Even at that hour of the night, there was a flurry of activity. Couples strolling home from dates, people walking their dogs, twenty-somethings trying to hail taxis, just starting their Saturday night. In the middle of it all, Perry dropped down on one knee and asked me to be his wife. The small crowd of onlookers cheered when I said yes, and he'd pulled me into his arms for a long, deep kiss.

I opened my eyes to face Gideon. "A few months later, his father died. We came back to London for the funeral and to help his mom with the arrangements and estate. When it was time for us to go back to New York, he told me he wanted to stay a bit longer to finish researching *Elizabeth*. Days turned into weeks and weeks into months. I thought once he finished writing *Elizabeth* he'd come back."

Gideon's voice softened and lowered. "I'm guessing he never did?"

I shook my head no. "He was invited to the Olivier Awards last year. There was already some buzz on *Elizabeth* and they asked him to present. I offered to fly in for it but he thought it'd be better for him to go on his own. Afterward, the press dubbed him one of the most eligible bachelors in London. I mailed him back the engagement ring a few weeks later. We haven't spoken since... well, until tonight."

I looked up, expecting to see Gideon turning on his heels to head back down the steps. Instead, he offered his hand to help me off the ground.

"Ready to see what's at the finish line?" he asked.

"You sure you want to?"

"I'm positive," he answered.

I nodded, and we raced up the last few flights. We reached the top and leaned over the railing to catch our breaths. We were almost a hundred feet above the cathedral floor, with the most incredible view of the entire chapel—the black-and-white checkered floors, the enormous archways, and glowing candlelit chandeliers.

"Now this *must* be the best view in the house," Gideon said.

I pointed to some pews toward the front of the large altar. "I'm guessing the viscounts sit somewhere over there and not up here in the cheap seats, though." I turned from the railing to face him. "While we're spilling secrets, anything you want to share with me on that front?"

He spun around and leaned back on his elbows. "I wasn't trying to dupe you. I just don't like to lead with my title," he said.

"Well, Viscount Satterley, heir apparent to the Earl of Harronsby, *is* kinda a mouthful."

He smiled. "Families like mine are about conditions and expectations. I spent my twenties trying to dodge most of them."

"So why are you working at Highclere Castle? Why not get out of the family estate business altogether?"

"Old houses like Badgley Hall are incredibly expensive to maintain. A lot of current-day owners can't keep up with the costs, so the estates end up getting sold to foreign buyers looking to recreate their own version of *Downton Abbey*. And when the sale doesn't quite cover the debts, the contents of the house get auctioned off. My parents are older, and it's my responsibility to try to preserve my family's legacy the best I can. In this case, that legacy comes in the form of a grand house and lands. But that doesn't make me better than anyone else. I sometimes worry that's what people assume when they hear my title. Isn't that what you assumed?"

"Me? No. I assumed it meant you had dragons and a moat," I teased.

He raised one eyebrow. "You do watch *Game of Thrones?* I knew it. Look," he said, stepping closer to me and taking hold of both my hands, "I'm sorry if you felt like I deceived you in any way. I promise I'm a straight shooter. What you see is what you get."

I motioned over to the Whispering Wall. "Should we try this thing?"

"Remind me how this works?"

I pulled out my map and read, "Whisper along the curving wall and someone positioned anywhere along that same wall should be able to hear you."

"Let's do it. I'll go this way, and you go that way," he said, pointing to two opposite sides of the room.

We took our posts, and from my corner, I could see him utter something into the wall. A few seconds later he came running over to see if I'd heard what he'd said.

I scrunched up my nose. "Experiment fail. I didn't hear a thing."

He looked around the vast space. "There must need to be more people in the room for the sound to reverberate off of," he guessed.

"The suspense is killing me, what'd you say?"

"I asked if I could see you again. I'd really like to see you again, Georgica."

"I'd like that too."

Chapter Seven

$\mathcal{A}$ few days and several more dates with Gideon later, I was back in New York City working on Victoria's wedding portfolio at G. Malone's design studio. A combination of jet lag and anxiety over the wedding gown had me up at four a.m., tossing and turning until I eventually gave up trying to fall back asleep, showered, and started my day. When Jamie walked into the studio at nine thirty carrying two cappuccinos, he was surprised to find me there. Lately, I'd been coming in sometime between eleven and noon and staying until all hours of the night.

It was still hard to be in my apartment alone. The space was less than six hundred square feet, but since Perry had moved out, it felt huge and lonely, like it'd swallow me up whole if I stayed in it too long. So, I threw myself into building G. Malone, spending as much time in the studio as possible, terrified the hurt of it all would paralyze me creatively, just as it had when things ended with Joshua and I got myself fired from Diane von Furstenberg. Up until now, I'd been able to channel my emotions into my work, and the brand hadn't suffered. But after this trip to London and seeing Perry with Annabelle Ellicott, I could sense that familiar ache rising from deep within my soul, threatening to grab hold of me. It was taking all I had to keep it at bay.

"Welcome home," Jamie said, kissing both my cheeks and passing me one of the steaming cups. He flung his coat and scarf over a dress form and pulled his stool up next to me. "Tell me everything. I've been dying to hear all about the date with Mr. Downton."

"Dates. Plural," I said, correcting him.

Jamie raised his eyebrows.

"We had a great time. We got to most of the spots on my sightseeing list and even hit up the Red Coat Club—ever hear of it? Pretty swanky place, right up your alley, actually."

He practically spit up his coffee. "Who'd you blow to get in there?"

"Jamie! Jesus! Gideon got us in."

"Who'd he blow?"

"Uh, nobody, at least not that I'm aware of. Turns out he's a viscount."

Jamie's eyes got huge. "Shut up! He's in line to be an earl?"

"How do you know that?"

"I watched all six seasons of *Downton* this weekend. Amazing, by the way. But a viscount? Wow, Gigi. Are you seeing him again?"

"Maybe. He told me he'd like to."

He pushed a piece of hair out of my eyes. "Then why do you look so miserable?"

"I ran into Perry and Annabelle at the club. She's…she's…perfect. Perfect hair, perfect clothes, perfect accent, pedigree, family. All of it perfect."

"She's not perfect, Gigi."

"Could've fooled me."

Jamie put his arm around me and squeezed. "Well, maybe design her a dress for the wedding that'll make her look a little less perfect."

"I'm not going to sabotage the wedding of the century."

"Who said anything about sabotage? Just design something with a few unflattering pleats," he said with a wink.

I spun the stool around to face my drafting table and flipped through the mostly empty pages of my sketchbook. Jamie and I'd been tasked with designing about fifteen looks for Victoria and another dozen or so for the other members of the bridal party. Essentially, we had to create an entire collection plus the finale look, the bridal gown. It was a daunting undertaking, and, at the moment, I didn't have a single clue where to begin. I pushed my sketchbook aside and picked up the stack of newspapers and magazines one of our interns had collected while we were out of town. Jamie and I liked to go through them once a week to get a sense of which designers certain celebrities were favoring and any emerging trends.

I thumbed through *US Weekly* and *People* then turned to the *New York Times*. Staring up at me from the Arts and Leisure section was the cover story on Perry that Alicia had told me about when I was in London. I peeked behind my shoulder. Jamie was wearing earphones, sketching away at his table, and a few interns were at their desks, answering emails. I turned back to the paper and started reading.

The reporter started the article with a deep look into Perry's childhood in Oxshott, spent surrounded by some of the greatest classical musicians of our time, including his father, Abe Gillman, the world-renowned violinist. Then the reporter dove into his "lost years," the ones he spent working as a counselor at a small sleepaway camp in Milbank, Pennsylvania, trying to complete his doctoral thesis. Perry was quoted saying, *"That was a difficult time in my life. I was running away from some personal issues and trying to find myself. I wouldn't say the time was wasted, but I wish I had more to show for that period."*

A hard, rough lump formed in my throat. I coughed to clear it, and all three interns turned to look at me. I gave them the thumbs-up, letting them know I was okay and turned my attention back to the *Times*. I turned to the last page of the article, which talked about Perry's creative process and all the historical research he did for *Elizabeth*, and read the last few paragraphs discussing his already acclaimed portrayal of Robert Dudley. Answering the reporter's question about whether he'd ever personally experienced the kind of fiery and passionate relationship

Elizabeth and Robert supposedly shared, he said, "*Some of the best relationships challenge you to be a better, different person. They're usually the ones where you don't start off on equal or sure footing but eventually, you find your way there. Those relationships are never the lasting ones, though. They require too much compromise, too many concessions. Some romances are intense and wonderful but are simply doomed from the start.*"

There they were, his feelings about us and our past relationship in black and white, out there for the world to read. I was folding the paper up to toss it into the wastepaper basket below my desk when the phone rang.

"Georgica Goldstein," I answered.

"Gideon Cooper," he replied.

I sat upright. "Oh, hi, how are you?"

"I'm great. I wanted to make sure you got home okay?"

"Yeah, thank you. It's an easy trip," I said.

"I'm glad to hear it. Any plans to come back across the pond?"

I glanced down at my computer and quickly scrolled through a series of emails from Gemma Landry with dates and details for my next meeting with Victoria. "It looks like maybe sometime next week, but nothing's definite. It's all still very cloak and dagger."

"I'm not sure I can wait that long to see you again. What are you doing this weekend?"

"This weekend? The one four days from now?"

"Yes, that very one."

"I was going to help my friend Jamie and his husband look at a few apartments, and I have an appointment to get my hair cut."

"Perfect, 'cause I just put a ticket on hold to come and see you. I'd land at half six on Friday night."

Gideon didn't just want to visit, he wanted to visit *this week-end*. Was I ready for that? Perry's cologne was still sitting on my bathroom vanity.

"He continued, "I had a wonderful few days with you in London and have some time off from Highclere. I want to get to know you better. Don't overthink it. I'm not."

I chewed on my bottom lip. "Let me see if I can cancel my plans. Can I call you back before the end of the day?"

"I'll be waiting," he said.

I hung up and walked over to Jamie's table. I tapped him on the shoulder. He took off his headphones and spun around.

"Do you and Thom still need my help looking at apartments this weekend?" I asked.

"What, do you have a hot date or something?"

I raised my eyebrows.

"Shut the front door. Who is it, that guy who's always checking you out at SoulCycle?"

"Gideon."

He put his hands over his mouth. "Viscount Gideon?"

"Viscount Gideon," I repeated. "He has some time off from work and wants to get to know me better."

"That's great, isn't it?"

"It's kind of fast, though, right? Don't you think it's sort of fast?" I looked down and into Jamie's eyes.

Jamie reached up and rubbed the small of my back. "It's time to move on, sweetie. We know Perry has."

Jamie was right. All these months, I'd wondered if Perry had started seeing someone else. I even convinced myself that, between the show and the press he was doing, he couldn't possibly find the time to devote to another relationship. I'd been wrong. He was in a full-blown relationship with someone. Well, not just *someone*, Annabelle Ellicott. Any hopes of a reconciliation were dashed when I heard him call her "darling."

I wandered back to my desk and pulled the large anthology on Elizabethan fashions from the Victoria and Albert Museum onto the drafting table. I grabbed a package of sticky notes from our supply closet and marked any image that was remotely inspiring. An hour later, with more than half the book tabbed, Jordana tapped me on the shoulder to ask if I wanted to prep for my appearance on *Top Designer*.

Jordana Singer had been my co-counselor and most trusted ally when I worked at Camp Chinooka. We kept in touch while she was in college, and she'd spent the last three summers and every semester break interning for G. Malone. She helped us build our social media platform, and when she graduated from Brown, Jamie and I hired her. Recently, we'd named her as Global Director of Brand Events. Our investors and advisory board thought we were crazy for promoting someone with so little experience, but her work ethic and commitment to building the company quickly made her invaluable. She lived and breathed G. Malone. So much so, I sometimes worried about the toll it was taking on her personal life.

It'd been Jordana's brainchild to reach out to the producers of *Top Designer* to see if they'd be interested in Jamie and me coming back to guest judge an episode. They jumped at the idea. As runner-up of the very first season, now running a successful design brand of my own, they thought my story would prove inspirational to the current contestants. It was also a great reminder to the audience that the show was really a launching pad to future success. Jordana was in favor of anything that would give G. Malone more national exposure and had fought for us to be on a two-episode arc.

Jordana had received a packet from production on the contestant challenge and my role as both mentor and judge. She said she wanted to go over the details, but I knew her real agenda was to coach me on ways I could insert the G. Malone brand into the episode. Although I'd agreed to go on the show, I was having second thoughts about my appearance. Being a contestant on *Top Designer* had opened the door to some amazing opportunities, but it also thrust me into a limelight I hadn't been ready for.

Part of the first wave of successful reality shows, *Top Designer* scored record-breaking ratings for its first three episodes. Immediately following the premiere, my phone was ringing with calls from magazines, newspapers, and entertainment shows for interviews. I was young and inexperienced in dealing with press and ended up putting my foot in my mouth more times than I cared to remember. The spotlight got too big and too hot, and I choked.

I was the projected favorite to win, and when it came time to put together that final collection, I froze. I went from having too many ideas to virtually none. At the final hour, I pieced together a runway show, but it was a poor comparison to most of the looks I'd created throughout the season. Kharen Chen was declared *Top Designer*, and the next day, I fell into obscurity.

A few weeks later, I got a call from Diane von Furstenberg's VP of Design asking me to join their team. Diane had served as one of the panel judges on several episodes and thought my aesthetic would work well in her brand. It was a fantastic opportunity that I completely took for granted. I was fired in less than a year.

I worried going back to the show would stir up all those feelings of insecurity and self-doubt. Ironically, when Jordana proposed the opportunity, Jamie had jumped at the idea he might get a chance to redeem himself on national television. This many years and successes later, he was still most famous for getting kicked off *Top Designer* because he couldn't construct a wedding dress out of toilet paper. It haunted him.

Jordana and I walked a few blocks over to our favorite food cart. We ordered two falafels and sat down on a nearby bench. Between bites, she gave me a rundown on the season's contestants. She pulled the episode challenge abstract out of a folder and handed it to me.

"You've got to be kidding," I said after I'd skimmed through.

Jordana wiped some tahini sauce off her chin with the back of her hand. "What?"

"They're recreating the Code Wed challenge?"

"Okay, so I know Jamie might not be thrilled, but think about how powerfully full circle it is. Yes, he got kicked off first, but now he's back and he's successful and none of it mattered. I mean, that's a compelling story line. Also, think about the replay value and all the buzz this will create if you're actually hired to design the most important wedding gown of the century. Talk about a twist of fate!"

I shook my head. "I'm not sure he'll see it that way."

She slid the abstract back into the portfolio. "I'll get him to see it that way. So, how was London—tell me everything. Do you think we got the gig?" she said, referring to the Royal Wedding.

"I can't believe you've managed to wait this long to ask me."

"If it was good news or bad news you would've told me by now. I figured we're still waiting to hear?"

The nondisclosure and confidentiality agreement allowed for Jamie and me to discuss the wedding with anyone from our company who we deemed needed to know. Jordana definitely fell into that category, but I wasn't ready to let her in on the big news just yet. I wanted to hold onto our secret just a little bit longer while I was still working out the different looks. Once the news got out, too many people would try to influence the designs.

"Still waiting. We should hear something soon, though," I said.

Jordana's green eyes were sparkling with possibilities. "Can you imagine what it'll mean to G. Malone if we're the house that designs Victoria's wedding dress?"

I took a long sip from my can of seltzer. "Pretty overwhelming to think about."

"It's pretty freakin' amazing, and I can say that because I saw your humble beginnings firsthand." Jordana wrapped up the last of her falafel and stuffed it into our makeshift trash bag.

"Ah, Camp Chinooka," I said. "I always miss it this time of year. Right when the weather's starting to warm up and you know summer's around the corner."

"Speaking of Chinooka..." she said, her voice trailing off. "You didn't see Perry, did you?"

"We ran into each other. *Verrry* long story short, I found out he's seeing someone new."

She reached over and put her hand over mine. "You know, I've always rooted for you guys, right from that first night he carried you home from Rosie's, but it may be for the best that you found out. Now you can hopefully close that chapter and start a new one."

We packed up our stuff and went back to the office. I started to clear my table of all the clutter, and peeking out from underneath the Elizabethan anthology was the Arts Section of the *Times*. I took one last long look at Perry's face on the cover and balled it up. I picked up my phone.

"You like Chinese food?" I asked Gideon after he picked up.

"Love it," he replied.

"Good, I have the perfect place."

"Want me to take care of the reservation?" he asked.

"Not necessary. It's first-come, first-served."

"Sounds like my kind of place. See you Friday."

"See you Friday."

Chapter Eight

Friday afternoon, at Jamie's insistence, I left work a little early for a manicure and blowout. He'd already come by my apartment early in the week to "style" me for my weekend, picking out outfits for every possible scenario. After binge-watching all of *Downton Abbey* and any other period pieces he could get his hands on from Netflix, he'd become pretty obsessed with the British aristocracy. The mere idea I could become a countess by marrying Gideon had him in a complete tizzy.

Alicia met me at our favorite nail salon for our manicure date. Although it hadn't been easy, time and forgiveness allowed Alicia and me to resuscitate our relationship. She and Joshua eventually came to a mutual decision not to get married, and over the last few years, the three of us had put most of the pieces of our friendship back together again.

I stopped to pick out a color, and Alicia waved to me from the back corner. I grabbed a wine-colored red off the top shelf and made my way toward her. I had to laugh. Only Alicia would be able to multitask her way through a manicure. She was using her foot to bounce the baby's stroller, snacking on some trail mix, and conducting a conference call all at the same time. She saw me and mouthed she'd be off the call in a minute.

Alicia had recently left her job in investment banking to work for a smaller private equity firm that agreed to let her work part-time. Part-time must have a different meaning in the finance world because she still put in well over forty hours a week. Compared to the almost eighty she used to work, though, she considered it a vast improvement.

I peered into the stroller. Sloane was sound asleep. I slid into the seat next to Alicia's and put my rings and bracelets into the small glass bowl on the station. The manicurist asked me to roll up my sleeves and slipped my hands into Borghese moisturizing gloves.

"Okay, call done. I'm putting it on silent for the next hour," Alicia said, putting the phone into her bag. "How are you? How was London? Tell me everything."

"It was a good trip," I said.

"Yeah?" she said, skeptically.

"Productive."

Her eyes narrowed. "You saw Perry, didn't you?"

"I ran into him. He's seeing someone new. That ship has sailed, sunk...and is now at the bottom of the ocean disintegrating faster than the Titanic."

She reached over and lightly stroked my arm. "I'm sorry."

"It's not like I didn't know it was over, but it was a different kind of finality seeing him happy with someone else."

Alicia turned back around to face the manicurist and pulled a nail polish out of her bag and handed it to her. "I'm sure she's just a rebound?"

"I don't think so. This has to be kept completely on the down low, but he's dating Annabelle Ellicott."

Alicia did a double take. "Annabelle Ellicott? I know her."

"Yeah, I guess she's pretty famous in her own right."

"No, like I *know her*, know her."

I yanked my hand out of the gloves and turned to face Alicia. "How do you know her?"

"We did that rotation program in London together a few years ago."

This small world I'd unexpectedly found myself in suddenly felt even tinier. Did everyone know Annabelle Ellicott? "Were you friends?"

"More friendly than friends, but we hung out a bit there and a few times when she came to the New York office. We've stayed in touch a little bit. The occasional holiday card and email." Alicia looked up at me. "What is it? You can't be upset I knew her six years ago?"

"No, I'm not. It just feels like Perry's everywhere. His picture. His show. His girlfriend. I can't seem to escape him."

"It just feels that way right now. It won't forever. You need to get out there, try to meet someone new. It's really the best way to move on."

The slightly irritated manicurist snatched back my hands so she could finish the manicure. Alicia and I continued catching up on my trip while the technician shaped, filed, and clipped my nails. She applied two coats of color and then shoved my hands under the ultraviolet light to dry.

I turned to Alicia. "I actually met someone in London."

Her face lit up. "You did? That's wonderful. What's he like?"

"He's a nice guy, but he knows Annabelle's whole family. He has for years. He'll be at the royal wedding, along with Perry. It's all just a little claustrophobic right now."

"I read today that Victoria's leaning toward Valentino. Maybe it'll be for the best if she picks him, and you can free yourself from all this hoopla."

Apparently, Gemma Landry's PR ploy was working, and people were buying into the idea Valentino would be the chosen designer.

"Maybe," I replied softly. "What've you been up to, aside from the obvious?" I glanced over at where Sloane was still sleeping.

"Just trying to figure out this working mom thing. It's as hard as people say."

"I'm sure. But well worth it."

Sloane started crying, and Alicia sprang up to get her out of the stroller. I motioned for her to sit back down, walked over, and picked Sloan up. I rocked her back and forth in my arms until she stopped fussing.

"You're a natural," Alicia said with a broad smile.

"I'm just dry," I said, holding up my hand to her. "Gel manicure."

She chuckled and leaned closer to the table. "I'm happy you met someone new. You deserve to be happy."

"I'd just like a few days where I don't think about Perry."

"Then don't sit here. He's on the cover of *Rolling Stone* and *Vogue*." She held up the two magazines.

"*Vogue*, really? A G. Malone design hasn't even graced the cover of *Vogue*."

I grabbed the magazine out of Alicia's hands before she could stop me. There was Perry, dressed as Robert Dudley, standing next to top model Chanel Iman dressed as Elizabeth I. "See what I mean? Everywhere."

She pried the magazine out of my fingers. "Go off the grid this weekend. Turn off your phone, your TV, don't get your mail or check your email. His face isn't on buses or billboards in Time Square...yet. Take a Perrycation."

"That guy I mentioned before, the one from London, he's coming to New York this weekend to see me."

Alicia carefully pulled out her wallet to pay. "That's perfect. Have fun and don't overthink it."

"That's funny, that's exactly what he said."

Alicia took Sloane out of my arms. "I like him already."

A few hours later, I was pacing around my apartment in a Jamie-approved outfit, waiting for Gideon. I poured myself a glass of wine and picked up my phone to check my email. Heeding Alicia's advice to stay off the grid, or at the very least Twitter, I quickly put it back down on the counter. I moved over to my drafting table, picked up my drawing pencils, and started to brainstorm ideas for Victoria's bridal party. My mind kept drifting back to Annabelle. Beautiful, self-assured Annabelle. I thought about Jamie's half-joking suggestion of designing something less than becoming for her and began to sketch the most hideous outfit I could come up with. Huge, puffy sleeves and a full pleated skirt that hit in all the least flattering places. I was having so much fun with my version of a "fashion don't" I almost didn't hear the buzzer ringing in the kitchen. I jumped up to answer it, and the doorman let me know Gideon Cooper was on his way up.

I heard the chime of the elevator door opening, smoothed out my dress, and walked to my front door to wait for him. He turned the hallway corner and spotted me, and a huge smile crept across his face. He looked adorable in a pair of fitted jeans, T-shirt, and slightly oversized gray cardigan. He was wearing his newsboy cap and had a beaten-up leather bag slung over his shoulder.

"Hey, you," I said, holding the door open so he could squeeze his suitcase through. "Sorry, it's sort of tight quarters."

"My fault. I should've gone to check in at the hotel first, but I couldn't wait to see you," he said, kissing me on each cheek.

I closed the door behind him. "You'll check in after dinner. Welcome to my humble, and I do mean humble, abode," I said, motioning around the apartment.

He slipped his coat off and folded it over a chair. "What are you talking about? I love it."

"It's a far cry from Highclere Castle or Badgley Hall, I'm sure."

"Yes, but Badgley Hall doesn't have a Gray's Papaya on the corner," he said.

I laughed. "Let me show you around. Couch. Bed. Drafting table. That's the door to my closet, and through there is the bathroom. Around that way is the kitchen."

"You forgot the best part," he said.

"What's that?"

He pulled open the blinds to expose my view of the city skyline.

"You're right, that is the best part. Can I get you a drink? Wine, beer, water?"

He motioned toward my glass. "Whatever you're having is great."

I poured him a glass of red and took a seat next to him on the couch. I folded my legs under me and asked him what sorts of things he wanted to do or see over the weekend.

"I'm at your disposal. I'm game for anything you had planned this weekend. I'll just tag along."

"I didn't have much planned beyond errands."

"Market and dry cleaners it is."

I tilted my head to the side. "I'm sure I can think of a few things more interesting than that for us to do." I stood up from the couch. "First things first, though, dinner."

"That's right, you promised Chinese food."

"And I deliver on my promises. Grab your coat. We're heading downtown."

Four subway stops later and we were on Canal Street, making our way to Mott. I'd made this journey dozens of times, and it still took me a few minutes to get my bearings in the heart of China-town. Gideon took my hand as we strolled through tiny streets filled with peddlers and merchants selling everything from fake handbags to live turtles. Gideon was riveted. He wanted to stop in all the stalls to examine the merchandise. I tried talking him out of an imitation iWatch until it became clear he could not be dissuaded.

"If it works, I just saved myself a few hundred quid, and if it doesn't, I have a souvenir of our first date in New York," he said, handing the vendor forty bucks.

I grabbed a paper fan from a basket by the register and handed the same vendor a five-dollar bill. "Now I have a souvenir too. Only difference, I know mine is going to work," I said with a wink.

We got to the restaurant, and Gideon started to climb the steps to the upstairs dining room. I took his hand and redirected him down the basement stairs.

Gideon wrinkled his nose and pursed his lips. "Where are you taking me?"

"Trust me," I replied, leading him into the restaurant.

We slid into the red faux leather booth as a waiter walked by and threw two waters, two menus, and a bowl of noodles and duck sauce on the white Formica table. Gideon handed me a menu and napkin from the dispenser.

"So, this place is…charming," he said, taking in the ambiance, or lack thereof. He grabbed a waiter who was rushing past by the elbow. "Can we get two glasses of Merlot."

"I've been coming here with my dad since I was a kid. Best Chinese food in the city. But just down here. The upstairs dining room is a totally different experience."

He leaned in and whispered. "You realize all the food is probably prepared in the same kitchen."

"Then something happens as they bring it down that flight of stairs, 'cause I swear, it tastes ten times better when you eat it off the paper placemats instead of the cloth tablecloths."

The waiter returned and set down two huge goblets of wine.

Gideon toasted to our weekend together then put down his glass. "So, what's good here?"

"Everything. I can personally vouch for the entire left side of the menu and my father can probably vouch for the entire right."

He handed me his menu. "Why don't you take the lead? I trust you implicitly."

I ordered us soup, egg rolls, dumplings, and a couple of dishes to share. While we waited for the food, he told me about his trip over and the woman who sat next to him on the flight who made no secret of the fact she'd be willing to join the mile-high club with him.

I took a sip of the wine. "How'd you decline her very generous offer?" I asked. "If you did, in fact, decline her very generous offer?"

"I thanked her for the proposition, but told her I was on my way to New York to see a girl I might be falling for," he said.

I lifted my hands to my cheeks and felt all the warmth from the wine rise to them. Gideon took hold of my hands and drew them back down to the table. We sat motionless, staring at one another, saying nothing. Then I heard a familiar voice calling my name from the doorway.

I slowly turned and saw my parents standing behind the small crowd of people who'd gathered at the take-out counter. My mother pushed her way through and over to our table. My father followed closely behind her. I stood up to greet them.

"What are you guys doing here?" I asked.

"Your father was in the mood for hot and sour soup," my mother said.

My parents' marriage wasn't so much complicated as it was unpredictable. They'd dealt with their share of infidelities and betrayals, but at the end of the day, there was no question they'd still rather navigate the world together than apart.

"Are you going to introduce us to your friend, Georgica?" my mother asked.

"Sorry. Yes, this is Gideon Cooper," I said. "Gideon, these are my parents, Kathryn and Mitchell Goldstein."

Gideon stood up and set his napkin on the table. He reached out to shake both of their hands.

My mother was looking him up and down, trying to size him up. I could almost hear the internal monologue as she tried to discern if he was a date or friend.

"How do you two know each other? Is Gideon a designer friend of yours?"

I was pretty sure that was my mother's not-so-subtle way of asking if Gideon was gay.

"I met Gideon in London last week when I was touring Highclere Castle. He's in New York for the weekend, so we're just grabbing dinner."

"The food smells wonderful," Gideon said. "I wasn't sure what I was in for when we took the stairs into the basement."

"Georgie knows this is the only dining room worth eating in," my father chimed in. He pointed to the large line snaking out the front door and up the stairs. "It's why there's always a wait."

"Do you want to join us?" Gideon asked. "We ordered way too much food for just the two of us."

"We'd love to." My mother slid into the booth next to Gideon.

My father crossed his arms over his body. "Kate, let's leave them to eat in peace."

"It's fine, Dad, just sit." I patted the seat next to me.

My father reluctantly sat down in the booth and picked up the menu to peruse it, even though he knew it by heart at this point.

My mother leaned into the table. "Highclere Castle. That must be exciting. Gigi and I are huge fans of *Downton Abbey*. Did you work on the show?"

"I run the Visitor's Centre," Gideon answered.

My mother couldn't hide her disappointment. Compared to Perry, now gracing the covers of magazines, in her estimation, I was taking a huge step down. I almost blurted out he was a viscount, just to put her out of her misery, but decided I'd save that nugget for another time.

"There was a big mix-up with the tour groups when Jamie and I were there, and Gideon saved us," I chimed in.

"That's nice," she said, dismissively.

I looked over to my father to salvage the conversation. He didn't seem particularly interested in Gideon, but for very different reasons than my mother. In the four years we were together, he'd come to love Perry like a son. They bonded over their appreciation of classical and jazz music and British history. I wasn't sure who took the break-up harder, me or him. I was hoping to spark some enthusiasm, so I turned the attention to Gideon's roots.

"Dad, Gideon grew up in South Gloucestershire."

My father took off his glasses and placed them on the table. "There's that manor house in South Gloucestershire, the one Henry VIII and Anne Boleyn stayed in. Remember, Kate, we took a tour of it?"

My mother turned to face Gideon. "Mitchell's taken me to more old homes than I can even count."

The waiter set the food down on the table, and we dug in. My father scooped a heaping spoonful of Moo Shoo chicken and set it on his plate. "What was the name of the estate? Do you remember, Kate?"

Gideon cleared his throat and answered, "Badgley Hall."

"That's right, Badgley Hall. Wonderful place. Do you know it well?"

"Pretty well, but we have a lot of notable houses in Gloucestershire. Highgrove House, Gatcombe Park. We're also pretty proud of our annual cheese-rolling festival."

"A cheese-rolling festival? Now, that's something I'd like to see," I said.

"We'll have to go, then." Gideon refilled my cup with tea and winked at me.

My mother caught our eyes locked together and said, "Did you get a chance to see *Elizabeth* while you were in London?"

I shifted in my seat. "Jamie and I were invited by Victoria Elli-cott. I left after the first act."

My mother's eyes opened wide. "Not as good as the hype?"

"No, it's better than the hype, actually."

"Our ticket broker is already on alert for when it opens here. I thought we might have an in, but doesn't look like it," she said. "Speaking of *Elizabeth*, I'm sure you saw the *New York Times* article by now." She lowered her voice. "It was you Perry was talking about, right? The relationship that was 'doomed from the start?'"

I picked up my glass and gulped down the rest of the wine. Gideon put his hand over mine and I caught my mother's disap-proving sideways glance. Well, at least now she knew he wasn't gay. The waiter came by and dropped the check on the table. My father reached over for it, but Gideon had already picked it up.

Gideon slid his credit card into the black leather holder. "I got this."

The waiter snatched it off the table and took it to the register.

"Thank you, Gideon," my father said.

"Yes, thank you," my mother repeated half-heartedly.

A few minutes later the waiter returned with the credit card and a pen. "Who is Vis-count Satterley?" he asked.

"It's pronounced VY-*kownt*, and that's me. I'm Viscount Sat-terley," Gideon said, sliding the black card back into his wallet.

My mother lifted her eyebrows and looked over at my father. Gideon winked at me, and with that one move, won us all over.

♛

"Did you see the look on my mother's face? Priceless," I said, as we strolled up Broadway.

Gideon laughed. "I don't use that move often, but when I do, it's supremely effective."

"Well, thank you. I didn't plan on you meeting my parents so soon. Or ideally, ever."

He shrugged. "Parents are parents. Mine are no picnic."

"Still, I'm sorry they were so tough on you. If you couldn't tell, they liked Perry a lot."

He nodded. "Yeah, I picked up on that."

"They're still holding out hope we'll reconcile. My mother is anyway."

He stopped walking and turned to look at me. "What about you?"

"We were done a long time ago. Meeting Annabelle just confirmed what I already knew," I said.

"His loss."

"We just met. How can you can be so sure?"

"Can I be totally honest with you?" he asked.

I chewed on the inside of my cheek. "Sure."

"I downloaded your entire season of *Top Designer* and watched most of the episodes on the flight over. I skipped to the finale."

"Ahh, I see. And?"

He leaned in and whispered in my ear, "You were robbed."

A warm rush charged through my body. I looked down at my watch. "It's still early. Anywhere you want to go? Might be tough to trump breaking into a church, but I'm game to try."

"I did read about this thing on the Highline I wanted to check out," he said.

"Let's go."

He took my hand, and we hopped into a taxi and over to the Highline, a public park built on a historic freight rail line elevated above the streets on Manhattan's West Side. It was a beautiful spring night, and the streets were packed. The taxi stopped as close to the entrance as it could, and we got out to walk the rest of the way. Gideon guided me through the crowds and up the two flights of stairs on Fourteenth Street and Tenth Ave to the Highline. Large telescopes were set up all along the footpath, and small groups were gathered around each one, taking turns looking through the eyepiece.

I did a full turn in my spot. "What is all this?"

"The Amateur Astronomers Association sets up these observation nights every week. That one's free," he said, directing us to an open telescope. "I read about it in my in-flight magazine and wanted to check it out. I'm kind of a nerd with this stuff. I've been into astronomy since I was a kid."

We tried adjusting the eyepiece, and one of the volunteers from the AAA came over to assist us. The volunteer turned the telescope up and to the right. "It's a pretty clear night. You should be able to see Jupiter and possibly all four Galilean moons."

I stepped back to let Gideon take a turn. He squinted into the telescope, and a huge smile spread across his face. He grabbed hold of my hand, held it tightly, and motioned for me to look. I crouched down and peered up into the lens. There it was, the whole universe lit up like Fourth of July fireworks. Jupiter and the Galilean moons were shining brightly in the navy sky.

Gideon knelt down beside me. "What do you think?"

"It's been a while since I looked at the stars," I said, thinking back to the evenings Perry and I laid on the Great Lawn at Camp Chinooka, staring up into the night. "Living in New York City, it's easy to forget they're still there."

He pulled me closer to him. "It's the light pollution. Makes it hard to see what's right there in front of you."

We were inches apart, both of us kneeling on the ground, people rushing by in every direction. Gideon brushed some hair out of my eyes and kissed me firmer and more intensely than the night at St. Paul's. He ran his fingers down my back and up my arms until he held my head in his hands. After a few more seconds he stood up, reached for my hand, and drew me into his embrace.

We'd spent these last moments observing space and all of its faraway objects, yet standing in Gideon's arms, I felt more connected and present in my own life than I had in months. I wasn't sure Gideon was the answer to getting over Perry or even should be, but allowing myself to believe moving on was even possible seemed like a good place to start.

We spent the rest of the weekend exploring New York and learning about one another. It was so incredible, he never did end up checking into his hotel.

Chapter Nine

Gideon left to catch his flight early Monday morning, and I rushed over to the Fashion Institute of Technology where *Top Designer* was still being filmed after all these years. Jordana had texted me over the weekend to let me know we had a call time of eight a.m. I was running about thirty minutes late. Fortunately, FIT was only a few blocks from my apartment, so I sprinted over. She was waiting for me outside the school's main entrance.

"I know, I know, and I'm sorry," I said between gasps.

"I texted you exactly what time you needed to be here if you wanted hair and makeup."

"I hope they started with Jamie."

"He isn't here yet, either," she said through gritted teeth.

"Is he okay? He's never late. Did you call him?"

"He's on his way." She looked me up and down. "Let's just get you into a chair. It's not really so much a question of want as need."

I pulled out my compact. "Do I really look that bad?"

Jordana tousled a few rogue strands of my bedhead. "Not bad, just unkempt."

I couldn't hide the smile that spread across my face.

"What? What's that look?" she asked.

"What look?"

Jamie walked up to greet us. "That look. You had a good weekend with the viscount, didn't you?"

"The who?" Jordana asked.

"I'll explain later. We should go inside."

Jordana shot me another confused look as we made our way into FIT's main building and down the hall to the auditorium where the show was filmed. Just being in the space instantly brought back a million memories from my first day as a contestant.

I remembered how we'd stood baking under the hot runway lights for what seemed like hours, when a production assistant finally appeared to tell us they were running behind schedule, dismissing the contestants back to the break room. The producers made it clear that we weren't allowed to speak to any of the other contestants until the first challenge was announced. We'd already been lined up for almost two hours in silence, waiting for the show's host to emerge from her dressing room.

After the PA walked away, most of the other female contestants (and some of the male ones) headed straight from the runway to the bathroom to freshen up and redo their makeup. I wasn't sure how much time we had, so I made a beeline over to the Nespresso coffee machine in the break room instead. Nerves had gotten the better of me, and I hadn't slept more than a couple hours. In that moment, caffeine seemed way more important than lip gloss.

"Show must have a healthy budget. That's a good sign. It means they expect good ratings," a male voice had said from behind me as I struggled to use the complicated coffee machine.

"Why do you say that?"

"A Nespresso machine's no joke. Those things cost a pretty penny," he said, reaching around me to readjust the settings I'd just entered.

"I wouldn't know. I haven't had my own coffee machine in a while. I'm living with a friend while I try to become rich and famous on a reality television show." I turned around and found myself face-to-face with one of the most impeccably dressed men I'd ever met. "Wow, did you design what you're wearing?"

"The suit's Dsquared. The shoes," he said, pointing down at his feet, "Louboutin. The shirt's a Jamie Malone, though."

"A Jamie Malone?"

He extended his hand toward me. "I'm a Jamie Malone. Nice to meet you."

"Ah. I'm a Georgica Goldstein, but everyone calls me Gigi," I said, taking his hand. "Are we going to get in trouble for talking? I don't think we're supposed to yet."

"Georgica like the Hamptons' beach?" he asked, ignoring my question.

"Just like it, actually. It's one of my parents' favorite vacation spots."

He leaned in close to my ear. "Don't tell anyone, but my real last name's Johnson. Jamie Johnson—how pedestrian, right? So I changed it. Valerie Malone served as my inspiration."

The name sounded familiar, but I couldn't quite place it. "I'm not sure I know who Valerie Malone is?"

"Tiffani Amber Thiessen's character on *Beverly Hills 90210*. The quintessential bad girl."

"I think she just goes by Tiffani Thiessen now. She dropped the Amber after *Saved by the Bell*."

He flashed a smile, impressed with my knowledge of pop culture. He leaned in to examine my dress. "DVF, right? Spring collection? Word of advice, don't ever attempt to design a wrap dress—you'll never do one as well as Diane."

I grinned and nodded in agreement. I knew we'd be fast friends.

"So, Gigi, where'd you go to design school?" he asked.

"I'm pretty much self-taught," I admitted reluctantly. "What about you?"

"Here, actually—top of my class. One of the producers was in the audience of my final exam runway show and asked if I wanted to audition."

"My best friend, Alicia, saw a casting call and encouraged me to apply. To be honest, I'm not even sure what I'm doing here. This is very much outside my comfort zone."

He smirked. "What is? Being followed by cameras twenty-four hours a day?"

"To start with."

"Small price to pay for a chance to show in fashion week and $100,000 to start your own line, though."

"Yeah, that's what Joshua said."

He shrugged his shoulders. "Who's Joshua?"

"Nobody," I answered without the smallest inflection.

Jamie gave me a knowing look, as if to say he could tell there was more to that story, but let it go. A few minutes later, the same PA came into the break room and announced they were ready and we'd start filming in a couple minutes. I threw the rest of my coffee out and headed back to the runway with Jamie. The PA lined us back up on our marks and gave a breakdown of how the scene would go. Then, Charlotte Cross—a top model who'd graced the cover of at least five of Europe's top fashion magazines that month—appeared. She looked flawless as all five foot ten of her came down the runway. When she got to the center, she proceeded to read our first challenge off the teleprompter.

"Welcome, contestants, to Season One of *Top Designer*. I'm Charlotte Cross. We're here at New York's Fashion Institute of Technology, where over the next twelve weeks, the fourteen of you will be competing for a chance to show your collections at fashion week and $100,000-prize to start your own line. You'll be taking part in design challenges meant to test your skills, creativity, ingenuity, and overall talent. Be true to your aesthetic, taste, and vision." She paused for what I could only assume was dramatic effect and said, "And now, on to your first challenge, which we're calling Episode Code Wed."

Jamie was smiling. I guessed we'd be designing some sort of wedding gown, and I could only assume this type of project fell right into his wheelhouse. I'd never designed anything on that scale and already felt out of my league.

"But here at *Top Designer*, nothing is as simple as it seems," Charlotte continued. "You will each be given a fabric budget of one hundred dollars to use at Ambiance Fabric. The rest of the dress has to be constructed using an alternative material."

She flashed a wicked smile and pulled it out of her suit jacket. "This is Charmin two-ply. That's right, your alternative material is toilet paper."

Jamie's smile quickly turned to dread. I had a feeling he was used to designing with more luxurious textiles.

"You each get a dozen rolls and two days to make the wedding dress of your dreams. The winner of this challenge will receive immunity and their dress will be showcased in the storefront of Kleinfeld's, New York's famous bridal boutique. Best of luck, designers," Charlotte said, waving to us. "See you at the show."

Charlotte walked off the set, and the fourteen of us were ushered over to Ambiance where we had 30 minutes to select additional materials for the challenge. Almost all the designers went rushing off to the section that had more typical wedding gown fabrics like taffeta, silk, and satin. They were beautiful textiles, but also very expensive. I knew the one-hundred-dollar allotment wouldn't go very far if I stuck to just those fabrics. Instead, I pulled yards of tulle and organza, lighter and cheaper materials. I had no idea how I was going to utilize them yet but figured the more fabric I had to work with, the better.

When we got back to FIT, the PAs led us to our workspace. Dress forms with each of our names were set up next to individual workstations. I took a seat at mine and waited for further instructions. None came. I scanned the room and noticed everyone else already frantically scribbling in their sketch pads. Jamie was up on his feet, draping muslin around his form, and at least three of the other contestants were furiously ripping pieces of toilet paper from the rolls.

Great. Not even five minutes into the competition and I was already ten minutes behind. I sketched out a few designs but wasn't crazy about any of them and tossed them to the side. I stared off into the room, rolling squares of ripped toilet paper back and forth between my thumb and forefinger before dropping them to the table, not one bit of inspiration hitting. The other contestants were already deep into their designs, shredding, fringing, and weaving their toilet paper into wearable art.

I'd be kicked off *Top Designer*. First. Maybe it would be considered more of a disqualification, anyway? Without a garment to show, I'd probably be spared the embarrassment of having to stand on the runway, and they'd just edit me out of this episode entirely. I laid my head down on my workstation.

Then, out of the corner of my eye, I noticed the pile of rolled up paper I'd been nervously dropping to the table. I picked my head back up and scooped them into my hands. Instantly, I was reminded of the summer at camp when my cabin was put in charge of running the very popular wedding booth. Even though the "marriages" usually only lasted until the end of the carnival, a two- to three-hour relationship at camp was equal to a six- to seven-month romance in the real world. My bunkmates and I took our responsibility as camp wedding officiants seriously. We created every necessary prop from fake wedding rings made of aluminum foil and rhinestones to a veil constructed out of tulle covered in glitter-dipped toilet paper rosettes.

There was the inspiration I'd been looking for. I'd construct the bodice for this gown using the allotted fabric from Ambiance and cover the skirt with larger hand-dyed toilet paper rosettes. I didn't have time to second-guess my decision and went for it.

Six hours later, I was half done with the dress and laying the roses out to dry across my workstation. I sprayed the top of each flower with glue and hand-dipped each one into my own mixture of iridescent glitter. If I could get the construction just right, I knew the lights would hit the dress in such a way that it would make a huge impact on the runway. I was feeling slightly more confident when I looked around the room and noticed nobody else had done anything remotely similar.

Poor Jamie just looked lost. Unraveled rolls of toilet paper just about covered every square inch of his workstation, and there was nothing pinned to his dress form. I walked over to see if I could lend any moral support.

"I was gonna go grab a coffee. Can I get you one?" I asked.

"I'm fine," he replied without looking up from his sketch pad.

I started to walk away but decided to double back. "You sure you don't want anything?"

"A loaded gun might be good."

"How 'bout a hot glue gun?" I said, holding one up.

He smiled and looked up from the table. "Have you ever seen *Gone with the Wind?*"

"Yeah, of course," I replied.

"That scene where Scarlett makes the dress out of the green velvet curtains keeps replaying and replaying in my head." He stood up from the stool. "Let's say I didn't actually complete a garment, I'd just be disqualified and edited out of the episode, right?"

I put my arm around him. "I think you should go with me to get a coffee from that fancy Nespresso machine I finally figured out how to work and then come back and look at this with fresh eyes."

A few hours later, Jamie pieced together a gown and was fitting it to his model. It was a mess, but at least he had something to show on the runway. My own dress came out better than I imagined. The sweetheart neckline and bodice gave way to a full skirt layered with hand-dipped glittering roses and rosettes. If you took a few steps back from it, you'd never know the dress was seventy percent toilet paper, thirty percent glue.

After the models finished in hair and makeup, we fitted them into our designs one last time and lined them up to go down the runway. Looking at the other gowns, I was impressed with the sheer level of ingenuity. Some of the dresses were literally held together by a thread, but the results were amazing. Jamie's, though, was a disaster. He'd used the squares of toilet paper almost like a patchwork pattern. It was a good concept, but the execution left a lot to be desired. He knew it. I could see it in his face as we sat down in the audience to watch the runway show.

When the show was over, Charlotte Cross introduced the impressive panel of judges, including Naomi Campbell and Diane von Furstenberg, and announced the contestants with the highest and lowest scores. She invited those designers to join her on the runway alongside their models. Jamie and I stepped back onto our marks from earlier that day and waited for the cameras to be repositioned for critiques.

The judges took their time questioning each of us about our looks. My whole body was shaking when Diane von Furstenberg asked me about my gown and inspiration. I had no idea if my scores had landed me in the top or bottom, and she wasn't giving much away. It wasn't until Charlotte Cross's icy stare gave way to a half-smile that I finally felt confident I wasn't going to be sent home first.

Next, the judges turned their attention to Jamie's design. Most of the toilet paper squares had fallen off his model during the runway show so that she looked like a half-naked molting bird. It was almost obscene, and I couldn't help but wonder if the show had the budget to pixelate out what couldn't be shown on network TV. Jamie was visibly sweating through his Jamie Malone original and looked like he wanted to die. I grabbed his hand for moral support. The judges dismissed us back to the workroom while they made their decisions.

The other contestants on the chopping block headed outside for a cigarette. Jamie was pacing in circles. After his third or fourth lap, I pulled him over to the couch.

"You're making me dizzy," I joked.

He lowered his head into his hands. "Sorry. I just can't believe this challenge is the reason I'm going home."

"You don't know that," I said supportively.

He lifted his head and raised his eyebrows. "Let's call this what it is. A total and complete disaster."

"For everyone. I doubt they'll even air this episode."

He cocked his head to the side. "You don't have to make me feel better. We just met."

"You're right. I don't have to, which is why what I'm telling you is the truth."

"Your gown was pretty spectacular, Gigi. You might take this whole thing."

"It was all smoke and mirrors. A little glitter goes a long way."

He sat back down on the couch. "Do you even get to be on the reunion show if you're kicked off first?"

The PA motioned for us to return to the studio. I turned to Jamie. "Hey, whatever happens, I'm glad to have met you."

"Ditto," he replied, putting his arm around me.

We went back to the runway and lined up next to our models. Charlotte Cross took her position in the center of the runway. She dismissed four of the designers as safe before announcing that I was the winner of the challenge and that Jamie was going home.

Charlotte gave us a minute to say our goodbyes. Jamie gave me a hug and whispered in my ear, "Scarecrow, I think I'll miss you most of all."

"I'm self-taught. I doubt I'll be here past the next challenge."

"You have immunity. You'll be here for the next challenge and a lot more after that."

"How do you know?" I said softly.

He softened his eyes. "My bets are on you, friend."

"Friend?"

"Oh yeah. For life."

♛

Jordana tapped me on the shoulder to let me know she'd smoothed everything out with the producers. As it turned out, the other two guest judges were also running a few minutes behind. A PA ushered Jamie and me into hair and makeup and handed us the day's schedule.

Jamie folded the schedule into his lap. "When did Jordana tell you?"

"On Friday, I swear."

"You didn't want to warn me?"

"She told me she was going to speak to you."

He picked up the schedule and held it in front of my face. "Episode Code Wed. Again? Really?"

I scrunched up my nose. "Okay, but in Jordana's defense, there's something poetic about you coming back to judge this challenge. Look at where we are, how far we've come."

"You are such a liar. I saw your face when you walked into the auditorium. You're just as freaked out to be back here as I am."

"It's fine. I'm fine."

"Sure, you are. What about seeing Trini again?"

Katrina Bower had started out her career at *Vogue* climbing up the ranks to editor-at-large. When I met her on *Top Designer*, she was serving as the Fashion Design Department chair of FIT and had been hired on as the contestant mentor on the show's first season. Her catchphrase, "Figure it out," quickly became synonymous with the show. She was tough but fair. Critical but supportive. Her advice and eye for fashion were always right on point. She was close friends with dozens of designers and was one of the few opinions Anna Wintour completely trusted. When I was a contestant, she'd constantly confronted me about my choices and designs, pushing me to create outside my comfort zone and challenge the boundaries of my abilities. Right before each runway show, I could tell just by the look in her eye if I was going to place in the top or bottom.

During my season, Trini came to check on my progress for the final episode and runway show. Within seconds of her looking through the racks of unfinished garments, I knew I was in serious trouble. She asked me to have coffee with her without the cameras in an effort to salvage my collection and point me in some sort of direction. And at that meeting, I completely broke down. The pressures of the show and how big it'd all become paralyzed me in a way I'd never experienced before. She did her best to coach me out of my slump, but it was too late. I didn't have nearly enough time to recover. I let my fans down, and worst of all, I let Trini down. Every few months I promised myself I'd send her a note or pick up the phone to give her a call, but I never did. It'd been years since we'd spoken, yet I still heard her voice in my head every time I put pencil to paper.

"It'll be nice to see her again," I said, turning from him.

One of the PAs poked her head in the room to check on our progress. "We'll need them on stage in fifteen. Is that enough time, Emily?"

The makeup artist glanced at Jamie and then over at me. "This one'll be done in five. I'll need some more time with her, though. She decided to show up with love bites all over her neck."

I grabbed a hand mirror off the station for a closer look. I pulled down my shirt and saw the two red blotches on my neck she was referring to.

Jamie leaned around for a better view. "Nice hickeys, G. Ver-rryyy classy."

"Jesus Christ." I looked up at Emily. "Can you cover these?"

She nodded. "I've covered up a lot worse. Don't worry about it."

Jamie laughed. "Good for Viscount Gideon. I thought he was all gentility and decorum."

I rolled my eyes. Jamie stood up and patted me on the back. "I'll let Jordana know you'll be a few more minutes."

Emily went to work with the cover-up, and I took my phone out of my bag. I opened up a text from Gideon that simply said, *Miss you already*. I smiled and slid down farther into my seat.

"That's a good smile," Emily said. "I have a feeling that who-ever's behind that smile is the reason for the extra makeup."

I turned my phone off, slipped it back into my bag, and swung back around to face the mirror. I leaned forward to examine her work.

"Looks so much better. Thank you for sparing me from *Top Designer* humiliation. For a second time."

"A second time?" a familiar voice with a soft Scottish accent said from behind me. "It wasn't all that bad, was it?"

I turned around in my chair. "Hey, Trini, long time."

She looked almost identical to when I'd first met her, still sporting her signature icy blonde pixie cut and oversized tortoise-rimmed glasses. She slid into the seat next to me.

"If I didn't know any better, I'd think you'd been avoiding me these last six years," she said.

"Probably because I've been avoiding you these last six years," I said with a playful smile.

She laughed. "How have you been, Georgica? Last time I saw you, you were pining away for that guy. What was his name?"

"Joshua."

She nodded her head. "That's right. Joshua. The love of your life."

"That wasn't love. I know that now. It was an all-consuming, life-altering crush."

"Something only a woman who's actually experienced love could know. So tell me—who is he?"

I took a breath. "There was someone, but that's over now. You would've liked him a lot. He takes risks in his work—pushes boundaries."

"Has it paid off for him?"

"Big time."

"What about your work? Taking chances?"

"G. Malone recently got offered a once-in-a-lifetime opportunity."

"I hope you said yes."

"Jamie talked me into it."

She looked around. "Speaking of, where is Mr. Malone?"

"Already out on the runway getting ready to relive his own personal nightmare, otherwise known as Episode Code Wed."

She leaned in close to me. "If it makes him feel better, I thought it was a terrible challenge then. And now. But," she said, standing up, "it's a fan favorite. Your toilet paper wedding dress is still the most talked about piece ever created on *Top Designer*. Not to mention Charmin paid for most of the advertising this episode. So, we do what we have to, right?"

"Right," I answered back.

She leaned in closer. "Don't be a stranger, Georgica."

"I won't."

"I mean it—let's grab coffee or lunch soon." Trini looked down at her watch. "The designers are probably in full meltdown mode backstage right about now. I should go talk them off some cliffs. See you on the runway."

Chapter Ten

"That wasn't so bad, was it?" I asked as we turned onto Seventh Avenue. "It was for sure better to be in the judge's seat than up there sweating on that stage."

"Yeah sure, all fun and games until we made that designer with the toilet paper wedding jumpsuit cry and sent him packing."

"You and I both know our decision had more to do with it being a jumpsuit than the fact it was constructed out of toilet paper."

Jamie snorted. "Where'd Jordana sneak off to? I didn't see her backstage."

"I think she went back to the office. She said she had some calls. Plus, I think she's a little afraid of you right now."

Jamie slipped on a pair of aviator sunglasses. "When you see her, remind her I fulfilled my end of the deal. One episode. They want you to judge the finale show, not me."

"I'll worry about my encore in a few months. In the meantime, have you checked your email?"

"Not since this morning, why?"

I turned my phone to him. He pushed his sunglasses up and onto his head. "Gemma's going to have to start giving us more than a few days' notice," he said after reading her note.

"I can't believe she really booked us on separate flights and at separate hotels. I thought she was kidding with all that. She asked to see the early sketches for the bridal party and Victoria's reception gowns. Not to mention the wedding gown options." I buried my phone back in my bag. "I don't have any of that done yet."

"It's a what, six-hour flight?"

"Seven"

"Bring your pencils."

"This is insane. They may as well have made us sign the contract in blood."

"Relax, Gigi, we'll figure it out." He took my hand as we crossed the busy intersection. "Let's pop in for a drink somewhere. We deserve it after our morning."

We stopped into a small Irish pub and ordered a round... which quickly turned into five. About three hours later, we stumbled out, piss drunk, having *almost* forgotten the events of the morning. Jamie was trying to convince me to go somewhere else for one more drink—his own version of a bar crawl. I looked at my watch and told him we should do the responsible thing and eat something to sober up and then head into the office for a bit.

We squeezed our way through the crowds lined up at the TKTS booth in the center of Times Square and crossed over to Forty-fourth Street, where there was a small crew readying the St. James Theater's marquee for a new show. Jamie grabbed my hand and rushed me past it.

I pulled out of his grip. "What are you doing?"

"Nothing. The restaurant I'm thinking of is up this way," he said, yanking me by the arm toward the corner.

"Oh my God, *ow*, Jamie, what's your problem?" I said, elbowing him off of me.

He pointed up to the marquee. "That. I was trying to avoid you seeing that."

I looked up at the massive billboard announcing that *Elizabeth*, starring Perry Gillman, would be occupying the St. James in the fall.

Jamie put his arm around my shoulder. "There's been press around this for months. You knew he was coming here."

"I didn't think about him in my backyard. I live six blocks away. I walk down this street at least four times a week."

"How 'bout that drink?"

I nodded, and we slipped into a dive bar off the corner of Forty-sixth and Eighth. The rest of the afternoon got a bit hazy after that. I remembered Jordana calling to check on whether we were coming back into the office and Jamie passing me the phone so I could tell her we were way too hammered to show our faces anywhere near there. I had a vague recollection of the bartender cutting us both off after our fourth Mind Eraser—a shot made up of Vodka, Kahlúa, and 7-Up that more than lived up to its name. After that, nothing, until I woke up on Jamie and Thom's couch the next morning with a throbbing headache, wearing only one of my shoes.

I rolled off the couch and crawled to the kitchen where Thom was busy making coffee.

"Morning, sunshine." Thom handed me a steaming mug.

I looked around. "Where's Jamie?"

"Well, as of around five this morning he was puking his guts up in the bathroom. I brought him a pillow and blanket. I think he's still asleep in there."

I sat down at the kitchen table. "We were hot messes yesterday."

"You were both curled up in fetal positions when I got home from the office, so, unfortunately, I didn't get a chance to see it firsthand. But, based on how Jamie looked this morning, I can imagine. He was so excited about going back to *Top Designer*. I'm guessing it didn't go well?"

"The contestants recreated Episode Code Wed."

He pushed his glasses down to the bridge of his nose. "Oh, Christ."

"Yeah, exactly."

Thom sliced open a bagel, smeared both sides with cream cheese, and handed me half.

"If he's serious about wanting a child, some of this behavior's gonna have to stop. He knows that, right?"

"I'm sure he knows," I said softly.

"Knows what?" Jamie walked into the kitchen to join us.

"That hangovers are for weekends, and today's a school day, young man. You better get yourself showered and into the studio," Thom said.

"I can't believe I have to be on a flight to London tonight," I said.

"Why do they need you back so soon?" Thom asked.

"Mostly to take measurements. We need the sizes of the bridal party and Victoria so we can get started. I'll fly out tomorrow and meet Gigi there," Jamie answered.

I rolled my eyes. "I still don't understand why we can't just go together. This whole thing is beyond ridiculous. Who even cares that we're designing the dress?"

Thom laid his hand on my forearm. "Everyone cares, darling. Everyone. Or at least everyone will care once news gets out."

Jamie slid into the seat next to me. "What are you complaining about? It's another opportunity to see Gideon, isn't it?"

Thom leaned into the table. "Who's Gideon?"

"Oh, didn't I tell you?" Jamie said. "Gigi's dating a viscount."

I shot Jamie a look. "I'm not dating anyone."

"Okay, Gigi's sleeping with a viscount. Is that better?"

I slapped my hand to my forehead. "Oh my God. No. Not better."

"You know if you marry him you become a countess, right?" Thom added.

"Did Jamie make you watch all of *Downton Abbey* too?"

"Make me? No. I'd already seen all of it. I knew it was just a matter of time before he'd come around to it."

"He's pushing me to start *Game of Thrones* next," Jamie said. "I don't know how I feel about all those moats and dragons though."

Thom threw Jamie a look. "When have I steered you wrong?"

"Never," he said, leaning into Thom for a kiss.

Thom stood up to clear my plate and coffee mug. He leaned close to my ear and whispered, "Countess or not, I'm just glad to hear you're starting to move on from Monsieur Gillman. It's about time."

I left Thom and Jamie's to head back to my apartment then fell asleep for a few hours and woke up with just enough time to shower and pack for my flight. In all the craziness of the day, I hadn't even had a chance to call Gideon and tell him I'd be in town for a few days. I picked up my phone to dial him and then decided it'd be more fun to surprise him in the morning with a call from London.

Two movies and lots of tossing and turning later, the pilot announced that the flight attendants should do their final sweep of the aisles, as we'd be touching down at Heathrow shortly. I readjusted my chair to its upright position and tucked my Kindle back into my tote. I closed my eyes and tried to forget how unprepared I was for the trip. Gemma'd been emailing me nonstop with changes to the dossier—additional events and inspirations. I was turning into Victoria's personal wedding Pinterest board. Her ideas were so all over the place they were almost giving me less of a direction instead of more of one.

After we landed, I stopped in the ladies' room to splash some water on my face and try to wake up. I did a quick wardrobe change in one of the stalls and emerged feeling a bit better. I slid on my biggest Jackie O sunglasses and pulled my carry-on into the terminal. As was my habit since I was a little girl, I liked to read off the destination for each gate, and then look at the people waiting to get on the flight, imagining all the possible reasons for their travel.

The first gate I passed was a British Airways flight to Nairobi. I noticed a young couple dressed almost head to toe in khaki. I guessed they were newlyweds, heading off for a fabulous honeymoon safari. I turned to the other side of the terminal, where people were waiting for an Air France flight going to Cannes. A beautiful and impeccably dressed young girl surrounded by Louis Vuitton luggage was talking on her phone and flipping through a magazine on her lap.

I decided she was a young starlet heading to Cannes for their famous film festival to debut in her first movie. Her agent had secured her a very coveted reservation at the *Hôtel du Cap-Eden-Roc*, and her suitcases were filled with borrowed gowns for the different premiers and parties.

The starlet put down her phone, picked up the magazine on her lap, and held it closer to her face. That's when I saw it. The cover of *Hello! Magazine* and the headline, "Victoria Ellicott Chooses G. Malone to Design Wedding Gown of the Century."

I dropped the handle of my carry-on, rushed over to where she was sitting, and tapped the starlet on the shoulder.

"Excuse me," I said, peeking around her neck.

She pushed her sunglasses on top of her head. "Can I help you?"

"Can I take a quick peek at that magazine?"

She held it up. "This one?"

I nodded. "That one."

"Uh, sure," she said, passing it back to me.

I practically ripped it from her hands and tore it open to the page of the article. It wasn't so much an article as a two-page spread all about Jamie and me, our brand, and predictions on what the gown would look like based on our past designs. There were interviews with some of the other contestants from our season of *Top Designer*, and even a quote from Trini Bower. I mumbled thank you to the girl, passed her back the magazine, and dashed over to the closest gift shop I could find.

I flew past the register over to the magazine rack. My face and Jamie's were everywhere, gracing the cover of several newspapers. I grabbed as many different ones as I could hold and tossed them at the salesclerk to ring up.

She rang them through the scanner. "You want all of these?"

"Yes, all of them."

"Long flight?"

I looked up. "What? Oh, sure, yeah, long flight."

"She's gorgeous, isn't she?"

I dug through my wallet to find the pounds I knew were mixed in with my American dollars. "Who is?"

"Victoria Ellicott. Do you know this G. Malone designer she selected? I've never heard of him. I thought she'd go with Mr. Valentino. His designs are so elegant and tasteful."

She handed the magazines back to me with the receipt. I stuffed what I could into my tote and the rest into my carry-on. I made my way through customs and as soon as I got the green light, I rushed out of the airport and into the black car waiting for me outside. As we pulled away, I tore into *The Guardian*. The article about Victoria and G. Malone was above the fold. I devoured it, trying to figure out who'd leaked the story. I didn't personally know any of the people quoted. Most were stylists and fashion industry insiders commenting on what an "outside of the box" choice G. Malone was. I threw the paper onto the seat and dug for my phone. There was only one person I could think of who could've outed us. The only person outside of my small, intimate circle who knew we were designing Victoria's dress. Gideon picked up on the second ring.

"Hello?" he said through a yawn.

"It's Gigi."

"What a nice morning surprise—although, what time is it for you? Three a.m.? Is this a booty call?"

"How much did you sell the story for?" I asked.

"What? What story?"

I took off my sunglasses and laid them on my lap. "Oh, don't play stupid with me. How much?"

"Am I still asleep? I literally have no idea what you are talking about?"

"It's everywhere. Everyone knows. I got off the plane, and it's the headline of every newspaper and magazine."

"Plane to where? Now you've completely lost me."

"London. I'm in London," I practically screamed into the phone.

"You're in London? That's fantastic. When can I see you?"

I dug my fingernails into the leather seat. "How 'bout a quarter past never."

"I'm so confused. Why are you so cross?"

"You told the press G. Malone's designing Victoria Ellicott's dress."

"I certainly did not."

"Then who did? Only a handful of people knew!"

His voice softened. "I didn't say a word, Georgica."

There was something in his tone and the way he sighed into the phone. I believed him. I heard a beep on the line and pulled the phone down to see who was calling.

I put the phone back to my ear. "Gemma's trying to get through. Can I call you back?"

"I don't know. Will you actually call me back?"

"Yes. I promise. I believe you. I'm sorry I overreacted."

"You can make it up to me with dinner tomorrow night. I'll come into town from Highclere."

"I might be on the first flight back to New York after Victoria fires me."

"She won't sack you. Just tell her the truth. That you don't know how it got leaked."

"That is the truth. I really don't know how it got leaked. I should take this call. I'll be in touch later." I hung up and switched over to Gemma. I took a deep breath and answered. "This is Georgica."

"Georgica, this is Gemma Landry."

"Hello, Gemma," I said in my most upbeat voice.

"How quickly can you be at Victoria's?"

"I'm in a cab now and heading to the hotel."

"Don't go to the hotel. Come straight here. Victoria wants to meet with you as soon as possible," she said before abruptly hanging up the call.

I started to dial Jamie but remembered it was only three a.m. back in New York. He'd certainly be sleeping, and even if I woke him, it'd take him at least a good half hour to be awake enough to help me piece together exactly what had happened. I turned off my phone, slipped my sunglasses back on, leaned back, and readied myself for the storm waiting for me in South Kensington.

Chapter Eleven

The taxi stopped in front of the Ellicotts' home in Kensington as I dug through my tote to find my wallet.

"Swanky address," the driver said.

"Uh-huh," I muttered as I pulled out my remaining pounds.

"Who lives here? Famous movie star or something?"

"Not a movie star, no," I answered.

"Then why all the paparazzi?" he asked.

I ducked down. "Shit. Where?"

He leaned forward on the steering wheel and pointed. "There are two there behind the lamppost and another one back by that hedge."

I peeked my head up. "They've got the house surrounded, all right."

"Are you the movie star? You look kind of familiar."

I passed him the money. "Me? No. I'm nobody."

I jumped out of the car and tore inside the gates before even one camera could get its flash off. Gemma was waiting for me in the vestibule.

"Victoria and Margaret are in the sunroom," she said sternly.

I nodded and made my way down the long hallway to them. When I walked in, Victoria and Margaret were already seated next to each other on the large toile settee. I parked my carry-on in the corner of the room and sat down in the miniature armchair across from them. Victoria gestured toward the tea set sitting in the center of the small table between us. I stood up, poured myself a cup, and sat back down.

"I hope your trip over was pleasant," Margaret said.

I took a small sip of tea and swallowed hard. "Yes, very pleasant."

"And the paparazzi outside wasn't too intrusive?"

"I made a mad dash to your door," I said, smiling. Neither one of their expressions lightened up.

Victoria cleared her throat. "I assume you know why you're here, Gigi?"

I fumbled with the teacup and saucer and placed it back on the table. "Of course, and I want to explain."

Victoria rose from her seat. "Annabelle, darling, come join us in here," she said.

I swiveled around in my seat. All five foot ten inches of Annabelle Ellicott was walking into the sunroom to join her mother and sister.

"As I was saying, I'd like to give my side of things," I said.

"I'm not going to mince words here, Gigi. I was incredibly disappointed to wake up and discover the whole world knows G. Malone's designing my wedding gown," Victoria said.

I let the fact she said *is* designing my wedding gown rather than *was* designing my wedding gown hang in the air for a moment before I responded. Finally, I said, "I can only imagine."

"As you know, I was hoping to keep my decision a secret a bit longer."

I looked over at Annabelle. She was daintily holding her cup of tea, nibbling on a biscuit. Her bouncy blowout was lying perfectly across her delicate shoulders.

"I can only tell you we've done everything possible to maintain discretion. I didn't even tell our Global Director for Brand Events we were chosen. Not only does she live for this sort of thing, but it would have been beneficial to tell her as soon as we signed the contract so that she could begin planning our brand's publicity strategy. But I didn't. I promise, I really don't have the first clue who let the cat of the bag. Maybe our phones were tapped? Jamie told me the paparazzi's been known to do that here."

Margaret chimed in. "It's done now. The news has been splashed everywhere."

I turned to face Victoria. "I understand if you want to break the contract with G. Malone. We didn't breach it, but I would understand."

"She doesn't want to break the contract," Annabelle said.

"The press is going wild over my pick of G. Malone. Anna Wintour herself called to congratulate me on my bold decision to go with a little-known up-and-coming designer rather than a more established house like Valentino or De La Renta."

We did design a winning Oscar gown. Up-and-coming isn't necessarily accurate, I thought to myself. "That's great news."

Gemma walked in from the room's entranceway. "We're fine to address the choice with the press as long as the actual wedding dress design doesn't get out."

"I promise to guard it all with my life," I said.

It was an easy promise to make, considering that at the moment, I didn't have much in the way of designs or sketches anyway.

Victoria relaxed her pose and smiled. "Good. I'm so glad this is settled."

"You must want to get to your hotel to check in and freshen up?" Margaret said.

"That'd be great. I'll plan on returning here at two like we planned?"

Annabelle stood up. "I'll walk Gigi out." Annabelle sidled up to me as we made our way back to the vestibule. "Mother and Victoria are always a bit dramatic. I hope you aren't too put off by everything."

"I stepped off the plane and saw my face plastered all over the airport. Hard not be a bit put off. I'm glad Victoria's willing to give us another chance though."

"Unfortunately, our whole family's had to get used to it since Victoria and Alexander put us on the map. It's part of the reason I don't want my relationship with Perry to be too public just yet.

"I can understand."

She smiled. "And I wish you'd told me we have a friend in common."

My stomach dropped. "Who's that?"

"Alicia Scheinman. She sent me a note over the weekend."

"Oh, right, she told me you two did a training program together a few years ago."

"She was so in love with our boss. We all thought she was going to move to London, but then she shocked us all by deciding to get back together with her ex. What was his name?"

"Joshua," I answered.

"That's right. Joshua. But that's not the man she ended up marrying, right?"

"No. She married someone else."

"Small world. And I hear you've been seeing a lot of Gideon Cooper?"

I jerked my head up. "What? No. I mean, yes, we have seen each other a few times. Where'd you hear that?"

"His sister. Linney and I go way back to boarding school at Mayfield. She wanted a little inside scoop on who has her brother all goggle-eyed."

"And what'd you tell her?"

"That you're absolutely lovely."

I checked into my hotel room and threw myself across the bed. Between the overnight flight and my chaotic morning, I needed a few minutes of shut-eye to get through the rest of the day. I hit the do-not-disturb button on the hotel phone and burrowed into the pile of feathered pillows at the top of the bed. My eyes had been closed for maybe two minutes when my cell phone rang. I rolled over, reached across the bed, hit the end call button, and rolled back. A few seconds later it rang again. I grunted and slid over to answer it.

"Hello?" I mumbled.

"Can you believe it? You're on the cover of *The Daily Telegraph, The Guardian, The Observer,* and *The Daily Mail*. And those are *just* the British papers."

"Jordana?" I murmured.

"When I sent out the press release last night, I had no idea it would get traction this quickly."

I quickly sat up and leaned back into the headboard. "*You* sent out the press release?"

"Of course. I knew it would be a big deal, but this is crazy. Oh my God, G. Malone's trending on Twitter," she screeched.

I got off the bed and began pacing around the room. "Why did you put out a press release? Who told you G. Malone was designing Victoria's dress?"

"Duh. You did, Gigi."

"No, I didn't."

"What, were you so drunk you don't remember?" she said, laughing.

It all came back to me like a flash—Jamie handing me his phone at the bar to tell Jordana we wouldn't be coming into the office and my subsequent rant about Perry's billboard in Times Square. Jordana trying to talk me off the ledge by rattling off a list of G. Malone's accomplishments and what an honor it was to even be in the running to design Victoria Ellicott's wedding dress. Then me telling her we'd already been chosen but leaving out the part that it was to be kept a secret. I'd been the one to breach the contract. Not Gideon, not Jordana—me. I spilled the beans.

I slapped my hand against my forehead and said softly, "I remember now."

"Now? What does that mean?"

"Nothing. Have you spoken to Jamie yet?"

"Not yet. I didn't think he'd be up this early."

"I'll give him a call."

"Great. I can cross that off my to-do list."

I couldn't help but imagine her sitting in her robe, checking things off a clipboard like when she was a counselor at Chinooka. "It's five a.m. in New York. How do you have a to-do list already?"

"I woke up to over fifty emails from publications and entertainment shows looking for comments or quotes from G. Malone. I think I'm gonna skip Flywheel this morning and head straight to the office."

"Jord, take a breath, okay? Maybe even try to go back to bed for a bit."

"I can't, Gigi. It's all so exciting. It's everything we've been working toward—making G. Malone a household name. Now it won't just be a household name—our little brand is going to have the spotlight of the whole world shining on it. Besides, I'm booked on the *Today* show this morning. They're doing a retrospective on royal wedding gowns and want me to comment on what direction G. Malone is going to take with Victoria's dress. What do you want me to say or not say? We should give a subtle hint about the design but also try to keep them guessing."

Considering my sketchbook was basically blank, keeping them guessing would be the easy part.

"You can say we're working to design a gown that complements Victoria's beauty and the traditions of the day."

I could hear her typing away on the other end of the phone. "Got it. That's a perfect soundbite. Okay, Gigi, I should run. I need to answer some of these emails and get over to 40 Rock for the segment. Let's debrief later."

She hung up the phone before I could even say goodbye. I cradled my head in my hands, building up the courage to call Jamie and confess that my gaffe had almost lost us the most important opportunity of our careers.

He picked up on the first ring. "Morning, or should I say afternoon? What time is it there?"

I glanced over at the antique-looking clock on the nightstand. "Almost noon."

"What time are you heading over to Kensington?"

"I was already there." I stood up from the bed. "So, I need you to not freak out about what I'm about to say."

"We got sacked, didn't we? I knew Victoria was gonna change her mind and want to wear an f-ing De La Renta. Fine. If she wants to look like every other cliché cookie-cutter bride and have that be what people remember about her, I guess that's her choice."

"What'd I just say about not freaking out?"

He huffed into the phone. "Go ahead."

"We weren't fired, but the cat's out of the bag. Everyone knows we're designing the dress."

"What?" he shrieked into the phone. "There were only a handful of people who knew. Who said something?"

I took a deep breath. "I did."

"*You* did?" he yelled back at me.

"You and I got way too drunk the other day, then we saw that marquee for Perry's show in Times Square. I guess it threw me more than I realized. I don't remember doing it, but apparently, I told Jordana about the wedding gown and then she took the story and ran with it. Our faces are all over the news. We're trending on Twitter."

"Jesus, Gigi. What'd Gemma say? Victoria?"

"They're upset the news came out so early but happy with the response it's getting. We've still got the gig if we want it?"

"What do you mean *if*? Of course, we still want it."

I laid back down on the bed. "Ignore me. I'm being stupid."

"I'm on the six p.m. flight tonight. Think you can avoid making international headlines again 'til then?" Jamie asked.

"Fingers crossed."

Chapter Twelve

Eight hours later, I found myself waiting for Gideon outside of Bob Bob Ricard, one of London's trendiest restaurants. He hopped out of a taxi and rushed to greet me with a long kiss—the kind you give to someone you haven't seen in months, not days. He smelled like the English countryside, fresh and clean.

He took my hand and led me inside the restaurant. It had a great roaring '20s décor and unique little touches like the 'press for champagne' buzzers at each booth.

"You know I'm just as happy with folding chairs and paper tablecloths," I said.

"Oh, I know, but since I haven't found a place to best your Chinese food yet, I figured I'd impress you with décor."

I pointed to the sign. "And a press-for-champagne buzzer."

He winked at me. "Well, that goes without saying."

The hostess sat us at a small electric-blue booth close to the bar. She handed us each a menu and encouraged us to press the tableside buzzer. I reached over Gideon's arm and pushed on it twice.

"Is this what it's like at Badgley Hall?" I asked.

"Do we have champagne flowing in every room of the house? No, we don't."

"I meant that on *Downton Abbey* they had that bell board in the servants' hall. The family could pull on a cord, and the staff would know which room they were needed in upstairs. A Victorian champagne buzzer if you will."

"I'm sure Badgley Hall had something like that at one time, but it's quite different living there nowadays."

The waiter came by with our two champagne flutes, and we ordered some starters. Gideon clinked his glass into mine and took a small sip.

I folded my hands on the table. "What is it like to live there nowadays? No army of staff to attend to your every need?" I teased.

He set the flute down. "We don't have any full-time staff with the exception of the groundskeeper and some other property managers." He leaned into the table. "You know, I have an idea. My parents are having a small get together this weekend, why don't you come?"

"Jamie comes into town tomorrow morning and we have back-to-back fittings with Victoria's bridal party."

He sat back again. "So, come for the weekend. Both of you."

"That feels like an imposition. I haven't even met your parents yet. It'd be strange to stay in your family's home," I said.

"The house is huge. They won't even know you're there. Invite Jamie to come along so you feel more comfortable. Unless, of course, you don't think he'd want to?"

Over the last week, Jamie had binge-watched every period drama set in England that he could get his hands on. No way he'd miss the opportunity to meet a real-life earl and countess in their natural habitat.

"I have a feeling I can talk him into it," I answered.

"Good."

The waiter brought out our baked oysters and truffled potato and mushroom vareniki. Gideon served us each some oysters and a few of the dumplings.

"Can I make a confession?" Gideon asked.

I looked up from my plate and nodded.

"I stopped by a market on my way here and bought any gossip magazine with a story about G. Malone on the cover just to see your face."

"You know what they say, don't you?"

He shook his head. "No, what do they say?"

"Today's headlines are tomorrow's fish wrap."

He snickered. "Who says that?"

"My father. It's something he likes to tell his clients. The ones in the most trouble, anyway."

"Didn't you tell me he's G. Malone's general counsel? What'd he have to say when he saw the news this morning?"

"He's our unofficial GC until we go public. *If* we ever go public."

Gideon pulled the stack of magazines out of his bag and held them up. "Oh, you'll go public, all right. You're designing the most important dress of this century. I'd be surprised if you don't have even more investors lining up as we speak."

There it was again. *The most important dress of the century.* I reached over Gideon and pressed down hard on the champagne button.

Early Saturday morning, Jamie and I left our London hotel to set out for South Gloucestershire. The agent at the car rental place told us the drive would take about two and a half hours and recommended we go with a convertible so we could really enjoy the views of the English countryside. Jamie jumped at the suggestion, hoping we could recreate his favorite scene from *Bridget Jones's Diary*, where Renee Zellweger and Hugh Grant go speeding off on their holiday with the top down.

Having been born and raised in New York City, my own driver's license now served as nothing more than identification. I hadn't driven a car in close to fifteen years, and my ineptitude had recently morphed into a full-blown fear. When we were dating, Perry had tried to reteach me. I was too afraid to practice in the city, so we borrowed my parents' car a couple of times and took it to the quiet roads in Milbank. Perry'd lean over my shoulder, directing every turn and occasionally taking hold of the wheel when I felt like the car was out of control. We'd end up pulling over and picnicking somewhere on the grounds of Camp Chinooka, which was mostly deserted during the off-season.

I tossed Jamie the keys to the car.

"You sure you don't want to drive?" he asked.

I rolled my eyes and climbed into the passenger seat. "I'm positive."

Jamie put the address into the car's navigation system and searched the radio for a station. He put the top down and handed me a baseball cap from his bag.

"Trust me," he said, putting on his own. "Otherwise we'll look like we just stepped out of a wind tunnel."

I slipped on the hat and tightened it in the back so it fit my head. "Thank you again for agreeing to come with me."

"Are you kidding? It's like we're going to Pemberley to see where Mr. Darcy lives."

"Mr. Malone, have you been reading *Pride and Prejudice?*"

Jamie handed me his phone. "Just the CliffsNotes. Tell me more about Badgley Hall. We should probably know what we're walking into."

I did a search and opened up their website. I clicked on the "House History" link and read aloud. "Badgley Hall lies in the heart of the Gloucestershire countryside and is home to the Earl and Countess of Harronsby. The House dates from the seventeenth century, and one of its most notable features is the moat that surrounds the house and immediate grounds." I looked up from the phone. "You've got to be kidding me."

Jamie raised his eyebrow. "Keep reading."

"The formal gardens cover twelve acres. They feature a yew hedge maze created in 1846 and a ridge and furrow greenhouse designed by Joseph Paxton, architect of The Crystal Palace."

I handed the phone back to Jamie. "Just turn the car around. This whole thing is ridiculous."

"What whole thing?"

"This world we're pretending to be a part of."

"Did you and I not just spend all of yesterday with the future Queen of England? We aren't pretending anything. Honey, this is real life. This could be your life—if you want it to be."

"Jamie, get a hold of yourself. Gideon and I have only been on a handful of dates."

"I know a smitten kitten when I see one, and that boy is smitten."

Close to three hours (and a couple of wrong turns) later, we passed the first sign for Badgley Hall. Jamie turned off the main road and onto a smaller one that took us past miles and miles of unspoiled woodlands until we reached the turnoff for the main estate. We snaked our way up a gravel drive leading to a stone bridge that crossed over the moat and led to the house. I used the term house loosely, as Badgley Hall could only be described as a castle, complete with three towers and stained-glass windows. Jamie stopped the car, pushed his sunglasses up over his head, and said, "Dorothy, I don't think we're in Kansas anymore."

I took in the imposing scenery and sank down in the front seat. "He grew up *here*? My six-hundred-square-foot apartment must've felt like a coffin to him."

"Or a breath of fresh air?" Jamie pointed to the massive front entranceway door, which looked like it was cracked open. "Someone's spotted us. We should get out of the car."

I removed my baseball cap and smoothed out my hair in the rearview mirror. Gideon hurried down the steps of the house to greet us with a warm, welcoming smile on his face.

"How was your trip?"

"Would've been nice if there was a Starbucks on the route, otherwise it was great," Jamie answered.

"I know. It's not like your American highways with rest stops along the way."

"I'll take rolling hills and pastoral views over the New Jersey Turnpike any day," I said.

"It really is gorgeous, isn't it? I've lived here my whole life and still find it awe-inspiring," Gideon replied. "Welcome to Badgley Hall," he said, leading us into the grand foyer.

Jamie and I set down our bags and looked straight up to the magnificent glass dome overhead.

"Gideon, this is…overwhelming. The moat and grounds were one thing, but this is too much."

"I promise, it'll get far less intimidating the farther into the house you go. My parents are waiting to have tea with us in the library." Gideon took my hand and led me down the hall.

I stopped in my tracks. "Your parents? How should I address them? How do you address them?"

"Well, I call them Mum and Dad, which you are more than welcome to do."

I shot him a look, letting him know that was less than helpful advice.

He scratched his chin. "The proper address, I suppose, would be Lord and Lady Harronsby, but quite honestly, they'd be more than comfortable with George and Amelia."

"Isn't there an option that falls somewhere in between those?" I looked over to Jamie for some support.

Jamie shrugged. "Just avoid using their names. It'll be like a game."

Gideon looked at us like we were both crazy and moved to hold open the door to the library, a gorgeous sunlit room with a roaring fireplace and shelves and shelves of antique books. The floor-to-ceiling windows looked out to the largest of the property's gardens. On the walls were portraits of people I had to assume were the past earls of Harronsby, and the ceilings were covered in frescoes by Italian masters.

I leaned in and whispered in Gideon's ear, "You're right. This is *muuucchhh* less impressive."

He smirked and put his hand on the small of my back to lead me farther into the room. "Mum. Dad. This is Georgica Goldstein and Jamie Malone."

A couple close in age to my own parents stood up to greet us. I could immediately see Gideon had inherited his coloring from his father, and his more striking features, like his piercing green-gray eyes and wide smile, from his mother.

"Nice to meet you both," I said, shaking hands with each of them, relieved Gideon had saved me from having to address them by name.

"Please, take a seat." Gideon's mother pointed to the small couch across from them. Jamie and I barely fit on it together.

"Gideon tells us you're from New York?" she asked.

"I am. I was born and raised there."

"I'm from a small town in Georgia, but I've lived in New York City so long now I consider it my home," Jamie said.

"And Georgica, your father's a top barrister?" Gideon's father chimed in from the far side of the room.

"He's a partner at a well-known law firm."

Gideon stood up to pour Jamie and me a cup of tea.

"Milk? Sugar?" he asked.

"Just milk, thank you," I replied.

"I'll take mine black unless you have two percent," Jamie said.

Gideon picked up the creamer. "The milk's from a farm on property."

I squeezed Jamie hard on the leg.

"Just black is fine," Jamie answered.

Gideon's mother gave me a small smile. "I hear you're designing Victoria Ellicott's wedding gown. That's quite wonderful. Have you always been into fashion?"

"No, not always," I answered. "I was overweight as a girl, so I started designing my own clothes when I couldn't find options in the stores I liked or that fit."

This time, Jamie squeezed my leg.

"I guess it was sometime during university that it became more of a career path and, of course, then I was on *Top Designer*, which sealed it."

"*Top Designer*? What's that?" Gideon's father asked.

"It's a reality show. A design competition," Gideon answered.

"It's where Jamie and I met," I said.

Gideon's mother picked up her teacup. "Did you win?"

"Uh, no. I didn't," I said.

"We don't watch much television anyway," she said.

I gestured to the windows. "Why would you when you're surrounded by such gorgeous scenery? Your home is incredible. It's breathtaking, really."

Gideon's mother stood and walked over to the window. "Yes, thank you. It's quite a lot to maintain, but we love it here."

"I can certainly see why." My eyes wandered over the intricate crown molding and the ornate patterns of the decorative tapestries.

Jamie set his tea down on a side table and turned to Gideon. "How does it work with the public? How do they explore a house you're actually living in?"

"Right now, the house is open during the week from April to October by guided tour only," Gideon answered.

"Is it strange to have people come in and out of your house like it's a museum?" Jamie asked.

"Not anymore," Gideon's father said. "We retreat to the family wing and try not to get mistaken for ghosts. Besides, Gideon has big plans to market the house for films and other events, so we better get used to it."

Gideon sat down in a large armchair beside us. "There's been a surge of interest in these houses for period dramas like your beloved *Downton Abbey*. I want to see Badgley House get its due. And what could be a more beautiful setting for a wedding than our gardens? We have to make money for the property or we'll be forced to sell."

"It's not as desperate as all that, yet, so let's try to enjoy a lovely weekend with your guests without all this talk of finances, shall we?" his mother said. "Gideon, why don't you show Georgica and Jamie to their rooms, and let's plan to congregate back here at six for drinks and hors d'oeuvres. I invited Linney and a few other friends to join us for dinner."

Gideon led us to the main staircase. I followed closely behind him while Jamie lingered at the foot of the stairs.

I walked back down to see what was holding him up.

"Hey, what are you doing?" I whispered.

"Waiting for Carson to ring the gong so we know to put on our formal dinner clothes?"

I hit Jamie softly on the behind. "Let's go, Lord Malone."

"After you, m'lady."

Chapter Thirteen

Later that evening, Gideon knocked on my door to escort me to dinner. He was wearing a perfectly tailored three-piece suit I immediately recognized as Ermenegildo Zegna, one of Jamie's favorite menswear designers. He'd slicked back his auburn hair just slightly, and for the first time since we met, was sporting a completely clean-shaven face. The rugged quality I'd come to associate with him had been replaced with a handsome and distinguished-looking man. I caught myself staring and quickly averted my attention to the bracelet I was struggling to close on my own. Gideon softly took hold of my wrist, fastened it, and gently kissed my hand.

I took a few steps closer to the full-length standing mirror in the corner of the room.

I smoothed out the one cocktail dress I'd packed. "I hope I look okay. You didn't tell me it was going to be a formal dinner party."

I'd accused Jamie of having a *Downton-Abbey*-induced freak out when he forced me to throw the dress into my suitcase. Now, I was extremely appreciative of his commitment to authenticity.

"You look great." Gideon took a seat on the bed. "I've been spending so much time at Highclere, I haven't been home in a while, let alone home with a girlfriend. I think my parents are just excited and decided to step things up a notch."

I turned from the mirror to face him. "Girlfriend?"

He looked up at me. "Oh, you caught that one? I thought it might just slide through."

I sat down next to him on the bed. "I like you a lot, Gideon. I think you know that. But we just…" my voice trailed off.

"We just met," he said, finishing my thought. "I know. And I also know you were very much in love with somebody else for a very long time."

"This isn't about him."

"Of course, it is. I'm the poor bloke who has to follow in the footsteps of Perry Gillman."

I rubbed Gideon's forearm. "If it's any consolation, he wasn't *that* guy when I met him. He was a summer camp counselor in the backwoods of Milbank, Pennsylvania."

"We can take it slow, Gigi. As slow as you want to. Just think about it," Gideon said.

"I promise I will," I answered.

Jamie peeked his head into the room to check to see if we were ready to go down to dinner. He was wearing his Tom Ford blue velvet smoking jacket with black satin lapels and matching pants. He only wore that suit on very special occasions and looked every inch in character.

I picked my wrap off the bed. "If I don't have the two most handsome dates tonight, I'll be very surprised. You both look amazing."

Gideon took my arm. "Shall we?"

We walked down the candlelit mahogany stairway to the library where some of Gideon's parents' guests had begun to congregate. Servers were walking around the room offering glasses of champagne and hors d'oeuvres.

I nudged Gideon in his side. "I thought you said you didn't have an army of staff?"

He leaned in and whispered in my ear, "It's called a catering service."

"Ahh," I said, picking up a flute.

We inched our way farther into the room, and Gideon introduced me to several of his parents' friends. It was obvious they traveled in a very specific social circle that included some of England's most prominent families. A few people recognized Jamie and me from the week's headlines and wanted to hear more about our plans for Victoria Ellicott's wedding gown. I quickly put down my champagne flute. In this crowd, it would be best if I stayed stone-cold sober and didn't risk any more slip-ups. I stood up on my tiptoes to look for Jamie and spotted him talking to Linney, Gideon's sister, and a few of her girlfriends. After another half hour or so of mingling, Gideon's father announced we should start making our way to the dining room for dinner.

Gideon and I found our place cards and took seats in the middle of the table beside his parents. Jamie sat down to the right of me, and the rest of the guests milled around, finding their assigned places. Just as I noticed the two empty chairs at the far end of the table, Jamie kicked me hard in the shin.

I lifted my leg up to examine it. "Jesus, Jamie, I think the spikes on your Louboutin's just punctured my skin. I might be bleeding."

"Perry and Annabelle just walked in," he whispered.

I threw my leg back under the table and looked up. Annabelle and Perry were making their way to their seats.

Gideon pulled me close to him. "Linney must've invited them. I had no idea they were coming."

I pushed my hair behind my ears. "It's fine." Jamie started to fill up my wineglass, but I put my hand over it to stop him. "I don't want to be drunk," I said.

Annabelle removed her wrap to reveal a tasteful slinky black cocktail dress that hugged her body in all the right places.

"You sure about that?" Jamie murmured.

I looked up at her again and tapped the glass. "Fill 'er up."

Perry took his seat at the end of the table and unfolded his napkin into his lap. He looked over and our eyes met. Gideon's father stood up and clinked his glass, breaking our gaze. Everyone at the table turned to face the Earl of Harronsby.

"Looking around the table, I see some old familiar faces and some new familiar faces. Amelia and I are delighted to welcome all of you to Badgley Hall. We are especially pleased Mr. Perry Gillman was able to join us straight off the stage at Her Majesty's Theater."

The room turned to look at Perry, who shifted uncomfortably in his chair, his face flushing.

"How many Olivier Awards is *Elizabeth* up for?" Gideon's father asked.

Perry cleared his throat. "Twelve, sir."

The table politely applauded his answer.

Gideon waited for the clapping to die down, then stood up next to his father. "A few of the Badgley Hall docents have graciously volunteered to give tours of the house and gardens this evening after dinner, for anyone interested in learning more about the house's rich history. I hope you take them up on their offer. For now, though, please enjoy dinner."

Gideon and his father both sat back down, and the servers brought out the first course—shrimp cocktail in antique frosted glass bowls.

I looked over at Perry, who was whispering something into Annabelle's ear. His wavy, dark hair was pulled back, emphasizing his chiseled features and long lashes. Jamie caught me staring.

He prodded me. "Gigi, your shrimp cocktail's gonna get…er… cold."

I turned my attention to my plate, using the small cocktail fork to pick up a shrimp. My hands were trembling so hard the fork dropped from my hands, crashing into the glass bowl. The entire table turned at the clang. Gideon clasped my hand and guided it under the table, where he held it firmly until it stopped shaking. Soup came next and I knew better than to even attempt it.

An hour and a half and several courses later, dinner finally ended. The guests retreated to the drawing room for after-dinner drinks. When Gideon went to see about organizing the docents for the house tours, I pulled Jamie over to the quietest corner of the room.

"When everyone takes off to explore the house, I'm just gonna sneak off to my room."

"You know Gideon's doing all this for you. To impress you. The dinner. The tours. It's all for you."

Jamie's words hung in the air as Annabelle came up behind him. I scanned the room for Perry and let out a breath when I saw him over by the fireplace, deep in conversation with Gideon's father.

"Lovely to see you both. Linney just invited us this morning, or I would've mentioned it at the fitting yesterday," Annabelle said.

"Perry was able to take the night off from *Elizabeth*?" Jamie asked.

"He's been pulling back on his performing schedule a bit since he'll be moving to Broadway in a few months."

"That's right, Gigi and I saw the marquee in Times Square just the other day. Didn't we, Gigi?"

"We did," I mumbled.

"It's all very exciting," she said, her eyes wide and shining with possibilities. "We're going in a few weeks to look at some apartments for when we move."

"We? You're both moving to New York?" I asked.

"It's easy enough for me to transfer to my company's New York office. I want to be as supportive as possible," she said.

I felt like she just sucker punched me in the stomach. In the beginning, Perry had pleaded with me to move to London while he was writing *Elizabeth*, but I couldn't leave G. Malone and everything I was trying to build. After years of flailing, I'd just found my way back to solid ground. I'd finally broken through my creative block and was pumping out some of my best designs. I was angry at Perry for assuming his work was somehow more important than my own and naively believing we'd find our way back together after we took time apart. Instead, we imploded.

Gideon came into the drawing room and announced the house tours would be setting off in a few minutes. He asked us to divide into groups of four and make our way into the entrance hall.

Annabelle excused herself to return to Perry, and Jamie leaned into me.

"You okay, kiddo?" he asked.

"I think I'll head upstairs," I said.

Gideon found his way over to us. He put his hand on top of my shoulder. "There you two are. I know this is uncomfortable for you, so go with the first group and I'll push Perry and Annabelle over to the third."

"Great," I said.

"Great," Gideon repeated and went to find them.

"What happened to going upstairs?" Jamie asked.

"You're right. I don't want to hurt Gideon. He's gone to a lot of trouble. I'll just take the tour and then head off."

"Well, I think I'll go join group two, far away from both you and Perry," Jamie said. "I actually want to learn about Badgley Hall."

I laughed and shook my head.

"What?" Jamie asked.

"You fought me tooth and nail about going to Highclere Castle for the *Downton Abbey* tour, and now you're a full-fledged Anglophile."

He leaned in and kissed me on the cheek. "When in Rome... or South Gloucestershire..."

I joined Group One as they were making their way up the main staircase to some of the bedrooms off the first-floor gallery. The docent took us through the bedrooms no longer in use by the family because of their historical significance. The first and most impressive was the room Henry VIII and Anne Boleyn had supposedly stayed in on their honeymoon tour. The walls were a deep crimson, and the four-poster canopy bed was draped with the most beautiful gossamer fabric. I snapped a picture of it on my phone for the inspiration board Jamie had put together for the royal wedding.

The docent led us back downstairs while reciting information about the servants' hall. Gideon had told me before *Downton Abbey*, nobody was particularly interested in viewing the downstairs quarters of these grand houses. After the airing of the show, it was the most requested tour. Gideon recently oversaw a full historical renovation to bring the kitchen back to its more original state, hoping it would be an additional draw for the house. I knew he was looking forward to showing off his achievement.

As we filed down the corridor, I could hear someone playing piano on the main floor of the house. I knew immediately it was Perry. Like the Sirens of Greek mythology who lured sailors to nearby shipwrecks with their enchanting music, I found myself called to him. I turned down the hallway and into the music room. Perry was alone, seated at the Baby Grand Steinway, head down, his fingers flying over the keys.

I slowly tiptoed into the room. "Debussy? Brahams?"

He stopped playing and looked up at me. "Gershwin, Gigi, always Gershwin."

"Seems like sometime soon the world will be saying that about Gillman."

He pushed his hair back and out of his eyes. "I don't know about that."

"I do," I said softly. I leaned down and touched his face. "It's been a long time since I saw you with your hair and beard this long."

"It's for Dudley—and with the transfer to Broadway, it doesn't look like I'll be able to cut it anytime soon."

"I like it. Reminds me of when you played The Fiddler at Chinooka."

He closed his eyes and sighed. "Chinooka." Then, as if snapped right back into reality, he said, "Annabelle told me we were going to dinner at her close friend's home. I didn't know this was the home until we pulled past the sign for Badgley Hall."

I walked to the far window. It looked out onto a large hedge maze that stretched far across the property. Even from this distance, I could see the maze was huge, dense, and complex. I wondered how long anyone had spent lost in it before they found their way to the center and eventually out the other side.

I turned to face Perry. He was still seated at the bench, his eyes firmly on my face.

"Back at Chinooka, you pleaded with me to be honest with Alicia about everything that had happened between Joshua and me. You said there'd be no closure for any of us without it. It's the same now, isn't it? You need to tell Annabelle who I am, so we can all move on."

"Is that what you want? To move on?" He stood up from the bench. "Never mind. The returned engagement ring answered that question for me ages ago."

"I just admitted what you were too much of a coward to say. We were done. There was no reason to keep pretending otherwise."

"No. You gave up on us," he growled.

"*You* gave up on us. With every unanswered call and each day that passed, you retreated farther and farther into your work. You forgot about the life we were building together, or maybe you decided along the way you wanted a different one. Well, congratulations. Annabelle told me she's moving to New York to be with you when the show opens on Broadway, so it looks like you two are all set."

From the far corner of the room, someone cleared their throat. We both squinted to make out who it was. Gideon emerged from the shadowy doorway and stepped into the moonlit room.

"I heard voices. I wanted to check to make sure nobody strayed too far from their tour," Gideon said.

"Sorry, mate. I saw the piano and couldn't help myself," Perry said.

"It's fine. We'll attach a plaque that says, '*Perry Gillman once played here,*' and we can charge more for the tour of the staterooms."

I appreciated Gideon's attempt to bring some levity to an awkward moment.

Gideon looked at his watch. "The docents should be wrapping up. I'll go check on the other guests and let the two of you finish up in here."

"Seems like a good guy," Perry said after Gideon was out of earshot.

"He is," I answered.

"And this place suits you, Princess," he said, using his provoking nickname for me from when we first met at Chinooka.

"Princess?"

"No, I guess you're right. Countess is probably more appropriate now," he said, brushing past me as he walked out of the room.

Later, after the rest of the guests retired for the night, Gideon came to see me. He knocked softly, and I got down off the bed and let him in. He was carrying a small tray with a brandy decanter and two glasses. He set them down on the nightstand.

"I thought you could use a nightcap."

"Yeah? Whatever gave you that idea?" I said with a half-smile.

He poured brandy into each of the glasses and handed me one. We clinked them together and each took a small sip.

Gideon took a seat on the bench at the end of the bed, grabbed my hand, and guided me beside him. He pushed my hair behind my shoulders.

"How you holding up?" he asked.

"Well, considering my ex-fiancé and his girlfriend are sleeping a few doors down from here, not too bad."

"Don't worry. I put them up on the other side of the house in the East Wing." He leaned in and whispered, "Rumor has it, it's haunted."

I smiled. "Why are you being so understanding about all this?"

"If you think it's easy to sit across the table from the guy who just graced the cover of *Rolling Stone* magazine and not feel like a massive wanker, it isn't. But, I like you, and I think you like me, and if we're going to have any shot at this, I'll just have to accept our paths are going to cross with theirs."

"Maybe not for too long. Perry's moving to New York in a few months. So is Annabelle."

"New York's not much bigger than London as far as certain social circles go," he said.

"I know that."

"Look, the question I asked you earlier tonight. Forget it. There's no reason to rush. I'm happy just getting to know you better and taking it as slowly as you need me to."

"Are you saying this because of what you walked in on with Perry and me?"

"It's obvious you still have feelings for him. Maybe it isn't love, but it's clear whatever he said tonight hurt you. It's written all over your face."

I looked down, afraid of what else my eyes might give away.

Gideon caressed my cheek, sliding his hand down so it cupped my chin. He pulled my face toward him and leaned up to kiss my forehead.

"Get some sleep. We'll talk more tomorrow," he whispered and left to go back to his own room.

I slid down into the big four-poster bed and stared up at the green crushed velvet canopy.

I closed my eyes and swore I could hear Gershwin's *Rhapsody in Blue* coming from the salon, its evocative melody creeping up the grand staircase and into my room.

Gideon was wrong. It wasn't just the East Wing that was haunted. This whole house was full of ghosts.

Chapter Fourteen

The next morning, all my bags were packed and ready to go before the sun was even up. I knocked on Jamie's door, hoping he'd be awake and we could make our apologies and leave before breakfast. I'd make my excuses to Gideon later, but for now, it was better to get as far away from Perry as possible. I knocked a few times, but Jamie didn't answer. I tiptoed into the room. Jamie was strewn across the bed, wearing nothing but boxer briefs. I tapped his shoulder. He grunted, rolled over, and burrowed deeper into the bed.

"Jamie," I whispered.

"Go away," he muffled through a pillow.

"I think we should get going back to London," I said.

He lifted his head and looked at the clock on the fireplace mantle. "It's six fifteen. Go away."

"We'll beat all the city traffic if we leave now."

He reached over to the nightstand and tossed a set of keys at me. "Drive yourself then. I'll take the train or catch a ride with someone later," he said.

I tossed them back at him. "You know I don't drive."

He grudgingly sat up and rubbed his eyes. "You can drive, you just don't like to. There's a difference. What's wrong?"

I sat down on the end of the bed. "Gideon has a full day of activities planned for everyone. *Everyone.*"

"Everyone? So, Perry and Annabelle are sticking around?"

"I was too afraid to ask Gideon. I didn't want him to think I care."

"But obviously you do care."

"Only because Annabelle doesn't know anything about our past. The more time we all spend together the more likely it is the truth is going to come out and then what?"

"Exactly and then what?" Jamie repeated back to me. "Christ, Gi, if you say something now it's going to look like you and Perry conspired to keep it a secret. You have to find a time and way to talk to Victoria about all this. I can't even imagine the shitstorm if the press gets wind of this before you've had a chance to come clean."

"I'll figure something out."

"You better. For both our sakes."

Jamie laid back down and rolled onto his side. I crawled into bed beside him. He handed me a pillow and I propped it underneath my head.

"Gideon asked me to be his girlfriend. I told him I needed some time to think about it."

"He's a good-looking, well-mannered member of the British aristocracy and he *really* likes you. What's to think about?

"I don't mean his pedigree. If he didn't have a title. If we weren't waking up in his..." I looked around before I finished my sentence. "Castle."

Jamie smirked and rolled back over to face me. "If you want to go back to London, I'll take you to the station later, but I think you should stay. Get to know Gideon better. Figure out how to answer his question."

I kissed Jamie on his forehead. "You're an incredible friend. You're going to be a wonderful father."

"I appreciate that. Now get out of my bed and my room. I need my beauty rest."

I left Jamie and went back to my room for my sketchbook before making my way outside to the gardens. The morning fog had just lifted, revealing meandering stone paths, bright pockets of flowers, and deep green lawns. I sat down on a wrought iron bench to take in the breathtaking scenery. There was so much to be inspired by—the grand house, the exquisite gardens, the rolling countryside—yet when I put pencil to paper, nothing.

I closed my eyes and couldn't help but imagine Victoria Ellicott standing at the back of Westminster Abbey, waiting to meet Prince Alexander at the altar. Seated along the aisles were foreign royals, celebrities, politicians, diplomats, family, and friends, all of them anxiously anticipating the bride in her show-stopping gown. The whole world gathered outside the church, clamoring to get a photograph of the iconic dress as Victoria emerged from the church an actual princess.

How could any design possibly measure up to the significance of that moment?

I tucked the pencil back into the sketchbook and leaned back to await a stroke of brilliance. Anything to pull me out of my block.

"Let's have a look," said a voice from above me.

Perry walked around the bench and sat down beside me. He was holding a composition notebook and pencil.

"What are you doing up this early?"

"I have some rewrites to do for when the show moves to Broadway. Apparently, the producers think I need to fill in more of the blanks for American audiences."

His dark, curly hair was held back with a blue bandanna, and he was wearing a beat-up T-shirt with the *Elizabeth* logo. He looked just like he had when I met him that first day at Chinooka, even down to the army-green cargo shorts. My breath caught in my throat. It was one thing to keep running into him in formal settings, both of us dressed to the nines, pretending to fit into our posh surroundings. It was quite another to see him like this, stripped of all formality. He was the Perry I fell in love with in the middle of the Poconos woods.

I laid my sketchbook on the ground. "Maybe you'll have better luck. I'm in a bit of designer's block. I thought coming out here might help."

He motioned to the house and hedge maze. "Something about this view has to be inspiring."

I shook my head. "I'm not sure I connect with it. Who lives like this?"

"Your boyfriend," he said flatly.

"You forget, I've been to your girlfriend's house. The views from there aren't half bad. Anyway, he isn't my boyfriend."

"No?"

My jaw clenched. "Even if he was, we're long past you having the right to care."

I bent to pick the sketch pad off the ground. I hugged it close to my body and turned from Perry.

He stood up, put his hand on my shoulder, and said, "Of course, I care."

That was rich coming from the man who'd unloaded our relationship woes in the *New York Times*. I spun on my heels and looked him straight in the eye.

"'Some romances are intense and wonderful but simply doomed from the start.' I'm paraphrasing a bit, but I think that was the quote you gave the *Times* about us, right?"

"Christ, Gigi, you read that?"

I crossed my arms over my chest. "It's the *New York Times*, Perry. *Everyone* read it. I especially appreciated having my mother quote it back to me verbatim."

"When I spoke to the reporter, I wasn't thinking about you *or* your mother. I wasn't thinking at all."

I shrugged my shoulders. "It's how you feel. I only wish you'd have shared it with me *before* the rest of the world—would've saved us both a lot of heartache."

"*Elizabeth* got so big so fast. I know I haven't handled all of it well." He rubbed the soft stubble on his face. "You know what I wish sometimes? That I could disappear back to Chinooka for the summer. That's crazy, right? I have everything I ever wanted..." His voice trailed off.

Almost immediately, he realized the callousness of his words and reached out to comfort me. I took two steps away from where he stood.

"That summer at Chinooka feels like a dream to me now," I said softly. "One of those amazing, once-every-so-often dreams where everything goes right and you wake up a new person. A few hours later, you can't even recall most of the dream anymore. But you hold onto that feeling as long as you can, savoring the little bits you do remember until eventually those fade away too and you're happy just to have had the dream at all. Perry, why haven't you told Annabelle about us? Really?"

"I should've. When we met, I told her I'd just come out of a long-term relationship, but I didn't tell her much beyond that and Annabelle never asked." Perry took two steps toward me and took hold of my hands. "That night in the club I panicked. I knew you were in the running to design Victoria's gown and I didn't want our past to mess it up for you."

I didn't know who to believe. The Perry who'd been by my side for four years cheering me on through each professional accomplishment. My unofficial collaborator, so sure of my talent and future success, he left no room for doubt. Or, the Perry who'd walked away from our partnership, convinced he'd be better off on his own.

I searched Perry's deep brown eyes for answers to the dozens of questions that had tortured me since we broke off our engagement. He closed his eyes and then as if forgetting where we were and the implications should we be spotted, Perry grabbed me by my shoulders and pulled me against his broad chest. I struggled against his hold, afraid of feeling too at ease in it. He whispered my name and I all but crumpled in his arms. He ran his fingers through my hair and kissed me hard. His beard grated against my skin, prickly and soft all at once—like Perry. I gripped his T-shirt in my hands as he drew me even closer.

I looked up into his eyes again but this time found myself staring at a reflection of my former self. The girl who, four years ago, almost extinguished everything good in her life by letting desire and lust overwhelm all reason. I was a guest in Gideon's home. Annabelle was sleeping a few yards away. This wasn't just reckless, it was selfish and I wouldn't be that person again. I pulled away from Perry's grasp.

Perry reached for my arm. "Gigi, please."

"Let me go!"

I ripped myself from his grip and hurried as far from Perry as I could. He called my name over and over again, but I refused to look back. Moments later, I was in the thick of the yew hedge maze, no clue where I'd come in and even less of an idea of how to get out. I walked down the pathways and passageways, moving deeper and deeper into the enclosure. I sprang up on my tiptoes, trying to locate any landmarks that might help me find my way, but the hedges extended well over my head. After several more wrong turns and dead ends, I was at the midpoint of the maze, staring up at a large fountain where water spewed from a statue of Janus, the Roman god of beginnings, transitions, and time.

When the Metropolitan Museum of Art opened its Greek and Roman wing a few years ago, I became a regular visitor of the galleries. Their gold bust of the god Janus was a favorite of mine. Depicted as having two faces looking in opposite ways, the sculpture was in the exact center of the gallery as if welcoming every sightseer—its younger face looking toward the past and its older face looking toward the future. I made a habit of greeting him on each and every visit.

Here in the Badgley Hall maze, Janus was gazing in each possible direction that might lead out from it. I peered left and right, trying to work out the correct route, but the passages looked nearly identical. I sat down on the edge of the fountain and thought back to what the docent had said about how these mazes were at one time used for secret romantic *rendez-vous* between the British aristocracy and their less-than-suitable lovers. I wondered how many had lost their way in these walls before realizing they preferred what they had on the other side?

I stood up and glanced in each direction again. Unless I wanted to camp for the night, I'd have to make a decision about which way to go. I started to walk toward one of the passageways and thought I heard Gideon's voice way off in the distance. Or was it Perry's?

I looked up at Janus, hoping for a sign, and then heard the voice again, louder and clearer this time. It was Gideon, crying out to me from somewhere inside the maze.

"I'm here, I'm here," I called back to him.

"Just follow my voice. I'll get you out," he yelled back. "Can you give me a landmark to help me figure out where you are?"

"I think I'm in the center. I'm standing next to the fountain and statue of Janus."

"Oh, easy then," Gideon shouted. "Go past the older face and down the passageway. Make two rights, a left, and then another right. I'll be standing there."

I followed his directions and emerged out of the last corridor. Gideon was waiting for me.

I threw my arms around him, and he yanked his cap off his head.

"My hero. How'd you know I was here?"

"The Gamekeeper saw you wander into the maze on his way down to the stream with the fishing equipment for later. He was worried you might be lost in there."

"I was stupid. I didn't have my phone or anything with me but my sketchbook. Left to my own devices, I'd have drifted around that thing for hours."

"I have a feeling you're more resourceful than that." He gestured to my sketchbook. "Get any work done?"

I turned the book to him and flipped through the empty pages. "At this rate, Victoria Ellicott may walk down the aisle naked."

"Well, that would certainly make a statement," he said with a wink.

I closed the book and tucked it under my arm. "So, fishing's on the day's itinerary?"

"Hunting, shooting, fly fishing. All part of life on these country estates. I arranged for the houseguests to get lessons this morning."

I glanced down at my feet. "I didn't bring my galoshes. Maybe I'll just hang at the house."

His expression softened. "I ran into Perry on my way out to find you. He and Annabelle are headed back to London this morning. You don't have to worry about anymore awkward encounters." He put his arm around me and pulled me close.

Without even thinking, I pulled away.

"What's wrong, Gigi?"

I squeezed my eyes closed and blurted out, "Perry kissed me. We were talking—actually fighting—and it just happened."

He rubbed the back of his neck. "I see."

"There's a lot of history, and I think he got swept up in the moment, that's all. But I wanted to be honest with you. I owe you that."

He turned from me. "You should go back inside and join the others for breakfast. I have to check on a few things."

I walked over to him. "Don't you want to talk about this?" I asked.

Gideon closed his eyes and clenched his jaw. "No."

I instantly recognized his reaction, the same one I'd seen so many times from Perry. Suppressing feelings, wanting to keep interactions brief and polite rather than causing a stir or making a scene.

I reached for his arm. "Gideon, please."

He put his flat cap back on and headed down the walkway toward the stream without another word.

The rest of the day, I wandered back and forth to the different activities Gideon had organized on the property, hoping to see him again. I fumbled my way through archery, skeet shooting, and fishing. I felt like I was back at Camp Chinooka, being forced to participate in sports I was completely hopeless at.

Jamie, however, was having the time of his life and, of course, was fully outfitted for the occasion in an elbow-patched Ralph Lauren tweed jacket, gingham-checked shirt, dark jeans, and a cap similar to the flat cap Gideon always wore.

I went down to the stream where Jamie and some of the other guests were getting a lesson in trout fly fishing. He was knee-high in the water, the instructor beside him showing him how to cast a line. I took out my phone, snapped a picture, and sent it to Thom. He'd never believe Jamie was fly fishing without the accompanying visual.

Jamie spotted me on the banks of the water and waded over. "Grab some coveralls and a pair of wellies and come join me."

I crossed my arms over my chest and shook my head. "I already flunked archery and skeet shooting."

"This is different. There's nothing to it. Stand here and enjoy the sounds of nature with me."

I eyed the muddy bank and the brackish water lapping upon the shore. "Umm…I'll enjoy them from right here, thank you."

"Gigi, stop being a princess and get in the stream with me."

I rolled my eyes and walked over to the equipment shed. I pulled on the waterproof overalls and yellow rubber wellies. I carefully trod down to a shallow part of the stream and eased my way in and over to Jamie. The instructor spotted me and brought over a pole. After giving me a quick lesson on how to cast, he moved over to check on some of the other guests.

Jamie and I stood in silence, waiting for something, anything to bite at our lines.

"How long are we supposed to stand here?" I whispered.

"I have no idea. Try to relax."

I tugged on my line. "Should we be moving around or something?"

Jamie glanced down at me. "Perry and Annabelle went back to London, right? Why so antsy?"

I didn't want to burden Jamie any more with my troubles, so I told him I was going to try to find a quiet spot to work on my sketches before heading back to the house to clean up for lunch.

I pushed my way through the current and back to the embankment where Gideon was lecturing some of the other houseguests about the type of stream we were fishing in.

He led the group down to the water. "This is a chalk stream. They get their name because they flow through chalk hills toward the sea. They're typically fairly shallow, although the ones here at Badgley Hall are a bit deeper due to our topography. There are two hundred and ten chalk streams in the world, and one hundred sixty of those are right here in England. Most importantly, they're wonderful for fishing."

I turned around and locked eyes with Gideon, who was finishing up his thought. "Chalk streams are known for their stable currents that vary only slightly over time. The temperature is steady and rarely deviates from ten degrees Celsius. Most unique is their transparent water, which is due to a lack of sand and sediment particles."

Stable, steady, and transparent. Gideon in a nutshell. In the short time I'd known him, he'd proven to be all of those things, and yet, I pushed him away with both hands. Was I crazy? Or worse, was I fooling myself to think I could ever really be over Perry Gillman?

Chapter Fifteen

Gideon avoided me the rest of the day, only making polite chitchat whenever his parents were nearby. I tried several times to talk to him and explain myself, but each time there was a small window of opportunity, he disappeared to do something for the estate. I thought I might have a chance to pull him aside after dinner, but as soon as we retreated to the library, Gideon excused himself, saying he had some emails to answer and calls to make. I stopped by his room on my way to mine and knocked, hoping he'd be willing to talk to me away from the rest of the guests, but he never answered. I finally gave up and went to bed.

The next morning, I finally got my opportunity. Jamie was packing the car for our return trip to London and I spotted Gideon way off in the distance. He was down at the edge of the property, setting up some small displays outside the Badgley Hall gift shop. I asked Jamie if we could hold off leaving and headed off to talk to him.

By the time I made my way down to the cottage, Gideon was already back inside, restocking shelves with Badgley Hall commemorative mugs, teapots, and strainers. He turned to look when the door chime rang.

"I know you're upset with me, but I wanted to come and at least say goodbye and thank you before we head back to London. Jamie and I leave for New York in the morning."

Gideon turned back around and continued stocking the shelves.

I walked farther into the gift shop and picked up a book titled, *The Secrets of Badgley Hall.*

"How much for the book?" I asked.

He turned around and glanced over at it. "You can just take it. The author didn't even include the most salacious stuff in that one."

I looked around at the old cottage, which had been converted to a quaint little gift and tea shop. "There's so much history everywhere. If these walls could talk…"

"The rooms…the walls…the hedge maze," he muttered.

"The hedge maze wouldn't tell you anything I haven't already," I said.

Gideon looked up at me. "Did I forget to commend you for your honesty? Thank you so much for telling me you kissed your ex-fiancé while staying at my home."

"I didn't mean it like that."

Gideon's arms hung down at his sides in defeat, his voice thick with disillusion. "It's my own fault. I pushed things too fast. I thought we were on the same page. But, we're not, are we?"

"I wanted to be. I thought there was a chance we could be. I never would have come here if I didn't."

I walked over to the corner of the store, where a telescope was propped up to the window, on display for sale. I knelt down and looked up through the glass.

"It was mine from when I was a kid. I used to take it up to the roof of the house to chart the stars. I don't have the time to devote to it anymore, so I decided to sell it."

I stood up, and Gideon brushed past me to readjust the telescope.

"If it means that much to you, don't let it go so easily. You'll find the time." I picked the book on Badgley Hall up from the table and hugged it close to my body. "This isn't goodbye, right? We'll see each other again?"

"I'm sure our paths will cross at Victoria and Alexander's wedding. Look for me up in the cheap seats," he said.

"Viscount Satterley in the cheap seats? I'll believe that when I see it."

"I think they reserve the front rows for dukes and Olivier Award winners."

"Perry hasn't won yet."

"He will."

Twenty-four hours later, I was back in my tiny apartment lying across the bed and trying to work out whether my bedroom in Badgley Hall had been larger than my entire home. It was. The door buzzer rang, and I sprang up to answer it. Jordana rushed at me as soon as I opened the door. She flung her coat and phone onto a pile of unread magazines and newspapers, sat down on the couch, and opened her laptop on my coffee table.

"Thank goodness you're back! We have so much to do."

I threw my hands up. "Easy, girl. I haven't even unpacked yet."

Jordana pushed my hands down and kept talking. "I spoke to Gemma, and she said you have a dossier with all the wedding details."

"You spoke with Gemma Landry?"

Jordana looked up from her computer. "She called me on Friday—wanted to make sure I had everything I needed to be able to field questions from the press. We hit it off like gangbusters."

I sipped on my coffee. "Why am I not entirely surprised?"

She ignored my comment and continued.

"We worked out our strategy for dealing with the press and agreed it was in everyone's best interest to give *Vogue* a bit of an exclusive on the gown. Anna Wintour has been such an outspoken supporter of Victoria's choice of G. Malone, it just makes sense."

"Victoria agreed to give *Vogue* an exclusive? I thought she wanted to keep the dress under wraps until the big day?"

"Victoria signed off on a cover story and spread to take place before the wedding to capture more stylistic elements of the dress but not to reveal the dress itself. Then they're going to run a follow-up article on the world's reaction to the gown following the wedding. You have a meeting with *Vogue* a week from…" She scrolled down to the bottom of her calendar. "Thursday."

Jordana pulled a notebook from her bag, flipped to the middle, and rattled off a list of things I needed to do to prepare for the meeting.

"They'll need an idea of the color scheme. For example, is the dress stark white or cream? If possible, they'd love a clue about the fabric choice. Lace? Satin? Taffeta? Tulle? Is the dress more whimsical or formal? Are you pulling any inspiration or ideas from history or past royal weddings? They also asked if you and Jamie would be willing to be in the actual photo shoot. I knew he'd be down for that but wasn't sure how you'd feel?"

"Umm, uh, sure—yeah, I guess that's fine."

She took out a pen and crossed that off her list. "Great. Anna's also asking for a lookbook as soon as we can get it to her."

"I thought the shoot was just supposed to evoke the feel of the dress. Why does she need a lookbook?"

"Gigi, it's Anna Wintour. I didn't ask questions. When do you think you can get that over to her?"

"I don't know. I'm pretty far behind."

"Okay, I'll let her team know you'll have something with you on Thursday," she said without looking up from her phone.

"Jordana, I'm not sure that's doable."

She stood up, closed her laptop, and stuffed it back into her very crammed tote. "You'll figure it out. I have to run. I have a million calls."

After a hurried air kiss goodbye, Jordana went back to the office, and I set up to work on designing Victoria's dress. I picked up my coffee mug, the one I'd bought at Highclere Castle, and set it down on my drafting table. I turned on some music and waited for the rush of adrenaline that comes after hearing you had to meet a completely unrealistic deadline. Nothing came. Not one iota of inspiration.

I never realized how many distractions could capture my attention while I was trying to focus so furtively on the empty pages of my sketchbook. The buzz of an errant fly zipping around in the hazy sunbeams streaming in from the bay window. The odor of frying oil and French fry grease floating up from the burger restaurant downstairs. The intermittent cool breeze of the small oscillating desk fan set upon my windowsill.

I stood up and hit the blinking red button on my answering machine. Another distraction I couldn't ignore. Aside from telemarketers, my mother was one of the only people who still bothered leaving formal messages on it. I wandered over to the couch and sifted through the pile of mail, newspapers, and magazines from my few days away while the messages played. The first was from the New York Philharmonic asking Mr. and Mrs. Gillman if we wanted to renew our yearly subscription. *Not likely.*

The second was from my mother. She spent the first half of the message letting me know how disappointed she was to have heard the news we were designing Victoria Ellicott's dress from Matt Lauer *instead* of her daughter and the second half rattling off a list of all the prominent people who'd called to congratulate her on the news. Before hanging up, she casually mentioned not to pay any attention to the article in the *New York Post.*

I pulled the *Post* out from the bottom of the pile and quickly flipped to *Page Six*, the newspaper's famous gossip section. The headline read, "Royal Flush: Will Georgica Goldstein Blow the Opportunity of a Lifetime?" The article that followed recounted my disastrous breakdown during the *Top Designer* finale and subsequent loss. I read through the story and scanned the accompanying pictures—photographs of some of my best and worst designs—then leaned back into the couch hoping it might swallow me whole.

Over the last four years when bouts of self-doubt crept up and out of the depths of my consciousness, Perry had been a few feet away cheering me on—forcing me to push those insecurities aside. I looked over to the corner where his keyboard once sat and hurled the newspaper at the empty wall. I walked back over to the drafting table turned to a blank page of the pad, and sat back down. I picked up a pencil and suddenly felt like my hands were going numb. I put the pencil down, shook them out, and tried to pick it up again. This time, I couldn't even grip the pencil and it fell to the floor. I watched as it slowly rolled past my feet and behind the far leg of the table.

When I lifted my head up the room was spinning. My breaths, more like gasps, were fast and irregular, and I was certain I was about to pass out. I climbed off the stool and squatted on the floor, my knees to my chest, rocking back and forth, praying the feeling would pass. Finally, when the familiar tingle of pins and needles started creeping back into my hands and my breathing slowed to its normal rhythm, I opened my eyes. The room was still turning but started to come into better focus. I shifted onto my knees, and only when I was sure I was stable, pulled myself back up to a standing position.

I peeled my T-shirt away from my body. It was almost completely soaked through with sweat. I pulled it up over my head and tossed it onto the couch. Standing in nothing but my bra and a pair of leggings, I scoured the room for my phone.

I picked it up off the kitchen counter and searched my contacts. Even after all these years, I couldn't bring myself to delete her information. Before I could second-guess myself, I hit the call button. Trini picked up on the first ring.

"This is Trini," she said.

I cleared my throat. "It's Georgica Goldstein."

"Gigi, how are you? What a funny coincidence, I was just speaking with Anna about you."

"Can we meet? Have lunch? Coffee? Whatever works for you?"

"Is everything okay?" she asked.

"Yes. No. I don't know."

"Okay. Let's meet in an hour at Abraco on East Seventh by my apartment."

I hung up and changed clothes. I was still shaky, so I called for an Uber to take me downtown. When the car pulled up to the coffee house, Trini was waiting outside for me. As soon as I saw her, I broke down in tears. She rushed to the car and helped me climb out and get inside. We sat at a small table in the back, and Trini called over the waiter. She ordered a pot of chamomile tea and two scones.

I wiped my eyes with the back of my hand and my nose with the cloth napkin from the table. Trini sat back in her chair and waited for me to compose myself. I took a few deep breaths to slow down my heart, which was beginning to race again. The waiter brought the tea, and Trini poured some into a cup, added a touch of milk, and slid it in my direction. I took a small sip and placed it back on the table.

"Do you know why the English put milk in their tea?" she asked.

I shook my head no.

"In the seventeenth and eighteenth centuries, the china cups tea was served in were so delicate, they would crack from the heat of the tea. Milk was added to cool the liquid and stop the cups from fracturing."

"You'd think I'd know that after all the time I've spent in London the last few years."

Trini poured some for herself, leaned back in her chair, and folded her hands in her lap. "So, what's going on, Georgica?"

I hesitated for a moment before all my frustrations came spilling out like a stream. "I put pencil to paper and nothing comes. It's like the finale of *Top Designer* and my last few months at Diane von Furstenberg all over again, only now, the whole world is gonna find out I'm a big fraud."

"Do you remember what I said to you all those years ago, when you were struggling with your final collection on *Top Designer*?"

"Figure it out?"

She laughed. "Yes, my annoyingly famous catchphrase, but I believe I said a bit more than that."

I moistened my lips. "I'm sorry, I don't remember."

"No, I didn't think you would."

The waiter brought the two scones in a basket with butter and jams and set them down at the table. Trini reached in, split one in half, and covered it with strawberry jelly.

She took a bite and said, "You were deeply in love with that guy, but he was dating your good friend. As I recall, you went on *Top Designer* to get away from him."

"I was trying to escape from a lot of things back then. Law school. My parents. Basically everything in my life, but yes, Joshua was the single biggest reason."

Trini nodded as she continued to nibble on her scone. She laid it back down on her plate and brushed the crumbs from her fingers. "It was about six years ago we sat at the table in the back corner, and I tried to talk you off a ledge."

"I didn't realize this was the very same coffee house we met at during my *Top Designer* breakdown."

"I'm not surprised. To say you were hysterical would be an understatement. You could've won your season. Easily. You know that, right?"

I shook my head. "There were so many talented people on the show with experience and education. I didn't know what I was doing half the time."

"Exactly. You worked completely on instinct and slayed each challenge. But then, right when you were at the finish line, you buckled."

I clasped my hands together and rested my chin on top. "I remember."

"At first, you blamed your creative block on the press, the time constraints of the show, a lack of technical training. But then you turned the conversation to Joshua and your friend. What was her name?"

"Alicia."

"Right. Alicia. You told me all about how you met each other at camp as kids. How you'd been in love with Joshua your whole life, but he didn't feel the same way. And as you prattled on and on about your perfect friend and perfect Joshua, I realized I wouldn't be able to help you out of your hole. You'd already convinced yourself you were the runner-up long before we ever announced that Kharen Chen was the winner."

I started to object, but she continued talking right over me.

"When I heard you'd started G. Malone, I hoped you could finally see yourself for the talented designer you are. But looking at you now, I still see that scared girl who didn't believe she could possibly be anybody's first choice."

Trini's words hung in the air as the waiter came by with a fresh kettle of hot water. I reached for it and burned the tip of my thumb and forefinger. Tears sprang to my eyes, the searing pain of the injury releasing all my pent-up emotions. Suddenly, I was sobbing. Trini came around to my side of the table and wiped my eyes with her cloth napkin. She knelt down and took my head in her hands.

"Georgica, my darling, you're the only person standing in the way of your success," she said in her soft Scottish accent.

I looked straight into her eyes. "If that's true, how do I fix it?"

"What'd you do after Diane von Furstenberg?"

"I left the city. I left everything. Alicia. Joshua. I ran away."

She pushed a piece of hair out of my face and tucked it behind my ear. "Where'd you run?"

"My childhood summer camp. I needed a break from the background noise. I went looking for quiet."

Trini returned to her seat. "I assume you found it?"

I nodded yes and thought of Perry. "That and a lot more."

She looked at me, her eyes wide as if I'd just resolved my own predicament.

"I can't go work as a counselor at Chinooka again," I said.

"No, of course not. But go to that camp of yours for a few days. Clear your head. You can't hear your own voice with all the chatter. Find that quiet again. You'll come up with the design."

"What if I can't?"

"The world will keep on spinning. It's just fashion, Gigi. Just a dress."

"What would *the* Anna Wintour have to say if she heard you talking like this?"

She waved her hand in the air. "Oh, she's heard me talk like this. Plenty of times."

Trini stood up and threw down some money for the bill. "Ready to go?"

"Yeah, I think I am," I said, already imagining the warm welcoming gates of Camp Chinooka. It was time I visited home.

Chapter Sixteen

wo days later, I was in Thom's car heading to Milbank, Pennsylvania. Jamie'd offered to make the trip with me, knowing how much I hated driving, but I needed to do this alone. I'd heeded Trini's advice and reached out to Gordy Birnbaum, Chinooka's director, to see if any of the off-season cabins were available for the week. He booked me into one of the refurbished ones and let me know he'd also be up for a few days to check on some of the camp's improvement projects before it opened for the summer.

Once I made it out of the city, the driving wasn't too hard. I programmed the GPS to direct me through more of the back roads and less highway. It just about doubled the length of the trip, but I was happy to turn up the radio and take in the scenery. I stopped twice, each time in a small town with a pretty main street that reminded me of the road trips I sometimes took with my parents to Martha's Vineyard. Right before the turnoff for Milbank, I pulled off to a grocery store to load up on provisions for the week. I wasn't sure how long I was staying and wanted to make sure I was stocked up.

I pushed the cart up the aisles, grabbing cold cuts for sandwiches and a bag of coffee. I'd already bought fruit and vegetables from a farm stand a few exits back, so I picked up a bag of lettuce, some plain yogurt, and granola to go with them. I walked down the candy aisle and smiled when I spotted a big chocolate bar on a low shelf. I tossed it into the cart and immediately doubled back to find a bag of marshmallows and a box of graham crackers.

I loaded the bags into the trunk, turned off the GPS, and drove slowly through the main square of Milbank. There were some small but noticeable changes to the town. A few mom-and-pop shops had been replaced with some larger chain discount stores. I was relieved to see Rosie's was still standing, glad this summer's crop of counselors would get to experience my favorite dive bar and a Chinooka mainstay.

As if on autopilot, I turned the car toward the small gravel road that led to the front gates of the camp. As soon as I saw the familiar distressed wood sign with gold letters that read Camp Chinooka, I rolled down the car windows and breathed in the air. There was something so distinctive about the way the sweet, woody scent of the birch trees mixed with the crisp air of Lake Chinooka that brought me right back to my childhood. I pulled over at the gatehouse, and Herb Henley, the older gentleman who ran The Canteen with his wife every summer, came down to greet me. He was holding a clipboard and a map of the grounds.

I stepped out of the car and told Herb my name. He checked it against his list and handed me a set of keys. He rattled off a series of instructions and rules about what was open on the property and what was off limits. I was free to use any of the canoes or kayaks at the lakefront as long as I signed them out. I could also use any items in the arts and crafts cabin, minus the kiln, as well as any of the equipment on the athletic fields. The Canteen would be open for a few hours at night and was stocked with snacks, basic toiletry items, and medications if I needed something.

He let me know there was a Renaissance fair taking place in a neighboring town, and many of the attendees were staying at Chinooka. I shouldn't be alarmed if I saw other guests wandering around the property in period costume.

I thanked Herb and reminded him I'd worked as Head Counselor of Cedar a few years earlier. He didn't remember me until I mentioned I'd worked alongside Perry Gillman a few summers ago. After that, he wanted a full report on how Perry was doing since he'd left Chinooka and made me promise to say hello the next time I ran into him.

I got back into the car and drove up the road, following the numbered cabins. As soon as I started inching closer to the Birch cabins, I realized where I was going. Of course Gordy would put me up in Perry's old cabin. It was the nicest one, and he probably thought he was doing me some sort of favor by letting me use it.

I almost turned the car right around to ask Herb to find me somewhere else, anywhere else, I could stay, but he'd already told me they were sold out of cabins due to the fair. I turned the car off and unloaded my groceries and bags onto the porch. It was close to seven, and the sun was just starting to set over the lake. I leaned over the railing to watch, having almost forgotten how magical the view was from Perry's cabin. I used to tease Perry that winning the Gordy so many years in a row had earned him Chinooka's deluxe accommodations. Now, staring at the sun-streaked colors reflecting off the ripples of the lake and back into the trees, I knew for certain. Gordy hadn't just rewarded him with deluxe accommodations but a million-dollar view to match.

I pushed my way inside the cabin and turned on all the lights. The furniture had been rearranged slightly, and some rugs and other decorative pieces had been added, but otherwise, everything looked the same. I opened the refrigerator and unpacked my groceries. I put the veggies and yogurt into the refrigerator to chill and grabbed an apple out of the small canvas tote they'd given me at the farm stand. I took a bite and went in search of a TV. I'd come to Chinooka looking for quiet, but this was maybe too quiet.

There was a satellite dish on top of the cabin so knew the TV was here somewhere. Most likely just well concealed for the guests who actually wanted to be at one with nature. I went into the main room of the cabin and over to what most resembled an entertainment center. Starting with the top cabinets, I found a remote and channel guide. A good sign. As I worked my way down, I uncovered a TV and a DVD/VCR combo. I turned to the bookcases, which were well stocked with movies on disc and tape and ran my finger down a row of classics from Casablanca to West Side Story.

Then I looked on the shelf below, and there was Perry's old turntable. The record player he'd shipped over from London along with dozens of his favorite vinyl records. He must've donated it to Gordy along with most of his collection, which was piled next to it. Recordings of Debussy, Copland, Stravinsky, Schubert, Berlin, and, of course, Gershwin. I pulled the 1924 recording of Gershwin's Rhapsody in Blue out of the sleeve, blew off some accumulated dust, and set it on the turntable.

As the iconic clarinet solo rose above the rest of the orchestrations, I was transported back to the first night Perry and I spent together in this very cabin when he pulled out his violin and played most of the concerto from memory. Back then, we were so blissfully happy in our hideaway. Far from the mistakes of our past, it felt like anything was possible. Perry was finally able to finish his thesis, and I broke through my year-long design block. Chinooka had been our refuge, and we were each other's salvation.

Voices outside the cabin snapped me right back to the present. I lowered the volume and stepped out onto the deck. About half a dozen people sat around a large bonfire down toward the lake. I rummaged around my suitcase for my Camp Chinooka Staff sweatshirt and slipped it over my head. I dug through a few drawers in the kitchen until I found a flashlight and tucked it into my pocket for the walk back.

I followed the well-carved path down to the shore and saw a group of people probably a little younger than my parents milling around the campfire and dock.

"Mind if I take a seat?" I asked one of the couples sitting closest to the fire.

A larger man with a reddish beard slid down to make room for me. "The more the merrier," he answered and extended his hand. "I'm Alan."

"Gigi" I answered, taking a seat beside him.

"Are you here for the fair?" he asked.

"Just hiding out for a few days." I held my sweatshirt away from my body, so he could see the Chinooka emblem. "I used to be a counselor here."

"This place must be pretty great in the summertime when it's overflowing with kids and activities."

I smiled. "Yeah, it's pretty special. Are all of you here for the Renaissance fair?"

"We're part of a traveling theater troupe hired to perform at the fairs. Sometimes Shakespeare. Sometimes Marlowe. This festival I'm Henry VIII in *A Man for All Seasons*."

I tossed some branches into the dying fire. "Oh, right. The red hair and the beard and everything. I see it. That's great."

"It isn't *Elizabeth*, but so far, the audiences seem to be enjoying it. Hey, did you know the composer of *Elizabeth*, Perry Gillman, was a counselor here? We ran into the camp's director earlier. Talked our ear off about it. Speak of the devil, there he is. Gordy, come join us," Alan shouted over to him.

Gordy trudged over to the campfire, and I stood up to greet him.

He pulled me in for a big bear hug. "Gigi, it's been too long."

"How've you been, Gordy?"

"I can't complain. How've you been?"

"I'm good. Everything's good."

He narrowed his eyes. "You can't lie to me. I've known you since you were nine years old."

I looked down at the ground. "To tell you the truth, I've been better."

"You know what you need, don't you?"

I shook my head.

"S'mores." He looked up and back toward the camp's Great Lawn. "Too bad the kitchen and Canteen are closed."

"I have all the ingredients back in my room. A Chinooka camper is always prepared."

He laughed, and I hustled back to the cabin. I grabbed the chocolate, marshmallows, and graham crackers and hurried back down to the lakefront where Gordy was building the fire back up. Most of the other guests had gone back to their cabins for the night. Only Alan and a woman he later introduced as his wife, Linda, stayed behind.

I passed around the supplies, and Gordy handed out small branches. We each loaded our sticks with marshmallows and held them over the flames. When mine was mostly toasted, and on the verge of charring, I pulled it out of the fire and squished it between the two graham crackers and piece of chocolate. I took a bite and let the melted marshmallow ooze out the sides.

"Taste as good as you remember it?" Gordy asked.

"Better," I answered.

He motioned toward the trail. "Let's take a walk."

I followed him away from the lake and up to the Great Lawn. We sat down in the far gazebo, the same one where I'd said good-bye to Joshua and tried to rekindle my friendship with Alicia. Gordy stood up and pointed to some of the improvements he'd made to the camp over the last couple of years since I was a counselor. A new putting green, squash court, and computer lab. Then, he told me about the most shocking improvement of all. He'd finally agreed to remove the shower houses and had installed showers in each bunk. Part of me was sad that future Chinookans wouldn't have the same authentic camp experience I had, but, deep down, I knew it was probably a much-appreciated upgrade.

"Now you tell me," Gordy said, sitting back down, "what are all the improvements in the life of Ms. Georgica Goldstein?"

"You know about Jamie and me designing Victoria Ellicott's wedding dress, right?"

"I live in Milbank, not under a rock. Of course, I know about it. I was even quoted in the Milbank Monitor. Once they got wind of the fact you once worked here, they came to interview me. I dug up a picture of the dress you designed for *Fiddler on the Roof* and they published it alongside the article. I have a copy somewhere in my cabin. I'll look for it and bring it to you tomorrow."

"Well, there you go. You know everything that's going on with me."

"What about you and Perry? Last time he wrote me, you two were engaged." Gordy lifted up my left hand. "No ring?"

"I broke off the engagement."

"I'm sorry to hear that. Nobody rooted for you two more than me. I even imagined you might get married here. Maybe down by the lake or in the amphitheater?"

"I would've liked that. I think he would've too."

Gordy leaned in closer. "What happened?"

"We both got swept up into our work, then his father died. Things changed for us after that."

He sat back up and straightened his posture. "Did you know Perry's father well?"

"No, I actually never met him. His father traveled so much for his work that, unfortunately, I never got a chance to."

Gordy took off his glasses and cleaned the lenses with the bottom corner of his shirt.

"Perry loved his father. Idolized him."

I tilted my head to the side. "First violinist with the Vienna Philharmonic. Tough act to follow."

He slipped his glasses back on. "After Annie's accident, things changed between them. I don't know if his father blamed Perry for what happened, but they became somewhat estranged. His father hated that he kept returning to Chinooka. Pleaded with him to just stay in London and finish his degree."

"Perry felt so much guilt over what happened to Annie. I'm sure he pushed his father away the same way he pushed away everyone else." I couldn't help but recall how closed off and detached he was when we first met.

"Maybe? From what I gathered from our correspondence, they still weren't on the best of terms in recent years."

I shrugged. "He never liked to talk about it, and I didn't pry. I know his father wasn't happy with Perry's decision to move to

New York to be with me. He'd set him up with dozens of auditions for different symphonies around Europe, but Perry didn't want to play other people's music, he wanted to compose his own."

He smiled. "That's our Perry.'

I shrugged. "Not exactly my Perry anymore."

"There are a lot of bends in the road, Gigi, but if it's meant to be…" he let his voice trail off.

"To be honest, I'm not sure it is. Or ever was."

Gordy put his arm around me. "You said you needed to come up to do some work for a few days. How I can help?"

"Big Bertha still in the arts and crafts cabin?"

"Of course, she's practically the camp mascot."

"I'll pay her a visit. Hopefully, the old girl can inspire some ideas."

"If not, maybe watching the Camp Chinooka Centennial production of *Fiddler on the Roof* will help. If you ask me that was some of your best work."

I raised my eyebrows. "There's a video of the show?"

Gordy walked to the entranceway of the gazebo. "In your cabin. I left it there for you earlier in the week when I heard you were coming."

"Hey, Gordy, not too many people know about me and Perry and our history. I don't think either one of us expected our paths would cross again so soon. For everyone's sake, it's probably better if the past stays in the past."

Gordy put his hand up. "Say no more. I understand."

"Thanks."

"Welcome home, kid."

I walked back down to the campfire and picked up what was left of the marshmallows, chocolate, and graham crackers. I looked over my provisions. Enough for at least one, maybe two, more S'mores. I loaded the marshmallows onto the stick and thrust it into the flames. When they were good and gooey, I pulled them off and smashed them into a sandwich. I ate them slowly, savoring each and every sticky bite.

I pulled my knees up to my chest and watched as the once proud and glowing inferno began to give way to soft, half-hearted crackling deep within the blaze. As I consumed the last bits of the s'mores, the fire diminished to embers. I walked down to the shores of Lake Chinooka and filled up a bucket with sand, then poured it over the campfire pit just as Perry had done back when we were counselors.

The fire turned a deep orange as it crawled across the blackened logs giving way to ash. I watched as it fought to come back to life, but eventually, it sucked in its last gasp of oxygen and then dwindled to nothing more than a wisp of smoke.

Chapter Seventeen

The next morning, I set out for the arts and crafts cabin to find Big Bertha, the old Singer sewing machine that once belonged to Gordy's grandmother. When she died, long before I was even a camper, Gordy couldn't bear to part with the machine and had found it a home at Chinooka. I taught myself to sew on Big Bertha and constructed many of the costumes for the centennial production of *Fiddler on the Roof* on her. Gordy told me last night that my work on *Fiddler* had inspired a new generation of campers to become interested in fashion design. To encourage them, the camp purchased brand new electric sewing machines and even set up a small workshop so the kids would have a place to create. Even though Big Bertha retired from Chinooka the same summer I did, she'd always have a home in the arts and crafts cabin.

I walked into the studio and looked around. Hanging from the walls were all the past winning Color War plaques by year. I counted back to the banner from my last summer at Chinooka, when Perry was the captain of the Villains team and I was the captain of the Heroes. The Villains plaque featured different bad guys from comics, movies, and TV, depicted in black-and-white mug shots. Their names and prison identification numbers were printed below each portrait. The word *Villains* was spray-painted across the plaque in bright blue. It was still irritatingly clever. Perry's team truly deserved the win.

I went to the back of the studio where the additional work-space had been added for the new sewing machines, dress forms, and drafting tables. Big Bertha was propped up against the far wall, almost as if she was the one in charge, supervising the other sewing machines. I ran my fingers over her iron frame and sat down. I pumped the foot pedal a few times and thought back to the dozens of afternoons I'd sat in this very seat, turning out piece after piece, wondering how I was going to break the news to my mother that I wanted to be a fashion designer and not a lawyer. Back when I was just a camper here, I didn't have the first clue what that really meant, or how competitive and difficult a road it would be to become one. All I knew was I had millions of ideas, and fashion was the medium I best expressed them.

But Trini was right. At some point along the way, I'd convinced myself that someone else's vision *had* to be more brilliant and their execution more refined than mine. Whether it was losing *Top Designer* in the home stretch or concealing my feelings for Joshua, whenever the spotlight shone too big or too bright, I ducked out of it. Now, with the eyes of the world on me, I was doing it again.

I grabbed a sketch pad and some pencils from the shelf and stuffed them into my bag. I walked down to the lake and sat on an old wooden chaise lounge and pulled out my phone to scroll through Gemma's most recent emails to see if there were any new developments. She'd sent over updates to the dossier including an additional meet and greet with foreign dignitaries and heads of state—bringing the grand total of wedding ensembles to fourteen. The wedding dress, plus thirteen additional looks.

When I finished, I tucked the phone into my bag and leaned back on the chair. After spending last weekend in gray and dreary England, the sun felt fantastic on my skin, and I soaked in the Vitamin D. I was starting to doze off when I felt a tap on my shoulder. I blinked my eyes open.

"Gigi, right?"

Nodding, I propped myself up on my elbows, using my hand as a visor from the sun so I could see her through the glare.

"I'm Linda, Alan's wife. We met last night. Do you happen to know if the Canteen's open? I'm looking for some Band-Aids."

Linda was dressed as Elizabeth I for the Renaissance fair. As was typical for Elizabeth, the dress was white, symbolizing virginity and purity, with long sleeves as well as neck and wrist ruffs. It was gorgeously hand embroidered with all sorts of colored thread and decorated with fake diamonds, rubies, and sapphires. Linda'd clearly been laced into a corset and was wearing several petticoats under the gown.

To complete the authenticity of her appearance, she was even wearing replicas of the ruby and diamond ring containing a miniature enameled portrait of Anne Boleyn and the watch encased in a bracelet given to the Queen by Robert Dudley. It had been the first known wristwatch in England and a detail Perry desperately wanted to include in *Elizabeth*. I'd helped him find the right moment in the second act and he came up with an incredible duet between Elizabeth and Dudley about time and missed opportunities.

"No, I don't think it's open until later. I might have some in my cabin, though."

"That'd be great. These shoes are giving me the worst blisters."

I looked down at her period kitten heels. "Those do not look comfortable."

"They're not."

Linda slipped off her shoes and held them as she followed me back to my cabin.

When we got inside, I poked around the bathroom and through all the drawers of the small cabinet under the sink.

"Found them." I passed her the tin box.

"Bless you." She pulled two out and placed them over two sizable blisters on each of her heels. "I should be able to get through the day now."

"Want to borrow some flip-flops? I don't think anyone will see them under that skirt."

"We try to remain as authentically dressed as possible. It's all part of the experience."

"You look pretty on point. I've actually seen the real version of the dress you're wearing on display at the Victoria and Albert Museum. It's different, though, to see it on an actual person and not on a dress form. This might sound weird, but would you mind if I sketched you in it?"

"Are you an artist?"

"Fashion designer."

She grabbed my arm. "Wait, are you *the* Georgica of G. Malone? The one designing Victoria Ellicott's wedding gown? Gordy was going on and on about you when we first got here."

"That's me."

Her eyes got huge. "Alan and I are true Anglophiles, still, by anyone's standards, getting asked to design the dress for the future Queen of England is a real honor."

"Thank you. So, it's okay if I sketch you?"

"Are you kidding? Wait 'til I tell the girls at the fair. Where should I stand?"

I picked up a pad and pencil off the couch. "Right there's fine."

Linda scooted back a few inches and then contorted herself into an over-exaggerated pose, careening over a chair, her hips and butt in the air.

"You can just stand how you normally do. I'm trying to capture the essence of the dress."

"Do you know much about her?" Linda asked.

I looked up from behind the sketch pad. "Who?"

"Queen Elizabeth."

"Probably not as much as you do, but I know a bit."

"I think I fell in love with her as a girl. I read a book about her relationship with Robert Dudley and was hooked."

I motioned her to slide over. "Can you turn a bit to the right?"

"There's just something so tragically beautiful about two people who long to be together, who love each other but can't make it work because of obligation and ambition. You know who captured that sentiment perfectly?"

I exhaled. "Perry Gillman in *Elizabeth*?"

"Yes! Oh, that's right, Gordy mentioned he worked at the camp here a few years ago. Did you two know each other?"

"Can you turn a bit more to the left so I can get the dress's train?"

Linda complied and shifted all her weight to the other leg.

"That's perfect—stand just like that," I said.

"Did you know Perry Gillman?" she asked again.

"A bit, yeah."

"Gordy said he's not the least bit surprised at how successful he's become."

"No, me neither."

Linda looked down at her watch. "Are we almost finished? I told Alan I'd try to make the afternoon performance of *A Man for All Seasons*."

"I'm all set," I said, closing the sketch pad. "Thanks for your help."

"Can I ask what you're using the sketch for?"

"Honestly, I'm not really sure yet. I'm hoping it triggers some sort of inspiration."

"Well, if anyone can, it's Elizabeth."

"So I hear." I smiled and handed her back her shoes from the counter. "You sure you don't want to borrow my flip-flops?"

"Nah, I'm okay. The corset's the real bitch anyway."

Later that night, I wandered over to The Canteen. A few of the Renaissance fair guests were hanging out in costume at the picnic tables in front. They waved as I walked past to the ordering counter. I tapped the bell, and Rita opened the shutters.

"Hiya, hon, what can I get ya?"

"Hi, Rita. I don't know if you remember me, but I'm Georgica Goldstein. I was a counselor here a few years ago."

She looked me up and down and narrowed her eyes before opening them wide. "Of course, you were the counselor who was friends with Jamie Malone from *Top Designer*."

"I was on the show too," I mumbled.

"How's he doing?" she asked over me.

"He's great," I answered.

"Glad to hear it. What can I get you?"

I ran my finger down the laminated menu. "I'll take a Chipwich."

"Coming right up."

I took the ice cream over to an empty picnic table and sat down. I pulled the sketch of Linda out of my pocket and used a rock to smooth it out across the table top. It was a beautiful gown. Regal and majestic, but also feminine and delicate. There was so much about the dress that reminded me of Victoria, but it didn't quite capture her modern and classic style. I folded the sketch up and stuffed it back into my pocket. I finished the Chipwich and wandered down to the amphitheater.

Alan and the other members of his theater troupe were rehearsing *A Man for All Seasons* up on the stage. I took a seat in the audience and watched the scene from Act I when Henry VIII visits Sir Thomas Moore at his home to make the case for his marriage to be annulled, so he can marry Anne Boleyn. Alan was actually really good—all of the actors were. When the scene was over, I stood up to applaud them, and Alan came down off the stage to say hello.

"Linda told me you saved her life today," he said.

"I gave her a couple of Band-Aids, that's all." I motioned to the stage. "You guys are great. I've only ever seen the movie version of the show, not the play."

"Not to take anything away from Paul Scofield and Orson Wells, but I think our cast is pretty fantastic. It's also this setting—what show wouldn't be special here?"

"We put on *Fiddler on the Roof* here back when I was a counselor. We staged the wedding scene in the round with the chuppah right in the middle of the amphitheater and votive candles up and down the two main aisles." I pointed to the long walkways that separated the audience so he could see the exact spot.

"Sounds really special."

"Yeah, it was. Anyway, I'm glad I ran into you. I wanted to say goodbye. Gordy said you guys head home tomorrow?"

"Not home, just on to a different festival, but we're leaving Milbank in the morning. What about you?"

"I'm not sure. I suppose I'll have to go back to the real world eventually."

"Or you can join the circus like we did. Every few weeks a new town and a new character to play." He lifted some hair off my shoulders. "With your dark features, you'd make a wonderful Anne Boleyn."

"Tempting…very tempting."

Alan laughed and pulled me in for a hug before leaping back up onto the stage. I stayed and watched for another half hour or so and then left to walk around. I hadn't been back to Cedar yet and wanted to see how the old bunks were faring. I pushed open the door to Bunk 14 and was hit with the familiar smell of mildew mixed with stale musty air. Bare bunkbed frames lined the walls while the mattresses were housed in a shed off the athletic field for the winter.

It was hard to believe twelve of us had lived in this small space for eight weeks. No wonder Jordana and I were still such close friends—we'd spent almost two months with our beds practically touching. I couldn't help but think of my campers and especially Madison who wept in my arms the last day of camp. She'd be around seventeen now, going into her senior year of high school. I wondered if she and Alex Shane had stayed in touch? Would she come back to Chinooka to work as a counselor now that she was old enough? I hoped so.

I walked into the bathroom and turned on the lights. It all looked the same with the exception of the added shower stalls. I laughed to myself remembering my nightly sprint from the old shower house into the bunk, with nothing between me and the world but a towel and a prayer.

I left Bunk 14 and sat down at the same picnic table where I'd spent so many nights sitting OD. The same spot Perry confessed his secret about Annie and how she died. That moment had been the turning point in our relationship, both of us finally admitting why we'd abandoned the real world for the refuge of Camp Chinooka. Things seemed so complicated back then, but really, they were simple. We were two people desperately trying to reinvent ourselves and start over again.

Now, there were obligations and expectations. There was press and pressure. There was so much more to lose and we both felt it. People say there's always one summer that changes you. For me, it was my last one at Chinooka. Everything fuzzy in my life had finally come into absolute focus and I went home a different person.

Was it too much to hope these grounds could work their magic a second time?

When I got back to the cabin later that night, I searched the shelves of the entertainment center for the recording Gordy said he'd left for me. Wedged between *Exodus* and *Gone with the Wind* was the Camp Chinooka Centennial performance of *Fiddler on the Roof*. I popped the DVD into the player and waited for the unmistakable haunting melody of the opening overture. I closed my eyes and listened to Perry's violin cadenza as it soared out over the audience and settled in the Chinooka woods.

I watched a few of the numbers from the beginning of Act I and then fast-forwarded to the wedding scene. The men coming down one side of the candlelit theater and the women down the other. Then, the bride, escorted by her mother and father, gliding down the center row. The wedding dress I'd designed especially for that moment was even more spectacular than I remembered. The dress itself was constructed in three complex parts: the lace bodice with an attached underbodice, a pleated silk faille skirt that incorporated a smoothing petticoat, and a pleated silk faille cummerbund.

One of my favorite things about the dress was its back. Jamie was of the firm opinion that the back of a wedding dress should be as interesting as the front; after all, the bride spends most of the service with her back to her guests. This one had a gorgeous lace train that cascaded down the bride's back like a waterfall.

I paused the video and moved closer to the TV. I pulled out the folded-up sketch of Linda and held it up beside the paused frame. There was something so classic and elegant about the dress I'd created for the show and something so stately and imposing about the Elizabeth gown. It hit me—Victoria's dress had to fall somewhere in-between. It needed to be both contemporary and sophisticated but also harken back to the traditions and institutions of the British crown and noble queens that preceded her future reign. I picked up my pad and began scribbling furiously.

The wedding gown was the first look to come pouring out. I took elements from each design and married them together to create something brand new. I incorporated the long sleeves and wrist ruffs from the Elizabeth gown and then came up with my own twist on the embroidered corset that was more modern and sleek. I looked back over to the sketch of Linda and studied the placement of the rubies, sapphires, and emeralds on the Elizabeth dress. The jewel tones weren't quite right for a wedding gown, but the general effect was magnificent. Maybe I could come up with a different play on it? I reached for my colored pencils and drew large pink, canary yellow, and diamond stones on the collar and cuffs of the dress and scattered a few more down the train.

I was in an almost manic state, flipping back and forth from page to page grabbing elements from one look to incorporate into a different one, each look and ensemble building off the one before like a crescendo. Over the next few hours, I knocked out an entire lookbook. By the time the sun rose, I'd completed sketches for all fourteen of Victoria's garments.

I got dressed, cleaned out the few items in the refrigerator, and packed up my belongings. I lifted the old turntable back onto the shelf and slid the records back into their sleeves. Debussy, Copland, Stravinsky, Schubert, Berlin, and finally Gershwin. I locked the cabin, carried my mug of coffee out to the porch, and stared out to Lake Chinooka.

The lake was completely still. The only noises were the sailboats as they rocked against the dock and the water as it lightly lapped onto the shore. Trini was right. Here, in the middle of the Poconos, away from the bloggers, fashion commentators, tabloids, and gossip columns, I could finally hear my own voice again.

I hurried to find Gordy before I took off to the city. He was putting a fresh coat of paint on the trim of the dining hall's main door.

He climbed down off his ladder as soon as he spotted me. "Heading back?"

I nodded.

"Get everything you needed sorted out?"

"And then some."

He smiled. "I'm glad."

I dug into my bag and pulled out a bag with what remained of my s'mores ingredients—a half-finished bag of marshmallows, two chocolate bars, and a box of graham crackers. "I figured you or one of the guests could use this."

"Nah, I have my own stash. Why don't you take them home with you?"

"S'mores made in the microwave just aren't the same as the ones made on a Chinooka campfire," I said.

He shook his head in agreement and I passed him the bag.

"Anytime you ever feel like you need one…"

"I'll know just where to come."

I gave Gordy one last hug goodbye, threw on my aviators, and drove out of the gates of Camp Chinooka.

Chapter Eighteen

fter I dropped Thom's car back at the garage, I headed to my apartment to change clothes and put away my things before going to the studio. I'd called Jamie on the drive back from Milbank to let him know I'd broken through my creative block and was ready to work. He praised every deity under the sun and told me he'd meet me there with coffee and bagels from H&H.

I stopped at my mailbox to grab the couple of days' worth of mail I'd missed and tucked the pile under my arm. I pulled my suitcase off the small elevator and down the narrow hall to my apartment while peering into my bag to find my keys. They were at the bottom, crammed between my wallet and passport holder. I yanked them out, and when I looked up, saw Gideon sitting on the ground, fast asleep against the front door to my apartment.

After rolling my bag closer to him, I cleared my throat a few times until he opened his eyes. "What are you doing? How long have you been here?"

"I landed around six this morning. I've been sitting here since seven thirty"

He stretched his hand up for help off the ground. I grabbed it and used my weight to pull him up. He brushed off his pants and rubbed the back of his neck. He was eyeing my suitcase.

"I've been out of town the last couple of days."

"I know, Jamie told me. I called him when I got here and discovered you weren't."

"Were you planning to wait here until I got back?"

"I didn't really have much of a plan. I just wanted to see you—talk in person."

I pushed open my front door. "You must need a drink or the bathroom. Something. Why don't you come inside?"

Gideon swung his bag over his shoulder and then pulled my suitcase into my apartment. I turned on the lights and went into the kitchen and switched on the coffee maker. When I came out, he was standing by the window.

"Can I ask where you've been?" He lowered the blinds back down.

"I needed to get away for a few days. I went up to my summer camp. It's mostly empty this time of year, so I was finally able to focus on Victoria's dress."

"That's where you met Perry if I remember, right?" he said softly.

"It's my little corner of the world. That's all."

Gideon shoved his hands into his pockets. "You know, I never thought I'd be this guy."

I took a seat on the couch and folded my legs underneath me. "What guy?"

"The guy who's so blind with jealousy he can't see what's right in front of him."

"I put you in an impossible situation, but it's over with Perry. It's been over for a long time."

Gideon sat down beside me. He took my hands into his. "I want us to work. What do I need to do?"

I pulled my hands back. "Gideon, Badgley Hall is your whole world, and my life is here. I've been down this road before. It won't work. I know you believe the obstacle is Perry, and maybe he's a part of this equation, but our lives, yours and mine, are very different."

"You can't tell me you didn't fall a little in love with Badgley Hall?"

"Of course I did," I answered, knowing we weren't *just* talking about Badgley Hall.

Gideon continued, "I shouldn't have shut you out the way I did. An unfortunate trait of families like mine. We don't know how to handle our emotions, so we pretend not to have any."

He offered me a smile and put his arm out. I crawled into the small nook between his shoulder and chest.

"I'm sorry about what happened with Perry in the garden," I whispered.

He kissed my forehead. "I know, just try not to let it happen again."

"I promise."

He took my hand into his own. "Are you game to give this a real go, Gigi?"

"I mean it, Gideon. As much as I might want to, I'm not sure the distance is going to work and I don't know if I can go through that again."

"Look, I just need to get Badgley Hall up and running. Once it's fully operational, I won't need to be there all the time. I could move to New York and travel back and forth between the two places."

"Is that realistic? Badgley Hall isn't just your business, it's your home."

"Don't they say home is where the heart is?"

I exhaled. "I'm not sure it's as simple as that."

"Maybe it isn't. But we won't know until we try. What do you say? Do we give it a shot?"

I looked into his beautiful eyes. Why was I fighting this so hard? Here was someone wanting to commit to me, ready to do everything in his power to make us work. Gideon was kind, handsome, smart, worldly, and funny, with a title to boot. We obviously had chemistry. He was a good kisser and from a respected family. He had a castle and a moat and was practically Prince-Freakin'-Charming, for God's sake. What else was I looking for? Sure, we didn't have the same fiery dynamic Perry and I had. But where had that gotten the two of us? Nowhere. We'd burned that relationship to the ground.

"Okay," I answered.

Gideon did a double take. "Okay?"

"Okay, let's give it a shot."

He grabbed my chin and pulled me in for a deep kiss. After he drew back, I rolled over to face him.

"What do we do now?" I asked.

Gideon sat up straighter. "I know you think I flew three thousand miles just to work things out with you, but truthfully, I was craving egg rolls and Moo Shoo chicken from Wo Hop."

"So, the truth comes out. It was Chinese food that called you across the pond?"

He nodded and nestled back down into the couch.

"Well, it's a little early for me, and besides, I have to go into my studio for a few hours." I picked up my sketch pad from the coffee table. "I finally broke through my block. Maybe we can take a raincheck on the Chinese?"

"How 'bout this? I'll stay here, watch some Netflix, and try to get some shut-eye since I didn't sleep on the plane. We'll meet up later for dinner?"

"Sounds perfect." I eased back into his arms where I stayed until he fell into a deep sleep.

About an hour later, I left Gideon still asleep on the couch and headed to the studio to meet Jamie. When I walked in, he was standing with his back to me at a dress form, draping it with the material we'd selected for the bridal party. "How's the viscount? I wasn't sure you'd make it in. Honestly, I was hoping you wouldn't—it'd mean there was still a chance for you guys."

I set my bag and coat down on the chair beside him. "We're good, actually."

Jamie whipped around and pulled a pin out from between his lips. "You are?"

I chewed on my bottom lip. "I think we're gonna try to make it work."

"Well, hallelujah." Jamie lifted up the dress form and pretended to dance with it. "When you told me you were going to spend a few days at Chinooka clearing your head, I just assumed you'd come back with Perry Gillman on the brain."

"I won't lie, it was hard being there. Gordy put me up in his old cabin, of all places. I think he thought he was doing me some sort of favor letting me stay there."

Jamie rolled his eyes. "Good old Gordy. How was Chinooka? Did you have the place to yourself?"

"Actually, there was this theater troupe staying on the grounds for a Renaissance fair a few towns away. Their commitment to that world was something else."

"My parents liked all that stuff. They went to the Renaissance festival every year in Fairburn, Georgia."

"You never really talk about your parents."

"My dad was a glassblower, and my mom gave demonstrations on how to use medieval and Renaissance looms. We had a few looms—kept the biggest ones in the barn. She weaved some outrageous stuff. Clothes, tapestries. All really intricate and really beautiful. I used to incorporate her pieces into my own designs. I'm pretty sure those are the garments that got me into FIT."

Jamie's parents were extremely conservative and very religious. When he was a teenager, he came out to them as gay and they basically disowned him. He moved himself to New York City and worked his way through FIT. As far as I knew, he hadn't communicated with his family in several years, and he rarely, if ever, talked about his childhood in Georgia. It was still a very open wound I knew hurt him to the core.

"Sounds like they were really talented people. Apple doesn't fall far from the tree."

Jamie took the pin he'd been rolling between his thumb and forefinger and pushed it into the pincushion. "They were. So," he said, changing the subject, "tell me more about these vagabonds staying at Chinooka?"

"I met this one couple, Alan and Linda. He was performing as Henry VIII in *A Man for All Seasons*, and she works the fair circuit playing Elizabeth I."

Jamie raised his eyebrows. "Ironic."

"I know, tell me about it."

"Did they help Stella get her groove back?"

I pulled out my sketch pad and flipped to the page with Victoria's wedding gown. "This is what I came up with—a dress loosely inspired by Elizabeth I and the gown we created for *Fiddler on the Roof*."

Jamie took the pad out of my hands and laid it on his drafting table. He turned on the small attached lamp and leaned in to look it over.

"This is magnificent. Has Victoria seen it yet?" he asked.

I shook my head. "I wanted you to see it first."

"The back is just…it's…it's a work of art." He looked up at me. "How long are you thinking the train should be?"

"About nine feet."

He pointed to the top section of the dress. "What's that detail on the bodice?"

"Alan told me about the Royal School of Needlework, based at Hampton Court Palace. Apparently, they're known for creating perfect replicas of antique textiles. I want to incorporate the embroidery from Elizabeth I's coronation dress but in a more modern way. Hold on, I have a sketch of it somewhere in here from when I was at the Victoria and Albert Museum."

"Very cool. What are you thinking for the fabrics?"

"I know we talked about looking at some options from Italy and Spain, but I think I want to use all UK-sourced fabrics. I'm going to reach out to the Cluny Lace Co. in Derbyshire for samples. Their Leaver Lace is unparalleled."

"And the stones on the cuffs and collar?"

"I'm not sure yet. How strict do you think the rules are about disassembling the Crown Jewels?" I teased. "Maybe we can reach out to the Swarovski people?

Jamie put the sketch back down on the table. "Looks like we have quite a bit of work to do these next months."

"That's the understatement of the century."

"Good, I'll need a distraction while I'm waiting."

My brow furrowed. "Waiting for what?"

"To become a dad. Our surrogate's three months pregnant. We're having twins in November."

"Jamie, why didn't you say anything?" I put my hand over my mouth.

"It was a little touch and go. The surrogate had some bleeding, and we were waiting for all the tests to come back."

I threw my arms around him. "That's the best news I've ever heard."

"Thom's over the moon. He's already picked out names and private schools."

"Of course he has. What about you? How are you feeling about it all?"

"I'm thrilled! But twins? I was worried about screwing just one kid up."

I cocked my head to the side. "You won't screw anyone up. Look how well you raised me."

"Gigi, do you really think I can do this? Be someone's father?"

"Unquestionably."

Jamie laid his hand over his heart. "I hope you're right."

I shook my head. "I am right."

"Right about what?" Jordana asked as she walked into the studio.

"Looks like I'm gonna be a dad," Jamie said.

"Oh my God," Jordana said as she rushed over to hug him. "When? How?"

"November. We used a surrogate. We're having twins."

Jordana stepped back. "Did Thom get the Dalton applications done yet?"

"They're on his desk," Jamie answered.

Jordana laughed. "This is gonna be quite the year for G. Malone. Speaking of which, Gigi, how's the lookbook coming? Anna's office called again for it. Apparently, she'd like to have it ahead of the meeting so she can be prepared with notes."

"Anna Wintour's evaluating the book? Does Victoria know?" Jamie asked.

Jordana shrugged her shoulders. "Victoria knows. She's fine with it."

"Do we get a say in this?" I looked over at Jamie. "What do you think?"

"It's Anna Wintour, Gi. If she loves it, great. If she doesn't, well then, fuck her."

"Excellent. Thank you for your two cents."

"What do you want me to say? I'm really not worried about it. The wedding gown is beyond."

"You finished the sketch of the gown?" Jordana screeched.

I picked up the pad and handed it to her.

Jordana looked it over and shook her head. "Holy crap, Gigi, this is the most exquisite dress I've ever seen. What about those gems around the collar, what are you thinking you'll use for those?"

"I thought we could reach out to Swarovski. Maybe even Cartier or Tiffany?"

"Oh, we can do better than that. Who owns the crown jewels? The royal family or the government? I'll send Gemma an email."

♛

Jamie and I spent the next few days in the studio, finalizing the wedding looks and coordinating with our production team to ensure we could get the fabrics and materials we needed in time. We barely left the space long enough to shower and grab a quick bite before coming right back to the office. Gideon told me he was happy to wander around the city and hit up some museums and shows while I was working. He even dropped takeout from Wo-Hop off at the studio for us one night when we were too wrapped up to leave for dinner.

I promised Gideon I'd make it up to him over the weekend with a getaway trip to my parents' house in East Hampton. It was the perfect spot for two people looking to escape the hustle and bustle of the city for a few days while still having access to great shopping, restaurants, and beaches. May was still considered off-season in the Hamptons so I hoped we wouldn't have to deal with the same crowds and traffic as in the height of the summer.

We caught the last Jitney out of the city Friday night. A little over two hours later, it dropped us in front of The Palm Restaurant on Main Street where we grabbed a taxi to the house.

My parents' summer home was no Badgley Hall, but it was absolutely beautiful in its own right. Situated on a remote corner of Georgica Pond, it was a charming cottage-style home my mother had spent the better part of the last two decades renovating and decorating. A few years ago, it had been photographed for an article in *Better Homes and Gardens* featuring Hampton's estates. Although our home was one of the smaller houses spotlighted, my mother's taste and ability to mix gorgeous vintage pieces with super modern ones made the house quite the showpiece.

I knew Gideon would love the quiet and serenity of the grounds and the pond. It reminded me quite a bit of some of the spots Jamie and I had driven through in South Gloucestershire on our way to Badgley Hall.

I was right. Gideon immediately responded to the property's rustic beauty, rushing down to get a closer look at Georgica Pond.

"So, this is your namesake? I can certainly understand why."

I took a few steps toward the shore. "My parents named me Georgica before they bought this house. The name was supposed to provide the inspiration to actually make the dream of living here happen. At first, they couldn't afford more than just the land. Then, each year, they added to the property and eventually got their dream of a home on Georgica Pond." I turned back to Gideon. "It's funny, I used to hate coming out here. Summer in the Hamptons was never my thing. I was more of a Camp Chinooka girl. But now, I'm proud of what they built. None of this was handed to them."

Gideon's posture stiffened. "Like Badgley Hall, you mean."

"No, no, I didn't mean it like that. I'm sorry. I wasn't even thinking of Badgley Hall."

Gideon dug his hands into his pockets and looked down to the ground. "A lot of people feel the way you do about inherited wealth and estates."

I tilted Gideon's chin up. "I'm so sorry. Open mouth. Insert foot."

He squinted and pointed to the dock. "Is that a rowboat?"

"My mother bought it as a gift for my father a few years ago."

"What do you say we take it for a spin?"

Right there—the difference between Gideon and Perry. A thoughtless comment like the one I'd just made would've resulted in a full-blown argument with Perry, who often relished in the push and pull of our dynamic. Gideon was more easygoing. Our connection was less kinetic, but in other ways, sounder. After Joshua, I'd convinced myself the only relationship worth having was a complicated one. Now, looking over at Gideon's warm, welcoming face, I wasn't sure why I'd ever bought into that notion.

After exploring some of Georgica Pond, we went back to the house to figure out our evening. I rattled off a list of nearby restaurants I thought would be Gideon's speed, but he surprised me and asked if he could make us dinner instead. I took him to my favorite market, known for their amazing seafood and produce. As soon as we walked in, he grabbed a cart and made a beeline to the cheese counter while I headed over to the wine section.

Gideon hadn't let me in on his menu, so I picked up a bottle of red and a bottle of white and put them into my basket. I wandered up and down the aisles, tossing in a few items for us for the weekend, and then made my way over to the checkout line to wait for him. I thumbed through a few magazines and then finally saw him emerging from the bakery section, his cart loaded with items.

My eyes widened. "What's all this?"

"I was a bit overwhelmed. The selection here is so much better than in the UK markets. This nice woman helped me streamline my menu." He pointed over to a woman a bit older than my mother who was checking out in a different line.

"Whoa, that's Ina Garten," I whispered.

"Who?"

"The Barefoot Contessa. She has a show on the Food Network. She used to have a famous market in West Hampton."

"What do you mean barefoot?" he said with his eyes fixed on her sandals.

"It was the name of her store, I think? Anyway, she helped you with the menu?"

He pulled a bunch of scraps of paper with notes all over them out from his pocket. "She did better than that. She wrote out a few recipes. We better get home and get to it unless you want dinner to be breakfast."

Gideon barricaded himself in the kitchen, absolutely refusing to let me in to help. Every fifteen minutes or so I shouted to him to see if I could do anything to help, and he'd shout back that he was fine. The banging and clanging of pots and pans had me thinking otherwise, but I let him do his thing. I wandered out to the pool area, sat down on a lounge chair, and pulled out my phone, which had been buzzing on and off for the better part of the last hour.

On the screen were half a dozen Twitter and text notifications. I opened the first one and quickly read the headline, "Elizabeth Wins a Record 9 Olivier Awards." I opened the article and scrolled down to the list of categories. Perry'd won Best Actor in a Musical and his co-star, Best Actress. The actor and actress playing Queen Mary Tudor and Sir Francis Walsingham won for Best Actor and Actress in a Supporting Role in a Musical. It also won for Best Set Design, Best Director, Best Theatre Choreographer, Best Costume Design, and of course, Best New Musical.

It was everything Perry had ever wished for and dreamed of when he started writing the show. My instinct was to call and congratulate him. Sure, we'd left things on less than great terms, but this feat transcended all that. I wanted him to know how incredibly proud and in awe I was of this monumental accomplishment. I'd just started dialing Perry's number when Alicia beeped through. I answered.

"Hey, how are you?" she asked.

"I'm good. I'm in the Hamptons with Viscount Gideon," I replied.

"I am going to require a full debrief when you're back in the city."

"Of course. How are you?"

"I'm fine. I was worried about you after all the articles about the Olivier Awards, but it sounds like you're totally handling things."

"Yeah, I just saw the news. Honestly, I'm thrilled for him. How could I not be? It's everything he's worked for all these years."

"Right, yeah. I knew you'd be okay with all that. I meant more the Annabelle stuff?"

My stomach dropped. "What Annabelle stuff?"

"Perry took her to the award show as his date. Their relationship is all over the news. If you thought the media was excited about Victoria and Prince Alexander, this is a whole 'nother level. Perry's so hot right now, and because of how guarded she is, Annabelle's love life has always fascinated the press."

I leaned all the way back into the lounge chair and sighed heavily into the phone.

"Gigi, don't let this ruin your weekend with Gideon," Alicia chided. "I know you. Don't start obsessively reading articles about last night. They're together. You've known for weeks. The fact the world now knows about it too doesn't change a thing."

"It doesn't?"

"It doesn't," she said resolutely. "Now go back to your duke or whatever he is, and try to forget about all this."

I hung up the phone and immediately typed Annabelle Ellicott and Perry Gillman into Google. I clicked on the first article in the *Daily Mail* and started reading.

Will the Ellicotts have a double wedding on their hands? It's been reported that Annabelle Ellicott is dating composer and creator of the West End hit Elizabeth, Perry Gillman. The gorgeous couple was photographed together at the Olivier Awards in London last evening. While Perry donned a classic tuxedo, Annabelle looked ravishing in a light pink Dior gown. Pulled from the spring collection, the sheer stunner had a bustier top and a full tulle skirt. This marks the first public appearance for the couple rumored to have been dating for several months now.

I stopped when I heard Gideon calling to let me know dinner was ready. I tucked the phone into the pocket of my jean jacket and went through the double French doors into the kitchen. Gideon was finishing plating the last of the dishes.

"What's wrong?" he asked. "You look like you've seen a ghost."

"Oh, I'm fine, just hungry," I answered.

"Well, I can remedy that," he said. "Grab this last plate, and let's head into the dining room."

"Want to eat outside, instead? It's warmed up a bit, and the sunset off the pond is something to see."

"Sure, I'm game. Let me grab the rest of the food and wine."

Gideon went to the dining room to collect the platters, while I set the outside table. A few minutes later he joined me, and we sat down to eat.

"That Ina Garten sure knows what she's doing," he said, serving me some incredible-looking salmon cakes.

I picked up a heaping forkful. "It seems you both do."

Gideon picked up his glass of wine. "A toast to us and a wonderful weekend away."

I put down my fork and lifted my glass to meet his. "To us," I said, clinking our glasses together.

Gideon pointed to my jacket. "Your pocket's vibrating."

I put my hand over it. "It must be Jordana."

Without even looking, I knew it was Jordana, calling to ask if I'd seen the news about Perry and Annabelle. I was positive she was already having a meltdown over all the possible PR implications if the press found out about my past relationship.

"Do you want to get it?"

I shook my head and turned my attention back to Gideon and Ina Garten's salmon cakes.

Chapter Nineteen

A few days later, Jamie and I were standing outside the new *Vogue* offices at One World Trade. The lookbook must have met Ms. Wintour's approval because Jordana let us know Anna didn't feel the need to personally meet with us and was comfortable with the shoot moving forward as planned.

An immaculately dressed assistant brought us into a gorgeous office with floor-to-ceiling windows looking out over the Hudson River. She offered us our choice of tea or coffee and told us Liza Lambert, one of the Senior Creative Directors, would be joining us momentarily. After she left the room, I looked down at my phone and read a text from Gemma, letting me know she and Victoria had landed at JFK about an hour ago and was on her way to the office.

I looked over at Jamie. He was pale and uncharacteristically quiet.

"You doing okay?" I asked.

"I've been dreaming of this moment since I was about ten years old."

I put one hand over Jamie's and used my other to skim through the latest issue of the magazine on the table. A few minutes later,

Liza Lambert came through the door, trailed by a few assistants and other *Vogue* staffers. Liza was the magazine's creative director and a well-known Manhattan socialite. My mother knew her a bit socially. They traveled in similar circles.

Liza introduced herself and took a seat at the far end of the table. She opened up a large leather portfolio and passed down a packet of glossy photos.

"Anna reviewed the lookbook and loved it," Liza said as she put on an incredibly chic pair of bejeweled reading glasses that only someone in her position could pull off. "The wedding gown was obviously designed to invoke an Elizabethan feel, but we just did that spread with Perry Gillman and the cast of *Elizabeth*. Even though it was one of our most popular issues to date, Anna doesn't want us to go down that road again."

Jamie cleared his throat. "Makes sense."

"We decided to shoot Victoria in the armor gallery of the Met. What you're looking at are renderings and test shots of the space."

Jamie's hands were trembling too much to look through the packet, so he slid it over to me, and I flipped through the pages for us both. As I was getting ready to turn to the last photo, Victoria and Gemma joined us in the conference room.

"So sorry we're a bit late," Victoria said, taking a seat. "Between the wedding and now this story about my sister and Perry Gillman, the press has been out in droves. We flew private, and reporters were still waiting for us right outside of customs."

"Not at all, we were just getting started." Liza leaned into the table. "Annabelle looked gorgeous at the Olivier Awards, by the way. She wore Dior, right? Perfection. How long have the two of them been dating?"

"A while. It's actually a really sweet story. He was camped out at the Victoria and Albert Museum doing research for *Elizabeth*, and Annabelle was there playing tourist on a rainy Saturday. They started talking and one thing led to another."

I sat upright. "When...when was that?"

Jamie shot me a look. He knew exactly what I was getting at.

"Oh, gosh, that had to have been at least a year and a half ago. I know. Isn't it crazy they managed to keep it under wraps as long as they did?"

A year and a half ago. Things between Perry and I had already begun going south, but technically, we were together when he started talking to Annabelle Ellicott.

"Crazy," I repeated.

"How are they handling the spotlight?" Liza asked.

"Annabelle's built differently than me. She wanted to keep the relationship quiet until after my wedding, but Perry really wanted her at the Oliviers with him. It's the only reason she agreed to go public."

He *wanted* Annabelle at the Oliviers with him? Last year when he was invited, he told me he was better off going on his own.

Jamie leaned close to my ear and whispered, "Breathe, Gigi, breathe."

"No chance of getting Annabelle into your shoot, is there? Anna suggested it this morning, but I wasn't sure how either of you would feel."

"No, she won't want to be a part of it. As you know, not her thing." Victoria answered.

Liza gave a half-smile. "Couldn't hurt to ask."

One of the *Vogue* staffers got up and handed Victoria and Gemma the same packet of photographs Jamie and I had in front of us.

Victoria held up the first photo. "Who did you book for the shoot?"

"Mario Testino," Liza answered.

A huge grin crept across Victoria's face. "He's the best."

"Absolutely. The concept of the shoot is the juxtaposition of the whimsical Spring Collection of G. Malone with the starkness of the Met's armor gallery. Since the wedding collection is a completely different direction, we aren't giving anything away, just playing off some themes."

"I love it," Victoria said. "Gigi, Jamie…what do you think?"

I was still reeling from Victoria's earlier revelation. Thankfully, Jamie took the reins.

"Sounds divine," he answered.

Liza made a few notes in her small leather notebook and then looked over at Jamie and I. "One of our feature's writers will be doing the accompanying piece about your rise to fame. We're thinking of calling the piece 'Non-S-TOP Designers,' a play on the fact you were both on *Top Designer*. Clever, right?" Liza flipped through a few pages of her notebook. "Jordana confirmed the interview for Friday. I think that's everything. Any questions?"

"Think now is the right time to ask to see the accessories closet?" Jamie muttered under his breath.

"I need to get out of here," I whispered back.

Jamie nodded in understanding.

"Wonderful. Victoria, we'll need you back here tomorrow for some fittings and a hair and makeup test. Gigi and Jamie, thank you again for your time. The spread's going to be fabulous," Liza said, rising from her chair.

I tried to make a dash for the door, but Gemma stopped me. She wanted to let me know she and Victoria were planning to come by the studio later in the day. They wanted to review the fabric swatches and the final sketch of the wedding gown. Liza pulled me aside after Gemma was out of earshot to tell me Anna absolutely loved the wedding gown and was going to make personal calls to Cartier and Harry Winston to see if they'd be willing to lend jewels for the dress's cuffs and collar. I let her know it wasn't necessary and we'd likely use semi-precious stones, but she insisted Anna wanted to be involved. I thanked her, grabbed Jamie by the hand, and headed directly to the elevator bank.

Jamie pressed the elevator's down button. "Don't do this, Gigi,"

"Do what?"

"Keep pushing on the bruise. What does it matter when Perry met Annabelle?"

"How could it not matter?"

"If anything, it's confirmation things were as over as you thought they were when you sent him back the ring," he said.

The elevator came, and we stepped onto it.

Jamie lowered his voice so the other riders wouldn't hear. "If you keep down this road, this whole thing isn't going to work. We have almost six months until the wedding. Six more months of fittings and meetings with Victoria and Annabelle. I never should have let you talk me into keeping quiet about you and Perry. Jesus, Gigi, can you imagine what will happen if it ever comes out that you and Perry were engaged and carried on all this time as if you were strangers? On top of it you're with Gideon now, right? What would your new boyfriend think of this obsession with your old one?"

"I'm not obsessed, I'm just in shock. I didn't know Annabelle entered the equation that early on."

The elevator doors opened, and we spilled out into the busy lobby. Jamie turned to me as the door closed behind us.

"Wake up, Gigi. She's not the reason you and Perry didn't work out. He chose *Elizabeth* over you. Not Annabelle."

"Georgica! Jamie!" A panicked British accented voice called over the crowd.

We turned around and spotted Victoria huddled by the security desk. We walked back over to meet her.

Jamie looked around the lobby. "What's wrong? Where's Gemma?"

"She stayed upstairs to go over a few more things for the shoot. I'm tired and wanted to check in and freshen up. She said our driver and security would be waiting for me downstairs, but I don't see anyone. I was about to go catch a cab, but then I was worried about the press waiting outside the hotel. Gemma was supposed to coordinate which entrance to use so I'm not sure what to do. She isn't answering her phone."

"The car probably couldn't stop and had to circle around. How about you come with us? We can drop Jamie at the studio and then I'll bring you back to my apartment. You can freshen up there."

She sighed. "That sounds wonderful. Thank you. I'll let Gemma know," she said shooting off a text.

Jamie ran outside the building and hailed a taxi. We rushed Victoria into it and gave the address for G. Malone. The cab dropped Jamie off so he could get a head start on organizing Victoria's preview and then I directed the driver to my apartment building a few blocks away. As we pulled up, Victoria rolled down her window to look in each direction.

I came around to her side of the car to help her out. "I promise you, there's no paparazzi here."

"I've unfortunately become accustomed to them hiding in the bushes or trees. Although the closer the wedding gets, the less they bother concealing themselves."

I rummaged through my bag for my keys. "I don't know how you handle it. Honestly."

"Some days I don't either, but then I remember this is Alexander's life. It's just as much a part of him as his smile. If I want him, I have to accept *all* of him, right?"

I smiled warmly and pressed for the elevator. When it came, we squeezed on with all of Victoria's luggage.

"My apartment isn't much bigger than this I'm afraid," I said.

"As long as you have a cup of tea and a loo, it's perfect."

We stepped inside and I directed her to the bathroom and then put a kettle on the stove for tea. I did a quick check of the apartment to make sure there wasn't anything of Perry's lying around. There wasn't a single item. Whatever he hadn't taken with him when he first left for London, I cleaned out after Gideon and I reconciled.

The kettle whistled and I pulled a small tray out from the cupboard above the sink. I set out two cups, the creamer, and sugar, and carried it out to my coffee table. I sat on the couch and a few minutes later, Victoria came out to join me. I offered her a piece of Entemann's coffee cake with her tea. It was the best I could scrounge up on such short notice.

Victoria took a small sip of tea. "This is lovely. I'm just glad to have a few minutes of quiet and a chance at some normal conversation that isn't centered on me or the wedding."

"If I knew you were coming I would've put out a better spread."

"No, it feels like old times. Like I'm back at university sitting with a good girlfriend," she said, looking more solemn.

"Are you okay?"

Victoria set her cup down on the table. "I was just thinking of a friend of mine. You remind me a bit of her. We haven't spoken in quite some time."

"I'm sorry, that must be hard."

Victoria shook her head. "So many of the girls in my circle treated dating Alexander as some sort of sport—capture the prince. This friend had real feelings for him though. They went out a few times, but he wasn't interested in her, not romantically anyway. When we got together she pretty much stopped speaking to me."

"Give her time to get used to the idea. She may come around."

"How can you be so sure?"

"I went through something similar with my closest friend, Alicia. I had a childhood crush on her boyfriend, Joshua. She didn't know or, if she did, she didn't acknowledge it. They broke up for a bit and I started seeing him. It almost destroyed our friendship."

Her eyes grew wide. "What happened?"

"It wasn't easy, but we worked through it. It's different than what it was before but better in some ways. More honest." I took a few forkfuls of the coffee cake and set my plate in my lap. "If you miss your friend, you should reach out to her. I know she'd be happy to hear from you."

Victoria picked up her teacup. "Maybe I will."

Victoria's phone rang and she reached into her bag to answer it. "It's Gemma. *Finally.*"

"I'll give you some privacy." I picked up the tray and carried it into the kitchen. I rinsed out the teacups and placed them back into the cabinet. A few minutes later, Victoria popped her head into the doorway.

"Gemma's swinging by with the car to bring me over to the hotel."

I opened up a canister to pour back the unused sugar. "Great. We aren't meeting at the studio 'til later so you'll have plenty of time to unwind."

"Thank you for this."

"It was tea and some store-bought cake. Really, it was nothing."

"Getting to feel normal for a few minutes isn't nothing. Not to me."

I smiled and poured the sugar back into the jar.

"Really Gigi, I hope we can be friends. I'd really like that."

"I'd like that too."

Jordana was waiting for me back at the studio. Before I could even throw my purse down on my chair, she grabbed my arm and dragged me into her office.

"What the fuck, Gigi? How long have you known about Annabelle and Perry seeing each other?"

I could've lied and said I found out on Page Six like everyone else, but I owed Jordana the truth. I scrunched up my nose and sank down into the blue crushed-velvet chair in the corner of the room. "A few weeks now."

"A few weeks? A few weeks? This is literally a nightmare. I am having a nightmare." Jordana closed her eyes and laid her head down on her desk. A few seconds later she lifted it back up. "If I'm dreaming, I want to wake up now, please."

"I found out after Victoria had already chosen us for the dress, and at that point, I wasn't really sure what Perry had told Annabelle about our past. It turns out, not much. I told Perry we should tell Annabelle, but he thought it was already too late."

"Isn't this the same crap you pulled with your friend Alicia and that guy you came to Chinooka to get over?"

I sat up, shook my head. "No, no, that was totally different."

Jordana shot me a look of disapproval. "Well, my job is to clean up these messes. So, pray tell, how do you suppose we keep the press from finding out you and Perry were once engaged?"

"How would they? We never put an announcement in the *Times*—even though my mother pleaded with me to submit one about a zillion times. We never registered. We never looked at any venues. I sent him back the ring. There's no record that Ms. Georgica Goldstein was ever going to be Mrs. Perry Gillman."

"What about the *Vogue* article?"

"What about it?"

"You can't talk about Camp Chinooka or how you and Jamie decided to start your own line after collaborating on costumes there."

"Why not?"

"Don't you remember Perry's article in the *New York Times*? The one where he talks about his lost years and the summers he spent at Chinooka? Don't you think someone might make the connection? Or at the very least, figure out that you two know each other?"

"Georgica, is there anybody else outside of your close friends and family who knows about you and Perry?"

"Gideon knows, but he won't say anything."

Jordana threw her head back dramatically. I put my hands on her shoulders. "Once all this wedding hoopla dies down, nobody is going to care about me. They'll only care about Victoria Ellicott, future Queen of England in a gown designed by G. Malone. We have too much riding on this now. I don't see another way. It'll be fine."

"I hope you're right."

I turned away from Jordana and felt a sharp tightening in my chest. I rubbed my hands up and down the soft velvet arms of the chair and laid them in my lap.

I exhaled deeply. "Of course I am."

Chapter Twenty
The Royal Wedding

Six months later, the "wedding hoopla" hadn't died down one bit. If anything, it'd reached a fever pitch. It felt like every news and entertainment outlet was reporting on royal wedding stories around the clock. Despite all the pandemonium, Victoria and I managed to develop a more genuine friendship, grabbing dinner or a drink each time she was in town. I was grateful to know Victoria beyond the royal façade and as a result was able to make some adjustments to the designs that further captured her essence.

In the last few weeks, Jamie and I hadn't slept more than a couple hours a night, most of the time just crashing somewhere in the studio when we were literally too exhausted to sew another seam or line another garment. But with the help of the artists at several ateliers across Europe—who feverishly stitched sequins and rhinestones and worked on embroidery and feathers—we completed the wedding collection in the nick of time.

Jamie rewarded himself with an Ambien, hoping that by the time we landed in London he'd be somewhat human again. It took me several tries to shake him out of his deep sleep. He finally started to come around as the flight attendants were coming through the cabin to remind everyone to adjust their seats and open the window shades in preparation for landing.

He stretched his arms up over his head. "I feel like Sleeping Beauty just waking up from a hundred-year nap," he said through a yawn.

"You were asleep before we even took off."

He rubbed his eyes and turned to me. "Did you sleep?"

I looked down at my watch. "I think I dozed for an hour or so."

"I told you to take an Ambien."

"And I told you the last and only time I took one on a flight, I woke up to discover I was covered in my in-flight meal, which I had zero recollection of eating. Besides, I don't think it would've helped. I'm too anxious."

"Why didn't you take a Xanax?"

I held up my fingers. "I took two."

"And only slept an hour?" He faced forward and stuffed his headphones back into his bag. "You need to relax. We have a few more fittings, and then, of course, we'll be on hand at the different events, but the hard part is over."

The plane pulled into the gate and I stood up to retrieve my bag from the overhead compartment. "Everything arrived to the space Gemma rented for us?"

Jamie scrolled to his email and held his phone up to me. "Confirmation right here. Everything was delivered and is there waiting for us to unpack it."

"Well, that's a relief. When does Thom get here?"

"The surrogate's been having contractions. He wants to stay local, just in case."

I shook my head. "I can't believe it."

"The timing's not ideal, but we'll figure it out. What about Gideon? When are you planning on seeing him?"

"With the schedule Gemma has us on, I may not have much time until the actual wedding. Did I tell you? Right after we finish up, Gideon's coming back to New York with me to celebrate his first American Thanksgiving."

"You probably did, I just can't keep anything in my brain that isn't wedding related. I still can't believe you're going on the arm of an earl."

"He isn't an earl yet. Anyway, at this rate, I might be going naked. In all the craziness, I didn't even think about what I'd wear. I don't have a dress for the ceremony or anything to wear to the reception."

Jamie pulled out his leather-bound dossier and turned to the third page. He pointed to the tenth line. "There," he said, "between the family tea and Victoria's hen party, a whole three hours on our own. I told you, by hook or by crook we'll find you a dress."

I held up two fingers.

"We'll find two dresses," Jamie said. "And a fascinator."

"Ugh, I look terrible in hats." I pulled the dossier toward me to get a better look. "Hen party? Victoria's having a hen party?"

"Look at the next line. Alexander's having a stag party, so I guess all is fair in royal love and marriage. From what it says here, it's gonna be a low-key night at her parents' house with her sister and closest friends. We'll be off duty, so plenty of time to find you something fabulous to wear to the wedding of the century."

We disembarked and pulled our luggage through the gate. Gemma had warned us there could be press waiting right outside the terminal and we should make as rapid an escape as possible if we didn't want to get caught in the crossfire of photographers.

We rushed through the terminal, which was bursting with royal wedding memorabilia. Every souvenir shop, newsstand, and even Starbucks was selling some sort of commemorative mug, plate, or T-shirt.

I asked Jamie if he'd mind if I stopped into one of the stores on our way out of the airport for a bottle of water. I grabbed a large bottle of Perrier, took it to the counter, and pulled out a few pounds to pay for it. The cashier rang me up, and when she heard my American accent, asked me if I'd be interested in a Victoria and Alexander commemorative teapot.

"I'm actually coming, not going—maybe I'll pick one up on my way out of town," I said.

"Makes sense. I'd wait to buy the version with her in the actual wedding dress too. Can I interest you in the issue of American *Vogue* with Victoria on the cover? We just got in a shipment of them. Can't keep 'em on the shelf."

"I already saw it back home. They hit the stands last week."

She handed me the bottle of water and receipt and wished me a good visit.

Jamie was waiting for me outside the store. "Gemma just sent me a text. There's a car waiting for us outside baggage claim under the name Abbott."

I did a double take. "How does Gemma know my mother's maiden name?"

"MI6? I have no idea? I have a feeling we're going to need to roll with things this next week."

We checked into The Savoy Hotel under two different pseudonyms and went to our rooms to freshen up before our first appointment at the makeshift studio Gemma had rented in Convent Garden. I fumbled with the key card until the sensor finally turned green and I heard the click of the door's lock opening. I pushed my way inside and was greeted by a huge, beautiful bouquet of flowers I assumed were from Victoria or Gemma. I opened the small card. They were from Gideon.

> Gi-
> May this week be the start of a brilliant new chapter for G. Malone. I couldn't be more proud of you.
> All my love and admiration,
> G

I smiled and picked up my phone to call him. "Thank you for my flowers."

"You're very welcome."

"One question, how'd you know where to find me? I'm staying under a pseudonym."

"I have my ways."

I imagined Gideon smiling coyly on the other end of the phone. "Linney?"

"Linney," he repeated. "She asked Victoria. Can I ask you a question?"

I moved the flowers over to the nightstand. "Anything."

"Who's Reid Codswild?"

"Reid's my middle name, and I can't believe you don't remember who Mrs. Codswild is?"

"Refresh my memory."

"When we met at Highclere Castle, you couldn't find my tour tickets. You gave Jamie and me the Codswilds' and told us to play along."

"That's right. How could I not remember? I thought maybe it was your porn star name. What's the game with that? I forget."

"I think you take your first pet's name and the first street you lived on. Mine's actually pretty good. Chloe Madison. What would yours be?"

"Hmmm, let me see...Napoleon Cheshire."

I sat down on the bed and slipped off my shoes. "Wow. What kind of pet was Napoleon, may I ask?"

"A horse."

"I should've guessed your first pet was a pony."

He laughed and said, "I picked up the issue of American *Vogue* about the wedding yesterday. I know Victoria was supposed to be the star of the magazine, but you looked gorgeous, and the article was great. Funny, honest, and the perfect amount of humility and self-deprecation. Us Brits eat that sort of thing up."

"I don't know how honest. I'm sure you noticed Jamie and I left out some key facts about how we came together as designers, and everything about Chinooka."

"I noticed, but nobody else would. This late in the game, some skeletons are better off remaining in the closet."

Maybe Perry had been right all along. Nobody else needed to get hurt by our mistakes. I was able to keep the job of a lifetime and he'd keep his relationship with Annabelle. By this time next week, Perry and I could go back to being mere acquaintances. The past would stay firmly in the past where it belonged.

I took a deep breath. "I just need to get through the next few days."

"Speaking of the next few days, when am I seeing you?"

I turned through the pages of Gemma's schedule. "I'm pretty much spoken for until the day of the wedding."

"Shame. Well, Ms. Codswild, what if I were to just show up at your door, unannounced?"

A smile crept across my face. "If Napoleon Cheshire were to show up, I suppose I'd have to let *him* in."

"Duly noted. I'll keep that in mind."

"I hope you do," I said. "Let me hang up, though. I have to meet Jamie in the lobby in half an hour, and after that, we're in fittings most of the day."

"Go. Go. I know you're crazy, but I'm glad you're here. I can't wait to have you on my arm in a few days," Gideon said before hanging up.

In the last few months, things between Gideon and me had really blossomed. He'd made several more trips to New York, and I'd made several visits to London, spending as much time with him as my busy schedule permitted. We found ourselves in an easy rhythm, and slowly but surely, I was falling for Viscount Satterley.

I unpacked and left the room to meet Jamie down in the lobby. He was sitting on a large leather sofa, holding two steaming cups of coffee.

"How'd you have time to do a coffee run?"

He handed me one cup. "Nespresso machine in my room."

"Remember that one in the break room of *Top Designer* you had to teach me how to use?" I peeked out the lobby's curtains and onto the street, which was swarming with paparazzi.

Jamie closed the curtain and took my hand to walk outside. "We've come a long way, baby," he said.

I took one more peek out the window and shook my head. "We sure have."

After a short drive, our black cab pulled up to the address Jamie read off Gemma's itinerary. Up until now, we'd been using Victoria's family home in Kensington for most of our meetings and all of our fittings. With so many relatives and friends coming in, it wasn't practical to keep working out of Victoria's sunroom, so Gemma had secured us a small studio. It wasn't much bigger than my apartment, but it was more than enough for our needs this week.

Jamie pulled the inventory sheet out of his dossier and started checking numbers against garment bags while I checked the accessories inventory list against the boxes stacked in the corner of the room. To my surprise, Anna Wintour had come through. A representative from Cartier was coming by later in the week to deliver several carats of jewels to be affixed to the collar and cuffs of the dress. The veil was just about complete, but Jamie wanted to see it on Victoria before finishing off the hems to ensure it laid just how he'd imagined.

"All good on my side," Jamie said. "All the dresses are here and accounted for."

I closed up the last box. "We're good here too. All the accessories and embellishments made it." I looked down at my watch. "Victoria will be here in about an hour, so let's unpack the wedding dress and have that ready."

"I was thinking the same thing. I'm hoping we can get away with one more fitting today, and then a final one on Thursday."

I crossed my fingers and held them up in the air. "As long as she doesn't have too many changes and hasn't lost too much weight since our last trip, we should be golden."

Jamie walked his phone over to me. "This is from last night. Victoria was at the Red Coat Club. She looks good. Maybe she's lost a few pounds, but nothing too drastic."

I took his phone and looked at the photo. Under the picture was the caption, "Victoria Ellicott spends one of her last single nights out on the town with sister, Annabelle Ellicott, and Perry Gillman."

I handed the phone back to Jamie. "Yeah, she looks great."

"What, what is it?"

"Nothing."

Jamie scrolled down past the picture. "Sorry, Gi, I wouldn't've shown it to you if I'd seen that."

"No, no, it's fine. I'm used to seeing their names together now."

Jamie rubbed my forearm and went back to his side of the room to begin unpacking the wedding gown while I set up the dress form. For the next hour, we worked in tandem getting everything organized for Victoria's fitting.

Forty-five minutes later, Victoria came rushing into the studio, Gemma and Annabelle close behind.

"I think we lost the paparazzi somewhere on Charing Cross Road." She gave me a double kiss on the cheek and pulled off her Burberry plaid poncho and sunglasses. She tossed them onto the table in the center of the room and looked to the doorway. "At least I hope we did."

Gemma sat down on the beat-up mustard-yellow settee the former tenants had left behind. "We did," she said. "Barely."

Annabelle took the seat next to her. I hadn't seen her in months—not since the weekend we spent together at Badgley Hall. She looked gorgeous. Her hair was a few shades lighter than her signature chestnut color, and her skin was perfectly sun-kissed like she'd just came back from a few days in St. Tropez or somewhere equally fabulous.

Victoria crossed the room to look over the racks of clothing. "I can't believe all this is for me. You both have absolutely outdone yourselves."

"Wait 'til you see the wedding gown," Jamie said.

Victoria clapped her hands together and squealed.

Jamie motioned for Victoria to follow him to the changing area, and I went to get my alterations kit from one of the boxes. Annabelle followed me.

"Gigi, what are you doing Tuesday night?" she asked.

Tuesday was the one night Jamie and I had free to go look for a dress for the wedding reception. "I think I have plans," I answered.

"With Gideon?" she asked.

"What? No." I was still thrown by the idea she knew so much about my current relationship, yet nothing about my prior one. "With Jamie, to do some shopping."

"Cancel them. I'm inviting you to Victoria's hen party."

"That's really sweet of you, but I know it's just close friends and family."

"No. It's all the people who love Victoria and who Victoria loves, *and* she loves you and Jamie. She wants both of you there."

"We're gonna be swamped with all this," I said, motioning around the room.

"You just said you were taking the night off to do some shopping. Victoria will be so disappointed if you can't make it."

Just as I opened my mouth to protest, Victoria emerged from behind the makeshift curtain in her wedding dress. Annabelle's mouth fell open at the same time as Gemma's.

"What do you all think?" she asked. "Not half bad, right?"

"Oh, Vic, there are no words," Annabelle said.

Gemma cupped her hands over her mouth. "Breathtaking, just breathtaking."

Victoria did a slow spin in front of the mirror. "It's an absolute work of art," she said, admiring it from every angle.

Jamie winked at me from across the room and I let out the breath I didn't know I was holding.

Victoria reached down toward the train. "I think we just need a few small adjustments here, and maybe back here."

I jumped up with my pincushion and knelt beside the dress to pin the hem. When I looked up, Victoria was fiddling with the collar.

Jamie came up behind her and flipped it up. "It should sit like this. The stones will be placed all around at the base of the neckline."

"Cartier really agreed to loan all those jewels to you?"

"I guess Anna Wintour really does have some pull," Jamie said, grinning.

Annabelle walked over to examine the dress more closely. "What happens to the gems after the wedding?"

"We'll replace them with semiprecious replicas of the real thing," Jamie answered.

I finished pinning the bottom and stood up to address her complaints about the extra material in the back and on the sides.

Victoria craned her neck around. "Show Annabelle the sketch that inspired the dress."

"That's okay, sometimes it's better when the magician doesn't reveal all her tricks," I said, avoiding eye contact with her.

"Please, Gigi," Victoria said, clasping her hands together. "I want her to understand the whole vision."

I went to my tote bag and reluctantly pulled out my sketchbook. I turned to the middle and opened to the page with the sketch of Linda in the Elizabeth gown I'd done at Chinooka.

"That's an Elizabeth I dress," Annabelle said. "I've seen it in Perry's research."

"Isn't it amazing?" Victoria said. "And this lace," she said, running her hand over the bodice, "was hand embroidered at the Royal School of Needlepoint in Hampton Court Palace."

Annabelle turned to me. "I didn't know you were an Elizabeth aficionado?"

I could feel my cheeks heating up. "Me either," I mumbled.

"We should find some time for you and Perry to connect. He's going to flip out when I tell him Vic's dress took its inspiration from an Elizabeth I gown."

Jamie put his hand on Annabelle's shoulder. "Maybe don't say anything. Let's see if he notices the subtle nod to her on his own."

"Of course," she replied.

Victoria turned to Annabelle. "Belles, did you ask them?"

"Ask us what?" Jamie answered.

"If you two will come to my hen party?"

"Really?" Jamie screeched.

"Of course. After all these months of working together, I consider you both good friends. I hope you feel the same about me?" Victoria said with a warm smile.

"Of course we do," Jamie answered before walking to the clothing rack and pulling the last garment bag off the stand. "I actually have a little surprise for you. I had a feeling you'd want something special for one of your last single nights. I whipped this up a couple weeks ago." He unzipped the bag to show off the dress inside.

Victoria flew off the pedestal and over to Jamie. "It's fantastic."

I picked up the gold-fringed dress and examined it. The workmanship was intricate and absolutely exquisite. "You just whipped this up?"

Jamie shrugged.

Victoria clasped my hand and then Jamie's. "Well, now it's settled," You're both coming. I won't hear another word about it."

And that was how I ended up at the bachelorette party for the future Queen of England.

Chapter Twenty-One

"What are we doing here? It's after nine—the store's not even going to be open."

"I may have done a little name dropping," Jamie answered. "Although I don't know why you didn't just take my suggestion and contact someone at British *Vogue*. I'm sure they would've hooked you up."

"I'm not going to this wedding as Georgica Goldstein, designer. I'm not looking to make a fashion statement. I just want my Cinderella moment—where she walks into the ballroom and catches the prince's eye. Although I guess in this case it's the viscount's eye."

"I get it," Jamie said. "Which is why I called and explained the situation. The owner said he'd keep the store open as late as we need so you can find something to wear."

I threw my arms around Jamie's neck. "You're the best. You know that, right?"

He winked at me. "I do know that. Now, let's go live out our *Pretty Woman* fantasy. The store is all ours."

I took Jamie's hand, and we walked into the swanky high-end vintage shop I'd found my Givenchy dress at months earlier. The owner and a sales clerk were waiting for us with two glasses of champagne.

"I pulled a few things I thought might be right," the clerk said. "They're hanging in the dressing room. If nothing's to your liking, I have another rack of options over there."

I looked over at Jamie, who lifted his glass in mock cheers. "Let the games begin," he said.

I walked into the dressing room, which was covered wall to wall in vintage couture gowns. I pulled the changing curtain to the side and hollered out to him, "I don't have the first clue where to begin."

"Go in alphabetical order—start with Chanel end with Valentino," he yelled back.

Not the worst strategy. I gently took a Chanel gown off the hanger, held it up, and slipped it on. It was a cream silk evening dress with a fringe skirt to the floor. It was sweet and demure. Jamie would hate it.

I came out of the dressing room, and Jamie put his hand up. "No."

"Really? I think it's kind of pretty."

"It is. But no," he said, shaking his head.

I did a turn in front of the mirror. "You sure?"

"It's cream, which isn't white, but it's still a no-no." He put his hand on the small of my back and shuffled me back into the dressing room.

I came out in several other options—Dior, Gucci, McQueen. Each dress met with some form of Jamie's disapproval. I changed into the last gown and yelled to Jamie from inside the dressing room.

"I'm all the way at Valentino, so I hope this is it."

I emerged in a gathered metallic silk gown with floral appliques, an open back, and a small train. Jamie stood to examine the gown up close before backing away to take the whole look in.

"Now that's a dress."

"You like?"

"I love. But there is one small problem with it."

I turned to examine the back of the dress for pulls or holes. "What's that? I don't see anything wrong?"

"You may outshine our designs *and* the bride."

I tilted my head. "Be serious. What do you think? It's too much, right?"

"Victoria didn't pick Valentino, but that doesn't mean you shouldn't. Go for it. *This* is your Cinderella dress. I can't imagine Prince Charming, er, or Earl Charming, not falling more in love with you after he sees you in this stunner."

After that, Jamie helped me select a tasteful dusty rose-colored Dior suit for the wedding ceremony, with a matching fascinator and a fun Stella McCartney dress for the hen party. We brought the garments up to the register.

I closed one eye and handed over my credit card. "Explain to me again how I can rationalize buying all this?"

"When the event's over, you'll sell it all on one of those designer resale websites. The dresses may even be worth more because they attended the royal wedding."

Jamie had a good point. The store's owner came out to take a look at my selections.

"Tell me quickly, what's the damage?" I asked the clerk.

"Don't worry about it. We want to lend you these items for the wedding," the owner said, handing me back my card.

"I can't accept all this. You forget I'm in your same line of work. I know how expensive these dresses are."

"For the person who dressed our future queen for her wedding, I have to insist."

"What an incredibly generous offer. Okay, well, let me buy the Valentino at least. I may want to hold on to that one for sentimental reasons," I said.

"Deal."

203

Two nights later, Jamie and I pulled up to the Ellicotts' home for the hen party. I was surprised to see so few paparazzi. Their home was usually swarming with photographers.

Jamie rolled his window back up. "Gemma planted a story that Annabelle was hosting the hen party in a private room at a nightclub in East London. I'd wager you'd find most of the London press camped out there."

As was our new routine, we made a mad dash from the car to Victoria's front door. Gemma let us in before we even had a chance to knock. Jamie handed her a large bottle of Cristal Rose Brut Champagne with a large gold bow tied around it.

"Here, these are for you," Gemma said, handing us each a sash that said *Hen's Night In* along with the date. She motioned for us to follow her into the formal salon.

"Gigi, Jamie—perfect timing," Victoria yelled from across the room. "We're about to play pin the crown on the prince." She pointed to a picture of Prince Alexander in a very skimpy European bathing suit that was hanging on the wall.

Victoria was dressed casually in jeans and a "Bride-to-Be" tank top and was holding court on one side of the salon while Annabelle was busy setting up activities on the other. Jamie took two glasses of champagne from a server and passed me one. I took it from him and wandered over to a bookshelf in a far corner. I picked up one of the crystal frames from the shelf and examined the photograph inside.

Annabelle crossed to me from the opposite side of the room. "That's my mother on her wedding day."

"When I met your mother, I thought Victoria was her spitting image. But in this picture, you look just like her."

Annabelle smiled, set the picture back down on the shelf, and turned to the room. "Who's ready to play the bachelorette version of The Newlywed Game? Vic, your seat awaits." Annabelle motioned to an armchair decorated to look like a formal throne.

Annabelle picked up a champagne and a pile of index cards from off the table. She downed the glass in two gulps and set it back down before reaching over to the serving tray for another one. She carried the cards and drink to the center of the room and asked everyone to gather round. Jamie took a seat next to Gemma and me on the couch.

"Let's find out just how well my sister and Alexander know each other. Vic, we asked Alex to answer a series of questions, and you have to guess how he responded."

Annabelle picked up a bowl of gumballs. "For each answer you guess incorrectly, you have to chew a piece." Annabelle looked down at her first card. "First question, where did Alex say you two met?"

Victoria narrowed her eyes. "He's going to say we met at his aunt's birthday party when we were about fifteen, but we really met in cotillion class when we were six or seven. He didn't want to dance with me. I was devastated."

"Let's see how Alex answered." Annabelle flipped to the next card. "He said, 'She doesn't think I remember, but we met in cotillion class. I *did* want to dance with her, but I was too shy and nervous to ask.'"

A collective *awwwww* reverberated throughout the room.

"That's sweet," Annabelle mumbled before throwing back her second glass of champagne and shuffling to the next index card. "Where did Alex say you shared your first kiss?"

"It was our second year of university. This is so embarrassing, but we were all out together at a pub and my roommate bet me I couldn't get Alex to kiss me. I didn't even like him, but I wanted to win the bet, so I walked right up and laid one on him."

Annabelle read off the card. "University. She came out of nowhere and kissed me hard. I was completely blown away by her confidence." She looked up and around the room. "Two for two. Pretty impressive. Now let's see if you get this next one right. What did Alex say is your worst habit?"

Victoria scrunched up her nose. "Probably that I run about ten minutes late for almost everything?"

Annabelle looked down and read, "He said you snort when you laugh really hard."

"I'm going to kill him," Victoria said through a shrieking laugh.

Annabelle passed Victoria the bowl of gumballs. "Take a piece."

Victoria popped a piece of gum in her mouth and Annabelle reached for another champagne. Jamie made eye contact with me and held up three fingers representing the number of glasses we'd seen Annabelle down in just the last few minutes. I shrugged my shoulders.

"Last question. What does Alex love most about you?"

Victoria motioned toward the bowl of gumballs. "Pass 'em over, I have no idea how he answered that one."

Annabelle went to pull out the next card and instead dropped the entire pile on the floor. Jamie jumped up to help her pick them up. She was clearly tipsy bordering on totally drunk.

"Sorry, just give me a second," Annabelle said.

Annabelle took another glass of champagne and finished it off while she reorganized the cards. Then she pulled a card out from the pile and waved it around. "Alex said, 'Fish n' Chips.' No that can't be the right answer. Where's the bloody card?" She asked looking back down at the ground.

I stood up to help her. I flipped through the pile until I found the card with the correlating response, then read it aloud. "Alex said he loves absolutely everything about you. From the way you cry at happy *and* sad movies to the way you light up a room. He loves that you still sleep with your baby blanket under your pillow and that you know all the words to Spice Girl's *Wannabe*. He loves the small freckle on your right shoulder and the one piece of hair you can never get to stay in place. He loves how kind and generous you are and the graceful way you've already managed to navigate the realities that come with marrying him. He loves that he fell in love with you at six or seven years old, but that it took another twenty years before you gave him the time of day. He'd gladly wait another hundred years if that's how long it took to make you his wife."

My eyes welled up. Victoria was blotting her eyes with a tissue and Annabelle had tears streaming down her face. She wiped them away and polished off one more glass of champagne. Gemma came in and announced the end of the game and that dinner was being served in the sunroom. Annabelle stayed behind to pick up a few more of the cards that'd scattered under Victoria's chair. I bent down to give her a hand.

"Here, I think these are the last of them." I handed the stack to Annabelle who was now leaning up against the wall. "You should probably try to eat something. Want me to bring you a plate?"

"I'm fine, don't worry about me," she said.

"You sure? I know firsthand how those champagne bubbles can sneak up on you."

She nodded and suddenly asked, "How are things going with you and Gideon Cooper?"

"Umm, good. We've been seeing each other a few months now. He asked me to be his date to the wedding."

"I'm happy for you. He's a solid guy. Things haven't been going so great with me and Perry," she said, taking a seat in the chair I pulled over to her. "Nobody knows. I didn't want anything to spoil Victoria's wedding and God knows, I don't want the press getting wind of it."

I couldn't believe what I was hearing. With all the recent pictures of them out together I'd just assumed I'd be seeing their wedding announced as soon as Victoria and Alexander's was over.

"I'm sure whatever it is will work itself out." I headed to join the others for dinner, but Annabelle placed her hand over mine and held it firmly in place.

"He doesn't want me to move to New York with him," she said, lowering her voice. "He thinks he'll be too busy with the show for anything or anyone else. He's worried I'll resent him for it down the road."

"You have your job here. Your family. Maybe he doesn't want to take you away from all that."

"He was engaged to someone a few years ago back in New York. He's never told me much about her and I never pressed. He told me it was completely over and I believed him. But, what if it isn't over?" She looked up at me.

My breath caught in my throat as a million different thoughts raced through my head. Why didn't he want Annabelle accompanying him to New York? Sure, he'd be busy and Broadway *was* a different beast to conquer, but still. Wouldn't he want his girlfriend by his side?

He couldn't still have feelings for me, could he? As quickly as the notion came to me, I tried to push it back into the recesses of my mind. We hadn't spoken once since that moment out by the hedge maze all those months ago. I was moving on with Gideon and he was seeing Annabelle Ellicott, the most eligible woman in all of England. We were over. My heart had finally come to accept what my brain had known all along—we weren't meant to be.

"I'm sure he just wants to focus on *Elizabeth*. You know how fanatical he can be about his work," I said.

Annabelle tilted her head to the side and narrowed her eyes at me. I quickly covered my tracks. "He's notorious for his work ethic, right? All the articles written about him this year mentioned that fact."

Annabelle softened her stance. "He is. I'm pretty sure he's still trying to prove to his father that he amounted to something."

"Well, there you have it. I'm sure he's just worried about how the show will play in the states. We Americans aren't as up on our British history as we should be. Let him get settled and I'm sure he'll change his mind about wanting you there."

She shrugged her shoulders. "He's coming to the wedding to keep up appearances, but after that I guess we'll see. The worst part is that I really do love him. He's the most infuriating person I've ever met, but I don't think I've ever loved anyone as much."

"Maybe absence will make the heart grow fonder?" I said, worried the hurt in my voice would betray my outward emotions.

She smiled. "You know what, I think I'll take your advice and go get something to eat. This is Victoria's night to act like a fool and embarrass herself, not mine."

"Good idea," I said. "I'll come join you in a minute."

Annabelle left to join the rest of the party and I sat down on the couch to collect myself. Jamie found me sitting there a few minutes later.

"You're missing all the fun. Gemma just pinned the crown on the "little prince." I don't think I've ever seen anyone turn that shade of red."

"I'll be right in," I said.

Jamie slid down beside me. "What's going on, Gi?"

"Annabelle told me she and Perry are on the outs. He doesn't want her moving to New York with him. She thinks it might have something to do with his former fiancée. The one she knows almost nothing about. I should've told her it was me. I should go tell her, right?" I crossed my arms over my stomach. "Did it just get really hot in here? God, I feel sick." I started to stand up but Jamie yanked me back down to the couch.

"The wedding is in three days. I'm sorry your conscience is eating at you right now, but take a Tums and deal with it. We are too far down this road for there to be any other option. Go get some air or wash your face. Do whatever you need to do, but I better see you in the other room for bridal bingo in five minutes, got it?"

"Got it," I mumbled.

"Good," he said and walked back into the other room.

Though Jamie's tough love act was a hard one to swallow, he was right. We both had too much to lose. We were in the final inning and keeping quiet was really the only option. I took Jamie's advice and returned to the party where bridal bingo was underway. Victoria'd changed into Jamie's gold-fringed design and was calling out wedding-themed words that the rest of the guests were furiously scratching off their cards. Annabelle was in the corner eating a plate of pasta. She'd switched out the champagne for a bottle of Perrier and already looked steadier on her feet.

After a few more rounds of bingo, Gemma announced there were cars waiting outside for anyone who wanted to continue the party.

Gemma tapped me on the shoulder. "Alex, Perry, and a couple of Victoria's other friends are at that new club in Soho, so we're heading over. They have a private VIP entrance in the back, so it shouldn't be too much of a hassle if you're up for it."

"I think I'm gonna head back to the hotel. It's been a long couple of days and the next few will be even longer."

"What about Jamie?"

I looked over to the doorway. Jamie had slipped on his blazer and was following Victoria out of the room.

"He's always up for a night on the town."

"Feel free to grab one of the cars outside to take you back to The Savoy."

As soon as I got back to my room I kicked my shoes off and slithered out of my dress. I wrapped one of the hotel robes around myself and called downstairs to order a burger and fries from room service. I popped the television on, turned up the volume, and went to the bathroom to wash off my makeup.

The Graham Norton Show was just beginning on BBC One. Graham Norton was my favorite talk show host, bar none. I loved the format of the show—celebrities casually hanging out on a couch, drinking and chatting with Graham while also interacting with each other. Graham liked to bring together different personalities, always resulting in funnier and more spontaneous exchanges than you tended to see on American late-night shows.

The voice-over announcer listed off the night's guests starting with Nicole Kidman and Daniel Radcliffe and ending with the one and only Perry Gillman. After I finished applying some facial moisturizer, I peered out from behind the bathroom door and watched Perry give Graham a bear hug before sitting down on the big red couch next to Daniel. I tiptoed out and sat on the corner of the bed to keep watching.

Graham went through his usual spiel asking the guests about whatever project they were promoting before sitting back and letting the guests talk to each other. Daniel Radcliffe gushed over

Elizabeth and asked Perry if he could write in a role for him for the Broadway transfer, even offering to play a piece of scenery just to be in the production. Perry laughed and said he might need to write a narrator into the show since the Broadway investors were pushing him to add in more backstory for American audiences.

Nicole Kidman jumped in, asking Perry what he knew about New York theatergoers and if he'd spent any significant time in the States. I held my breath as he talked about the summers he spent working as a camp counselor in a small town in Pennsylvania. He regaled the studio audience with stories about the Color Wars, Gordy, and his small but pivotal role in the annual Camp Chinooka production of *Fiddler on the Roof*. Then, Graham changed the subject to the royal wedding and the role Perry was set to play in it. He coyly answered a few questions about Annabelle. Just as he was turning the conversation to the performance he and the *Elizabeth* cast were planning for the after party, my hotel phone rang.

I reached over to the nightstand to answer it.

"Miss Codswild?" the operator asked.

"This is she."

"We have a Napoleon Cheshire in the lobby asking to see you? Is it okay to let him up to your room?"

"You can absolutely let him up." I leaned over to the remote and shut off the TV.

I quickly brushed my hair and spritzed on some perfume. I changed into a T-shirt and pair of jeans and straightened up the room. As I was stuffing the last carry-on suitcase into the closet, Gideon knocked on the door.

"Room service," he said, carrying a tray into my room. "I rode up with the bellhop, so I offered to bring it to you."

"Service with a smile. I like it," I teased.

"I waited for you at the club, but Jamie said you'd gone back to the hotel."

"I was tired from the week," I answered.

"I thought it might have had something to do with the fact Perry was also there?"

"I just wasn't in the mood to dodge paparazzi. I didn't even know you'd be at Alex's stag party. You never said anything."

"I think I was a last-minute addition, but how do you refuse a prince? I don't know why, but I got the feeling Perry was hoping you'd show up too?"

"He and Annabelle are having some issues. I'm sure he just wasn't himself."

Gideon raised his eyebrows.

"Annabelle had a little too much champagne and decided to unload on me," I said.

"Ahh, I see."

I pulled Gideon toward me. "Can we not talk about them tonight? I don't want to talk about Perry or Annabelle or Victoria or Alexander. I don't want to hear any more about weddings or royalty. I need a few minutes reprieve. If that's okay?"

"Of course, it is Miss Codswild."

"Thanks, Gid." I leaned up to kiss him.

"The name's Napoleon Cheshire," he said, picking me up and carrying me to the bed.

Chapter Twenty-Two

For the next few days, Jamie and I basically shifted into autopilot, jumping from one fitting to another—hemming, trimming, and cinching bridesmaid gowns and the remainder of Victoria's looks. Our workspace was a revolving door of the who's who of British society. I knew Jamie well enough to know he was still annoyed from our spat at Victoria's hen party. He punished me for my bad behavior by leaving for a coffee run right when Annabelle showed up for her final fitting. Maybe he hoped that by leaving us on our own I'd better appreciate the bind we were in because of the reckless decision Perry and I had made to keep our past relationship a secret.

Annabelle's maid of honor dress was really something special. Jamie'd taken the lead on it and absolutely outdid himself. The final product was elegant and sophisticated with a touch of bohemian whimsy. It was the palest shade of blush organza with similar jeweled embellishments to Victoria's dress placed only around the waist and down the back of her small train. It complimented every one of Annabelle's features without detracting from the bride. It was perfect. I unzipped it from the garment bag and brought it to her to try on.

She looked around the room. "Should I go behind there to change?"

"Sorry. Yes, of course."

A minute or two later, Annabelle came out from behind the curtain. She turned her back to me. "I need your help zipping up this last bit."

I pulled the zipper up the tight track and she turned around to face me.

"What do you think? It doesn't need much of anything, does it?" she asked.

I examined the dress from all angles. It fit her like a glove. Jamie really had nailed it.

I grabbed a pair of crystal-covered Louboutins off the table. "These are the shoes you're planning to wear right?"

She nodded yes and slipped them on. I lifted the bottom of the dress off the ground. "Maybe I'll shorten it another quarter of an inch just to be on the safe side. It's a long way up the aisle at Westminster."

"Ever been there? Westminster?"

"About a billion years ago on one of those greatest hits through Europe tours with my parents," I answered.

Annabelle stepped up onto the pedestal. "It's beautiful, but so the opposite of the type of place in which I'd want to get married. I used to tell Perry I wanted to elope in some exotic locale like Fiji or Bali. No obligations. No fanfare. Just us."

I thought back to the dozens of conversations Perry and I had about where we should get married. New York or London? In the city or the country? A big wedding or more intimate one? We could never agree, and after several rounds of arguments we always ended up tabling the discussion for another time.

"He humors me, but deep down, I think he's more of a traditionalist. He might even like a little fanfare," she added.

I smiled and knelt on the floor to begin pinning around the bottom of the dress.

Annabelle looked down to me. "Hey, Gigi, I wanted to apologize for laying all that stuff on you the other night at Victoria's hen party. We barely know each other and I could tell I made you uncomfortable. I had way too much to drink."

"We've all been there," I said, remembering the night I danced on the bar at Rosie's.

"It's not like me to come undone like that. I was upset about the fight with Perry and didn't have a chance to process my feelings about it. Anyway, he wants to table any more conversations about me moving to New York until after the wedding. I think it's probably for the best."

Jamie walked in balancing a coffee carrier in his hand. "What's for the best?"

"Just some girl talk," Annabelle responded.

"I'm all ears," Jamie teased.

Annabelle laughed and stepped down from the pedestal. "Are we done?"

"All pinned. Just be careful taking it off," I said. Annabelle went back to change and Jamie passed me a coffee.

"What's for the best?" He leaned in and whispered.

"Annabelle and Perry are tabling their issues until after the wedding."

Jamie raised his eyebrows. "Think we can do the same, Gigi?"

I put my hand on his shoulder. "Yes, of course, and I'm sorry,"

Jamie smiled warmly as Annabelle called out asking for some help getting out of the dress.

Jamie set his coffee down on the table. "I'll go."

He went to the back corner of the room and I slipped Victoria's cathedral length veil off the hanger. Jamie had finished off all the edges last night and added the small rhinestones to the very bottom of it. Our hope was that the natural light coming in from the church windows would reflect off of the stones just enough to give a hint of a sparkle without it looking overdone.

Trying on Victoria's actual wedding dress might be bad luck, but what harm could come from trying on the veil? I searched for the affixed hair comb and slid it into my own hair. I stood up on the pedestal and examined it from every angle. Even in this poor light, I could see it achieved the effect we were looking for—the sun bouncing off of every stone.

"Looks good on you," a familiar voice said from behind me.

Embarrassed, I pulled the comb out, wrapped the veil over my arm and turned around. Perry was standing in the doorway.

"Looks better on Victoria." I stepped down from the pedestal and placed the veil back on the hanger.

"Is Annabelle here? She asked me to meet her."

"She's getting changed. We just finished her final fitting."

"Everything ready for the big day?"

"I think so. We have one last meeting with Victoria later today about the wedding dress. She's already debuted a few of our looks. So far so good."

"And you're attending with Gideon?"

I nodded. "I'll probably be behind the scenes during the ceremony and early part of the reception in case of a dress disaster. I should be able to attend most of it though."

"We're performing a number from *Elizabeth* at the after-hours party."

"I heard. Which one?"

"*The Accession.*"

The song was an absolute masterpiece, contrasting Elizabeth's ascent to the crown with the different revolutions happening throughout England. Perry had mixed choral music from that time period with British new wave punk and created the most thrilling piece in musical theater of the last century—according to the New York Times theater critic. He'd worked on it for close to a year, asking for my input along the way. As soon as he finished it, we both knew he had a masterpiece on his hands.

"One of my favorites."

"I know," he said softly.

"Oh good, you found me." Annabelle emerged from behind the curtain. "Ready for lunch, darling?"

Perry nodded as Annabelle took his hand.

"See you at the wedding," Perry said.

"Yeah, see you there."

Chapter Twenty-Three

The morning of the wedding was a flurry of activity. Jamie and I left the hotel around 7 a.m. to meet Victoria at her parents' house. A courier escorted by armed guard had transported the wedding gown over from our studio the night before. The plan was for Victoria to have her hair and makeup done before getting dressed. Once Victoria was completely ready, she'd travel by processional from her home in South Kensington to Westminster Abbey for the ceremony.

Jordana had flown in the night before to deal with some press and to assist me on the chance that Jamie had to head back early for the babies' births. She'd insisted on staying in New York until the very last possible minute so she could manage all the other things going on with G. Malone. I appreciated her commitment to ensuring we had a fully functional company to return to when all the craziness of the wedding eventually died down.

When I walked into Victoria's bedroom, she was surrounded by what could only be described as a glam squad. She had three stylists working on setting her hair into rollers while the makeup artist and his assistant mixed foundation colors. I tiptoed over to her to let her know Jamie was steaming the dress out in the other room and we'd be ready for her whenever she finished. I turned to leave the room, but she grabbed me by the arm.

"Gigi, I am freaking out," she said.

I pulled over a chair to sit down beside her and took her hand. "Normal wedding day jitters, that's all."

She motioned around the room. "Does anything about this seem normal to you?"

"Yes, albeit on a larger scale. You can handle this. You love Alexander and he's over the moon about you. Just try to focus on him. Nothing else. Just you and him."

I started to rise from my seat and Victoria pulled me back down. "Can you stay here and keep talking to me? I need a distraction. Belle and Mum are busy readying themselves."

"Of course." I crossed my hands in my lap. "What do you want to talk about?"

"I don't know? Anything. Just distract me. What are you wearing tonight?"

"A gorgeous vintage metallic Valentino. I hope Gideon likes it."

"Do you think you and Gideon are in it for the long term? Do you see yourself getting married?"

"I don't know. I'm certainly very fond of him."

"That doesn't sound all that promising."

"He's great. He really is. We have some cards stacked against us though. His life is here. Mine is in New York. I don't know if we'll be able to overcome the distance."

"You should talk to Annabelle. She thought she had everything wrapped up with Perry and now who knows what's going on with them."

Jamie called out to let me know Jordana had arrived and wanted to do a run-through of the morning's plans. I asked Victoria if she'd mind if I stepped out for a bit to join them in the other room. Victoria reluctantly let go of my hand. One of the stylists quickly replaced it with a mimosa. She took a few small sips and handed it back to him.

I walked in while Jamie was lifting the gown onto the dress form. This was the first time Jordana'd seen the finished wedding gown complete with the borrowed Cartier jewels. Pure astonishment registered across her face.

"Oh my God. You haven't just outdone yourselves, you've maybe outdone every designer *ever*," Jordana said, her jaw practically on the floor.

"It's good, right?" Jamie said.

"No, it's not good, it's a game changer. I've been fielding calls from investors since it was announced G. Malone was designing the gown. Once they get a look at this dress, the brand's gonna explode. Brick and mortar stores, licensing deals…"

Jamie's phone went off and he pulled it out of his pocket. "It's Thom, I have to grab this," he said, answering it. "I'll be right back."

I stepped over to the dress form, smoothed out a few creases, and adjusted the lining while Jordana plugged her laptop into a nearby outlet and logged into her computer. A minute or so later Jamie stepped back into the room. His face was ashen.

I took two steps toward the door. "Is everything okay with Thom? The babies?"

"The surrogate's in active labor. I have to get back home as soon as I finish here."

Jordana jumped up. "I'll go speak to Gemma and see what we can be arranged."

After Jordana was out of earshot, Jamie said, "I'm pretty sure the two of them could run the world."

"And maybe should," I said, laughing.

Jamie rubbed his temples and surveyed the room. "I can't leave you here with all this."

"Yes, you can. We'll get Victoria dressed and then you'll head to the airport. I can handle the rest of the looks myself."

"I can't believe the timing of this. I had a front seat to the wedding of the century."

"You have a better spot waiting for you at home. Jamie, you're going to be a father."

Tears welled up in his eyes and fell down his cheeks. I wiped them away and leaned into his chest. He pulled me in for a warm hug. "I want you to be involved in their lives. What if we have a girl and she wants a woman to take her shopping for her first bra or prom dress?"

"She'll want you," I answered. "But you know I'll be there for anything you or they need."

Jamie kissed me on the forehead. "Who would've thought a chance encounter on reality TV would lead to all this?"

I smiled and went to check on Victoria. The stylists were finishing up her hair and the makeup artists were waving a fan in front of Victoria's eyes to dry her fake lashes.

"What's the ETA?" I asked.

"We need another few minutes to get the veil in," one of the stylists said.

"Oh, let me bring it from the other room." I went to retrieve the veil and carefully carried it to her.

Victoria called for Gemma. "Gem, can you get the tiara from the vault?"

"Tiara?" I said.

"Last night, Alex surprised me and asked if I'd wear the same tiara his mother wore when she married his father. Besides, now it's my something borrowed. This handkerchief is my something old. These earrings," she said, holding up a pair of diamond studs, "are my something new. And this garter," she said, flashing some thigh, "is my something blue."

I giggled and Gemma walked in with the jewel box and presented Victoria with the crown.

I leaned in toward Victoria to examine it. "It's perfect. We couldn't have designed a better compliment to the dress."

The stylist secured the tiara into Victoria's hair and then pinned the veil into place. Victoria stared at her reflection in the mirror.

"You look like a princess," Jamie said as he walked into the room. "Gigi, get this woman dressed and ready to marry her prince."

Two hours later, Victoria's car arrived at the Great West Door in front of Westminster Abbey. Between the nonstop chimes of the church bells and the wall-to-wall cheering of the crowd that'd gathered to catch a glimpse of their future queen, it was hard to hear even the person next to you. Gemma was shouting instructions to me for where I should go stand so I'd be able to do one final check of Victoria's dress before she walked into the church.

Victoria's father exited the car first so he could offer his hand to help her out while Annabelle waited by the stairs, ready to attend to the train. Annabelle looked absolutely stunning. Her hair cascaded down to her shoulders in soft waves. She'd opted for a bit more makeup than her usual more natural look. The dress, though, was the real star. It fit like an absolute dream, showing off every one of Annabelle's best assets. The photographers were going crazy snapping her picture while she stood half-posing off to the side.

The minute Victoria got out of the car, every single camera and head turned to look at her like a flock of birds changing direction. I'd spent the last six months working on every square inch of her wedding gown, but just like the rest of the world, it felt as though I was seeing it for the very first time. Victoria didn't just look beautiful, she looked regal. The sun bounced off the jewel clusters on the collar of the dress, hitting Victoria's face in such a way that she positively glowed. When she turned to wave to the stands, the crowd went crazy. Annabelle rushed behind her to lift the train as Victoria's father took her hand and led her up the small stairs to where the Archbishop of Canterbury was waiting to greet them all.

Gemma gave me a thumbs-up and I retreated to a hidden corner in the back of the church where Victoria and her father were preparing to start their long walk down the aisle to the altar. The service commenced with the procession of the King, Queen, and then the clergy. Once the processional got underway, I counted the rows and found Gideon, his parents, and Linney sitting right where he'd told me he'd be. I snuck around the side and slid into the bench beside them. Gideon took my hand and we turned to watch Victoria make her way to Alexander.

As a boy's tabernacle choir sang religious hymns, the bride made her three-and-a-half-minute procession through the nave of the church on her father's arm. At first, she looked a bit shaky and nervous, but then her eyes locked with Alexander's. After that, she practically glided up the aisle. I looked around the room to gauge reactions to the gown. Mouths were agape. I even saw Victoria Beckham hit David and point to the details on the back of the dress. I prayed Jamie had satellite TV on his flight back home so he could see firsthand how the world was reacting to our creation.

I scanned the room again and saw Perry sitting way up front with the rest of the Ellicott family. When Victoria passed, I watched his eyes study every inch of the dress before a small knowing smile crept across his face. He glanced over to where I was seated, and I quickly averted my eyes.

I turned to the front of the church as Victoria's father escorted her up the steps to the altar where Alexander was waiting in full military dress. According to Gemma, it was the customary attire for the royal family at formal occasions. He looked regal and debonair. I could almost hear the hearts of young girls breaking all over the world. "Love em and leave em Lex" was about to officially and forever be taken off the market. He took Victoria by the hand and they turned to face the archbishop while Mr. Ellicott joined his wife already seated in the first pew.

Jamie had been right. The back of the wedding gown was in many ways more important than the front. Every single pair of eyes in the room was focused on it. The transparent lace back with 58 buttons of organza, fastened by Rouleau loops. The soft pleats that unfolded to the floor, forming a Victorian-style semi-bustle leading to the almost ten-foot train. It was a stunning success.

The archbishop began the service by speaking to Victoria and Alexander's commitment and devotion to one another before launching into the main ceremony and vows. The couple promised to "love, comfort, honor, and keep" each other and then sealed their promise with the exchange of simple rings. I looked over at Gideon, who was spellbound. He squeezed my knee at least three times during the ceremony.

When the archbishop called up Alexander's first cousin to recite the famous passage from Corinthians about love, I stole a peek at my phone and scrolled through the first few texts from my mother, Alicia, and Jordana. The reviews were in, and according to all three, the wedding gown had been lauded as an undisputed accomplishment.

Fashion industry insiders *and* worldwide viewers were in agreement that Victoria's gown was a design masterpiece. Alicia sent me a direct quote from a prominent fashion site:

"This dress symbolizes a partnership in which the vision and dreams of Victoria Ellicott and all of England have been superbly interpreted and executed by Georgica Goldstein and Jamie Malone. Their understanding of fashion's role in serving and underlining this historic moment is truly unparalleled."

Tears flooded my eyes as I slipped the phone back into my clutch. Believing I was moved by the wedding ceremony, Gideon put his arm around me, pulled me into his chest, and kissed the top of my head.

The service concluded with prayers and exhortations by the archbishop. After the signing of the registers, Alexander and Victoria walked down the aisle, pausing briefly to bow and curtsey to the King and Queen. They were followed in procession by other members of the bridal party and their families, being joined at the door by the two youngest flower girls.

When we got outside, Victoria and Alexander climbed into an ornate carriage pulled by four white horses. A similar open carriage carried the rest of the bridal party while the other members of the royal family and Ellicott family followed in cars to the afternoon reception being hosted at Buckingham Palace.

As the church slowly cleared out, Gemma found me standing with Gideon and his family on the front steps. She let me know Victoria was all set with her dress for the brunch and I should plan to be at the Goring Hotel at 5:00 to help get her dressed for the evening's reception. Gemma generously reserved a room for me at the hotel so I could get ready for the party after I was finished. Gideon asked me if I wanted to join him and his family for lunch at the Ritz, but I told him I was anxious to get to the hotel to make sure all of Victoria's looks for the reception had been brought over. Without Jamie's reassuring voice there to tell me everything would be fine, I was a bundle of nerves.

Gideon kissed me and told me he'd be at the hotel later to escort me to the reception. I repeated I'd be fine to just meet him there, but he insisted on coming to collect me like a proper date. I waved his family off and stepped out of the way to let the remaining guests and wedding attendees pass. I took my phone out and read the simple four-word text message in all caps from Jamie who obviously had Wi-Fi on the plane.

GIRL, WE SLAYED IT.

I couldn't help but laugh out loud and wish my partner and best friend was here so we could celebrate this triumph together.

"What's so funny?"

I turned around. Perry was standing there, his hands in his gray morning coat, his wavy hair pulled back neatly off his face.

"Something Jamie texted me," I answered, slipping the phone back into my purse.

"Where is he? Back at the Ellicotts?"

"Back in the States. He and Thom are about to become fathers. Their surrogate's having twins any minute now."

His eyes widened. "That's incredible news. How's Jamie handling it?"

"You know him. He's being as dramatic as humanly possible right now, but when the babies get here, there'll be no better dad in the world," I said.

Perry smiled and nodded in agreement then came down a few more steps so we were face to face. "I'm glad you haven't left yet. I wanted to congratulate you on Victoria's dress. What a showstopper. Really, Gigi, it's far and away the best thing you've ever done."

"High praise coming from the man with a record-breaking number of Oliviers." I looked up into Perry's deep brown eyes. "I'm sorry I didn't call after the awards. I wanted to. I meant to. I hope you know your father would've been so proud."

"I appreciate that," he said before softly laying his hand on my arm.

I moved down to the next step and out of Perry's reach. "I should get going, I have a lot of things to do before tonight."

"Take a second. Look around at where we are. What do you think those two starving artists working in that crowded studio apartment in Hell's Kitchen would have to say if they saw us now?" He whispered in my ear.

I felt a lump rise in my throat. Hearing Perry talk about our years of struggling to make something of ourselves reminded me just how intertwined our pasts were. He wasn't just some ex-boyfriend of mine. He was the man I'd been planning to marry. Our ceremony wouldn't have been anywhere near as grand as the one we just witnessed, but the vows and promises we'd intended to make to one another would've been no different. I'd been ready to commit to Perry—to love, honor, comfort, and keep him. That is, until his actions forced me to let him go.

I turned to look at him. "I guess they'd be happy to know we both got everything we ever wanted."

"Did we?" he asked.

Gemma walked over and tapped Perry on the shoulder. "Perry, the family car's waiting for you," she said.

"Give me a moment, I'm just congratulating Gigi on her triumph."

"No, you should go. We're done," I said, retreating into the crowd that'd gathered on the sidewalk.

"Gigi," Perry called out after me, but I refused to look back.

Chapter Twenty - Four

A few hours later, Victoria was dressed in a strapless white satin and organza evening dress with a circle skirt and the same colored jeweled details from the wedding gown around its waist. After the grandeur of the morning, Jamie and I had agreed the reception dress should be more refined, emphasizing Victoria's classic beauty and style. It was simple but stunning.

Victoria's glam squad returned, working to transform her wedding day look into a glamorous evening one. They darkened her eye makeup and slicked her hair into a neat chignon. She looked right off the runway. She completed the look with open-toe gold Louboutins that gave her another unnecessary few inches in height.

"You should be all set." I stepped away from Victoria to look her up and down. "The hem's perfect and the fit—sublime."

"Thank you so much. Really. I don't know how you and Jamie managed to capture everything I wanted in these looks, but I've never felt more special or beautiful. Speaking of Jamie, any word from him yet?"

I looked down at my phone. "Nothing yet."

"Let me know when you hear anything."

Gemma poked her head into the room and let Victoria know she was needed for photos at the palace.

"As a thank you, I asked if my stylists could stay a bit longer and get you ready. I know I haven't left you with much time for yourself," Victoria said.

"That's very generous of you. Are you sure?"

"My pleasure. Didn't you say Gideon will be here at seven? You don't have a lot of time." She turned to her glam squad. "Boys, give this one the works. She deserves it."

Victoria left with Gemma as I sat down in front of the mirror. The hairstylist got to work pinning my hair into rollers while the senior makeup artist asked me what I was wearing to the reception. I described the metallic silk Valentino gown with its floral appliques and then remembered I had a picture of it on my phone. I pulled it out to show him and saw a missed call from Jamie and a text, which I quickly opened.

Welcome to the world Oliver Malone Beckett 5lbs 9 oz. and Clara Malone Beckett 6 lbs. 2 oz.

I squealed and jumped up from the chair.

"I have to make one quick call. I'll be right back," I said.

"How's the proud papa?" I asked as soon as Jamie picked up.

"When I saw the reviews of the wedding dress coming in on the flight I thought nothing could possibly top that moment, but the minute I held my children nothing else in the world mattered."

"Your children. Oh Jamie," I said, tearing up myself. "Everyone's okay? The babies are doing well?"

"They're perfect. Just perfect."

"And Thom?"

"Busy taking a million pictures. He'll send some over to you soon. What time is it there? Shouldn't you be getting ready for the reception?"

"It's six. Victoria just left for the palace. Gideon's picking me up in about an hour."

"So, we did pretty good today, partner?" he said.

I rubbed my hand over my heart. "We sure did."

"I have to go, Gi. Thom's parents just got to the hospital. Take copious mental notes on the party but more importantly the after party. I want all the dish," he said before hanging up.

I looked back down at my phone. Thom sent a text with about a dozen pictures of the twins. Jamie was right. They were absolutely perfect from their tufts of blonde hair right down to the small dimple each of them had in their right cheek.

I sat back down in the chair and apologized to the stylists. I scrolled to the picture of me in the Valentino gown Jamie'd snapped at the vintage store and showed it to the makeup artist.

"We should do a more natural eye but a bold red lip. Toni, are you thinking finger waves?" he asked the hairstylist.

"Totally," Toni answered. "This dress has a real 20s feel. Very old New York. I'm picturing a smoky club with jazz standards playing. Let's go for it."

I smiled. "Do I have any say in this?"

"No." They both answered in unison.

I leaned back into the chair and let the team work their magic.

Forty-five minutes later, Gideon knocked on the hotel room door. The glam squad let him in while I finished dressing in the bathroom. It was a good thing I hadn't had time to eat much all week. The dress closed within an inch of my life. I inhaled a few times to make sure I could breathe in it. Not well, but it'd have to do. I thought of Jamie's fashion mantra, "Style before a smile." You didn't have to be happy or comfortable in a couture gown as long as it looked fabulous. Gideon would have to be the judge.

I stepped out of the bathroom and did a full turn in front of him. "What do you think?"

"Forget whatever the Queen is wearing tonight, I'll be the one with the crown jewels on my arm."

I picked up my clutch from the nightstand. "That's a good line. How long have you been working on it?"

"Came up with it in the car on the way over." He stood to give me a kiss on the cheek.

I laughed. "You look incredible. That tuxedo's amazing."

Gideon smoothed out the jacket lapels. "My new stylist helped me pick it out."

"Jamie?"

Gideon nodded and I leaned over to straighten his bow tie. "There. Now you're perfect."

"If you say so," he said with a wink.

"Oh, I say so."

"We should get going if you want to see the bagpipers," he said, taking my arm.

The car drove through the crowds who'd gathered along the sidewalks and footways to catch a glimpse the royal reception guests. When we pulled up to the gates of Buckingham Palace, Gideon gave his name to a palace guard who let us through. The driver was then directed to the porte-cochère where a butler was waiting to greet the guests and announce the arrivals. Gideon climbed out first and extended a hand to help me. The butler asked Gideon for his name or title and then proclaimed the entrance of "Viscount Satterley and Ms. Georgica Goldstein."

It felt like a dream. The courtyard was aglow with candles, and servers walked around with trays of vintage pink champagne and peach Bellinis. Bagpipers played traditional English music as more guests were announced into the space. I looked around, recognizing many of the same faces from the morning's ceremony. Gideon pointed to the corner of the courtyard where his parents were standing with Linney.

We slowly made our way over to them, stopping to speak with several of Gideon's friends and acquaintances along the way. Gideon made a point of introducing me, not as his date but as the designer of Victoria's wedding gown. As guest after guest gushed about how much they'd loved the dress, Gideon couldn't conceal his pride and admiration.

"When we walked in the butler *should* have announced us as 'Georgica Goldstein, extraordinary designer and that schlub she let escort her,'" he said.

"Schlub's a little bit harsh, isn't it?" I teased.

Gideon surveyed the courtyard. "I might just be the luckiest guy in this room."

"I think Prince Alexander would dare to challenge you on that one."

"It is his wedding day so I'll let him take the title…just this once," he said with a squeeze of my hand.

After the cocktail hour, the guests were ushered toward dinner in the palace's ballroom, complete with two huge thrones at one end of the room for Victoria and Alexander and a grand piano at the other. Gideon and I searched the seating chart and found our names at Table 22 along with the rest of his family and some of their close friends. I couldn't help but glance around the chart to see where Perry was seated. He was across the room at Table 2 with the Ellicotts and some members of the royal family.

I took the seat next to Gideon and folded my napkin into my lap. A waiter placed a starter in front of us—dressed crab topped with lemon slices and served with a small cucumber salad. A sommelier came by to pour wine for the table, explaining he'd paired this course with an exquisite white Meursault Burgundy, a French wine that was one of Prince Alexander's favorites.

After the room was served, Victoria and Alexander were announced as the Duke and Duchess of Sussex.

I leaned into Gideon. "Why weren't they announced as prince and princess?" I whispered.

"You only carry prince or princess before your name *if* you were born into the role. Because Victoria is a commoner, she doesn't get the princess title in her own right."

"I wonder if she knew that before she agreed to marry him?" I joked.

"The king bestowed the titles of Duke and Duchess to mark their wedding," he added. "Not a bad consolation."

"Thank goodness I was issued an interpreter for this event. I would've been completely lost otherwise."

"I'll draw you a chart later."

"Thank you, Viscount Satterley heir apparent to the Earl of Harronsby." I nudged Gideon's side. "Did I say that right?"

"Perfectly."

"I'm going to go find the ladies' room, I'll be right back;" I excused myself from the table.

I wandered out of the ballroom and into a corridor. Large Old Masters paintings lined the long hallway. I recognized a Velázquez and Rubens. I was sure the one at the far end of the hall was a Vermeer but wanted to get a closer look. I leaned in to look for a signature or marking on the painting and knocked into the frame.

"Be careful with that one. You break it. You buy it."

"I was looking for the bathroom and apparently wandered into a museum," I said to Perry, who was watching me from the doorway.

"No, you're right, this is just the hallway to the bathroom," he said.

I raised my eyebrows. "Some hallway."

"I know. This is my fourth trip to the palace and I still can't believe I'm here."

"Me neither," I answered.

"Neither," he responded in his posh British accent.

"Neither, *neither*. Either, *either*," I echoed back to him in the same playful way we used to exchange quips.

"Let's call the whole thing off," he finished.

I snickered and looked at the ground.

"What? What is it?" Perry tilted my chin back up again.

"After you returned to London, I used to imagine you sitting in your house playing your Gershwin records, listening to that song and thinking of us. I say tomato and you say *tomahto*, right? I guess in the end the lyrics rang true. It *was* easier to call the whole thing off."

"Is that what you think? That it was easier? Saying goodbye to you was the hardest thing I've ever done."

"Really? It didn't seem so," I responded.

A guy with a headset popped his head out from behind the doorway. "Hey, Perry, they need you for sound check."

"I'll be there in a second, Chris," he yelled back.

"Go. Your performance is all anyone's talking about."

"I switched it up. We're not doing *The Accession* anymore."

"No? Which song are you performing?"

"*Dudley's Petition.*"

Dudley's Petition was a powerful love ballad between Robert Dudley and Queen Elizabeth. Dudley, growing desperate, decides to make one last, spectacular attempt to persuade Elizabeth to marry him. Pulling out all the stops, he invites her to Kenilworth Castle and stages several days of extraordinarily lavish entertainments at a huge cost. The Queen enjoys every minute of the visit but, in the end, cannot be dazzled into acquiescence. Although she loves Dudley fiercely, she knows marrying him will court disaster in her kingdom, sparking such intense opposition from Dudley's rivals that it might even spill out into civil war.

"I've never seen that one performed outside of our apartment," I said.

"You made a wonderful Elizabeth," Perry said with a playful smile.

"I made a terrible Elizabeth. Didn't you tell me in all your years of performing music you'd never heard anyone that off key?"

"Yes, true. But the enthusiasm you exhibited—no other actress has quite embodied the role the way you did."

"Not even Beyoncé?"

Perry leaned in close to me and whispered, "Not even the Queen B herself."

I raised my eyebrows. "I don't believe you, but I'll take the compliment and run with it."

"Really, Gigi, nobody's ever even come close to you."

"Perry, man, what's the holdup?" Chris shouted again from down the hall.

I glanced from Chris back to Perry. "Go. Don't keep your throngs of adoring fans waiting on account of me."

Our eyes locked for just a moment and then he was gone.

Chapter Twenty-Five

After dinner, dancing, and several toasts, most of the guests made their way into the throne room, which had been completely transformed into a cabaret-type nightclub complete with a stage, dance floor, and cocktail bars stationed in every corner. It reminded me of the Red Coat Club—probably because Victoria had commissioned their same design team to help create a similar feel.

I'd helped Victoria change from her evening dress into the party dress Jamie designed. It carried over the motif of the jewel-toned stones from the wedding gown, and he'd tactically placed jewels around the collar and hem of the dress for maximum effect. It was fun and flirty and totally different than anything she'd worn all week.

The glam squad took her hair down from the sleek chignon and flat ironed it perfectly straight with a middle part. I snapped a picture of her and sent it off to Jamie so he could see how the entire look came together. Alexander changed out of his formal tuxedo into a cool midnight blue suit with dark navy velvet lapels. Standing there together, he and Victoria looked like two movie stars out for a night in the big city.

Although the wedding hoopla would die down, I knew the interest in Victoria and Alexander never would. They were the true embodiment of a fairy tale. Modern royals who were beautiful, elegant, and worldly. I didn't envy the spotlight that would forever follow them and hoped Victoria would be strong enough to handle it. If these last few months were any indication though, she would be.

Gideon grabbed us each a cocktail from the bar and found us a high-top table to sit at close to the stage. Alexander walked out from behind the curtain and introduced the singer, Adele, to the crowd who went absolutely wild at the mention of her name. She congratulated Victoria and Alexander on their marriage and then went on to perform some of her biggest hits followed by a brand-new song she'd written just for the occasion.

I'd tried unsuccessfully for years to score tickets to one of Adele's shows, which typically sold out in a matter of minutes. Being able to hear her perform in such an intimate setting was once in a lifetime. I looked over at Gideon who was singing along to all the words, having a great time.

When Adele finished her set, she cleared the stage and Alexander came back up. She handed him the microphone, which he slipped back into the stand and pulled to the front of the stage.

"I am thrilled to introduce the next set of performers," he said. "Following their record-breaking wins at the Olivier Awards, please help me welcome my friend, Perry Gillman, and the incomparable cast of *Elizabeth*."

Alexander quickly vacated the stage as the entire cast of *Elizabeth* came down the aisles of the audience dressed as traveling mistrals and troubadours. Perry, as Robert Dudley was leading the charge to impress the actress playing Queen Elizabeth, who was reveling in the scene before her. The room was completely silent until Perry started singing with several members of the company joining in at different verses.

Perry'd written this specific song as a modern take on the madrigal, which he'd explained to me was a popular musical arrangement of the Elizabethan era consisting of several vocal parts with no instrumental accompaniment. Each vocal was carefully layered and harmonized to act as an instrument would if the song were being played by an actual orchestra. Even after several attempts to educate me on the complexity of the music theory involved in this piece, I'd never been sure I quite understood what he was try-ing to accomplish...until now. Hearing the song performed with the full chorus the way he must've imagined when he was writing the score was absolutely mind-blowing.

I glanced around. Every single eye in the place, including the staff, was transfixed on Perry, who was singing and dancing up the aisles, encouraging audience members to join him in merriment. He was doing all he could to woo his queen. Elizabeth though, wouldn't be persuaded, ultimately choosing ambition and the crown over love. She turned the heartsick Dudley down, finally and definitively letting him go.

When the scene was over, the entire room was on its feet applauding. I looked over to the front row where Annabelle was seated. Tears were streaming down her face and all the color was drained from it. I thought back to Perry's quote from that fate-ful New York Time's article: "*Certain relationships require too much compromise, too many concessions. Some romances are intense and wonderful but are simply doomed from the start.*" My breath caught in my chest. What if it wasn't me he'd been talking about? What if it was Annabelle?

I looked up at the stage. The cast was clearing off and just Perry and a few of the musicians stayed behind to act as his backup band. Alexander walked back to the microphone and thanked him for the incredible performance. He handed Perry a violin and the mic and stepped back offstage.

Perry waited a few more seconds to finish catching his breath then stepped closer to the stand and slipped in microphone. "I'm so honored the Duke and Duchess of Sussex asked me to per-form this evening. It's an absolute dream come true to be standing here, so thank you." Perry looked over to Victoria and Alexander.

He continued, "I haven't always been a Broadway guy. My musical roots and heart live a little closer to the jazz age. I hope everyone will indulge me a bit as I play some of my favorite standards for the happy couple." Perry nodded to the pianist onstage beside him. "It's been quite a while since I picked up a bow, so please excuse me if I'm a little rusty."

Perry put the violin to his chin and began playing the all-too-familiar first notes of Gershwin's *They Can't Take That Away From Me*. He looked out into the audience and I could feel his eyes searching for me. I closed mine and drifted back to Chinooka. I replayed the dozens of times I'd watched spellbound as Perry's fingers danced over the strings of his violin, private concerts performed just for me. When he got too tired of playing, he'd throw one of his records onto the turntable and we'd dance in his cabin until the sun came up.

I opened my eyes. Victoria and Alexander had taken to the dance floor and other couples were slowly moving to join them.

Gideon stood up and said, "Shall we?"

I accepted his hand and followed him out into the crowd. He pulled me close, wrapping his arms around me. I laid my head down on Gideon's shoulder.

"Have I told you how absolutely beautiful you look tonight?" Gideon whispered in my ear.

I picked my head up. "You may have mentioned it once or twice."

"Well, let me just say it again. You look gorgeous."

"You look pretty dapper yourself," I said, adjusting his bowtie. "I'm one lucky lady."

"I'm glad to hear you say it. After that performance, I might be the only person in this room who didn't fall a little more in love with Perry Gillman tonight."

I looked up at the stage. Perry'd put down his violin and was singing the last few lines of the song staring straight at me.

"No. Not the only one," I said, laying my head back down on Gideon's shoulder.

Chapter Twenty-Six

The after party raged on for several more hours with at least another half dozen international popstars taking the stage in celebration of Victoria and Alexander's wedding. We were enjoying the performances so much Gideon and I barely left the dance floor. When the blisters on the backs of my heels couldn't take it anymore, I asked Gideon if he'd mind taking a break. He grabbed each of us a cocktail from one of the corner bars and directed us out to the courtyard for some air.

We breathed in the cool breeze.

"This is better," he said.

"Have you ever seen so many royals in a mosh pit before?" I joked.

He passed me his phone. "Never, which is why I snapped a few pictures of it."

I shook my head and passed the phone back to him. "Your parents get back to their hotel okay?"

"I'm sure. They're staying just up the road. Are you still able to join us for brunch tomorrow morning?"

"I think so. I'm going to stop back at Victoria's room at The Goring tonight and make sure her clothes are laid out properly for tomorrow and her going away breakfast. After that, I'm a free woman. Hard to believe, but my job here is done."

Gideon set down his drink. "Speaking of jobs, I have some news I've been waiting to talk to you about. I gave my notice at Highclere last week. I'm moving to South Gloucestershire to run Badgley Hall full-time."

"That's great. It's everything you've been working toward, right?"

Gideon turned from me. "I used to believe that. Now it feels more like a big anchor around my neck."

I took two steps toward him and placed my hand on his shoulder. "What do you mean?"

He turned to face me. "I can't convince you to come with me, can I? I'll turn one of those musty staterooms into the most incredible studio for you to do your work. Hell, you can have a whole wing of the house if you want it."

"G. Malone's in New York. My whole life is in New York. Jordana's positive that after all the press from the wedding, we'll finally be able to take the company public. We talked about this, Gid. I can't just abandon all that to play duchess in South Gloucestershire."

"Countess," he corrected.

I cocked my head to the side. "You know what I mean. Anyway, I thought once you had the estate up and running you'd be able to spend more time in New York. Isn't that what we talked about?"

"Realistically, I'm not sure how long it's going to take to get Badgley Hall not just operational but also profitable."

Linney came outside to find us and let us know Victoria and Alexander were getting ready to cut the cake.

Gideon took my hand. "Tonight's been wonderful. Let's not ruin it. We'll talk more about this later."

"Gideon, my mind's not going to change."

"Are you both coming?" Linney yelled back to us.

We picked up our cocktails and hurried back inside where the cake cutting ceremony was already underway. Alexander was slowly feeding a piece to Victoria while the remaining guests picked up their champagne flutes to toast the happy couple once again. I spotted Perry at the bar at the far end of the room nursing a drink. A few minutes later, Annabelle found him. What at first looked like a small quarrel quickly flared into a larger argument, ending with Perry slamming his glass down on the bar and Annabelle storming off in tears. Fortunately, with all the activity centered on the cake cutting, nobody else in the room seemed to notice.

Alexander picked up the microphone and invited everyone to join him and Victoria outside for fireworks. As the room slowly emptied out, I glanced back over my shoulder. Perry was still seated at the bar, staring into the courtyard sipping on his whiskey neat. The moon was shining through the window, casting the most hypnotizing light across his bearded face.

I thought back to when he played The Fiddler at Camp Chinooka. The show had opened with Perry suspended at the top of the amphitheater, the moonlight pouring down like a spotlight. He danced and played his way up the aisles and stairs, finally settling atop the stage to observe everything below. We were a million miles from that night, but the look in his eyes was the same, cool and concentrated like he was trying to work out a problem with no obvious solution.

I followed Gideon out to the palace garden, which was set up like an old-fashioned carnival with booths and antique food carts. We stopped for two boxes of popcorn and a cone of cotton candy. Plaid blankets were laid out all along the grass and guests were being directed to different corners of the garden for the best views of the show. Gideon took my hand and we settled down together on a blanket on the far side of the lawn.

After the first few fireworks lit up the sky, Gideon pulled me close and kissed me harder and more urgently than ever before. Maybe to make me change my mind about South Gloucestershire? Or maybe in the hopes I'd forget we had that conversation at all? Either way, it didn't matter. I kissed him back equally hard, so he'd know I wasn't going anywhere. I wanted to be with him. We'd figure out how to make it work.

Gideon pulled me into his arms and wrapped them tightly around me. I leaned back into his chest and we watched the rest of the show. When it was over, we walked the lanes of the carnival. We stopped to play a few games and after several attempts, Gideon proudly knocked down a tower of clear milk bottles and won me a big stuffed teddy bear.

It was almost 3 a.m. and most of the guests were starting to leave. I looked at my phone and saw a text from Jordana reminding me that the representative from Cartier would be at Victoria's room at The Goring by 5 a.m. to collect the jewels from the wedding gown.

"Shoot, I have to get going," I said to Gideon.

"Victoria's still here. You have plenty of time to make sure she has what she needs for the morning."

"The Cartier people are coming to collect the stones from the dress at five. Since I basically signed my life away so we could borrow them, I better get going or you'll be visiting me in the Tower of London."

He shook his head. "You never did make it over there, did you?"

"Why do you say that?"

"It hasn't been in use as a prison since the 1940s."

"Next time I'm here, we'll make sure to take the proper tour," I said, kissing him on the cheek.

"I have some goodbyes to make and I want to make sure Linney gets off okay. Should I just meet you back at The Savoy?" he asked.

"I already let them know this morning that a certain Mr. Napoleon Cheshire would likely be paying another call and to let him up if he did."

A smile crept across his face. "Brilliant."

I rushed back to The Goring and laid out Victoria's dress for the going away breakfast and a few other options Jamie and I had whipped up as gifts for her to take along on her honeymoon to the Maldives. I slipped out of my Valentino, hung it back on the hanger, and changed into leggings and my favorite and most comfortably worn-in Camp Chinooka Staff T-shirt. At four in the morning, I didn't have to worry about too many people seeing me in such a non-glamourous outfit. After I was changed, I zipped the dress into a garment bag and placed it next to the rest of my bags to take back with me to The Savoy. I was glad that I'd decided to purchase the gown instead of borrowing it from the vintage store. This dress was going into my personal archives. One day, if I was fortunate enough to have a daughter, I'd show her what I wore when I attended the royal wedding on the arm of Viscount Satterley.

I went into the bathroom, pulled off my fake eyelashes, and washed my face. I took out the beautiful chandelier earrings Cartier had lent me along with the jewels and put them back into their box for return. I looked in the mirror and thought to myself, *"Okay Cinderella, time to turn back into a pumpkin."*

I heard a knock on the door and checked my watch. It was a good thing I'd hurried back to the hotel because the Cartier rep was about forty-five minutes early. I yelled out I was coming and wrapped my hair into a bun as I walked to the door. I unlocked the chain and opened it to find Perry standing there. His bowtie was unknotted and casually draped over his shoulders. The top two buttons of his dress shirt were undone and he was carrying his evening coat over his arm. His normally tamed curly hair was more disheveled than I was used to, waves sticking out in different directions.

"What are you doing here?" I asked.

"I needed to talk to you. Alone," he said.

"Jesus, Perry, I'm expecting someone from Cartier any minute now and Gemma warned there might be press staked out on this floor." I poked my head out of the door frame and looked down the hallway in both directions. "Someone could see us talking. You better come inside."

He stepped into the room and I quickly shut the door behind him. "How'd you even know where to find me?"

Perry laid his blazer down on the bed. "I heard Gemma talking to Victoria about her plans for the morning. She said you were here pulling some things together for her."

"I'm just about done. As soon as Cartier shows up, I'm leaving to meet Gideon at The Savoy." I handed him back his jacket.

Perry rubbed the stubble on his face. "Can I take a seat? I just need a moment." He motioned toward the bed.

I nodded reluctantly and he sat down.

I took two steps toward him. "Perry, what do you want? Why are you here? Really?"

"I miss you. I know I don't have any right to say that to you. And I know I made a million mistakes. But, there it is," he said, looking up at me.

I shook my head and sat down beside him. "Do you know how long I've waited for some sort of explanation for what happened with us? Every day I would think today's the day my phone's going to ring or Perry's gonna show up at my door to tell me he had some sort of temporary lapse in sanity. Anything that *might* help me understand how you could walk away from four years of our life together and never even look back."

"The first thing I did when I came back to London was go to my father's grave and make him a promise that if I couldn't get the show off the ground in one year, I'd return and audition with New York Philharmonic like he wanted me to. I planned on coming back to be with you and to marry you. But then, everything clicked. I put my head down and finished writing the show. This thing that I'd been dancing around and toying with for four years came together in just a few months."

Perry stood and walked to the window at the far side of the room then leaned back against the sill. The light from the nearby buildings was streaming in, framing his perfect silhouette.

He took a deep breath and continued, "I somehow managed to convince myself none of it would've happened if I'd stayed in New York."

I took a few steps toward him. "So, it's my fault. I was the person holding you back from your full potential. Is that it?"

"Do you know what is to have the person you admired most in the world, the person you spent your whole life trying to be like, die thinking you've made nothing of yourself?" He crossed the room and pulled me into his arms. "But I was wrong, Gigi. I'm telling you I was wrong. I'm not who I am *despite* you. I am who I am *because* of you. It was your face I saw when I was writing those duets between Elizabeth and Dudley. You are in every melody of that show. You're in every moment, every measure."

His words hung in the air as I looked at his beautiful face. He'd always be my Perry. The man who, four years ago, helped pull me out of the depths and put me back on a course to myself. I loved him. I might always. But, we were over. I'd known it as soon as I sat down in Her Majesty's Theater all those months ago, just like Annabelle had known it when she watched him perform tonight. Jamie was right. Elizabeth had been the other woman all along. With the ambition and passion that so consumed Perry, there wasn't room for anyone else now and there might never be. I couldn't take that chance again. I'd barely survived the fallout the first time.

"Please, Gigi. Please forgive me," he said, choking back sobs.

He pulled out the same ring he'd proposed to me with all those months ago and got down on one knee. He held it up to me, his hands trembling and his body unsteady.

"I'll be back in New York in a few months. We'll start over again. Let me show you I can be the man you believed I was. Please, darling."

I looked down into his big brown eyes. "It's too hard. I used to think it had to be that hard. I thought it was the constant push and pull, the give and take that brought out the best in each of us. I don't believe that anymore."

He stood up and opened up my clenched fist, took the ring out of the box, and placed it into the palm of my left hand. "I hurt you. I know I did. But if you let me, I'll spend the rest of my life trying to make it right. I love you. I never stopped loving you. Marry me. Say you will? It'll be different this time. I'll be different."

I closed my eyes and let his words wash over me like a rogue wave that appears without warning, crushing everything in its wake. "What about Annabelle?"

"It's done. I told her I was in love with somebody else."

"And what happens when the world finds out that person's me? Victoria's friend. Annabelle's friend. They'll assume we've been sneaking around behind their backs this whole time."

"We'll figure that part out. I don't even care. Let the world think whatever it wants. We know the truth."

"It's not that simple. None of this is that simple. I'm in a relationship with somebody else."

"Gideon's a good guy. I won't say otherwise. But what you two have, it isn't what we had."

I unfurled my fingers and looked down at the ring still nestled in my palm. It was still beautiful, the diamond as brilliant as ever. But, it was also still the symbol of every promise Perry had made and broken—along with my heart. I closed my eyes and extended my hand back toward him. "I can't accept this."

"Can't or won't?"

"What does it matter anymore?" I stroked Perry's cheek and brushed my hand over his full lips. "Go to New York. Make your mark on Broadway. Conquer everything you ever set out to."

"If this is really what you want, then why are you crying?"

I brushed the tears from my face. "I didn't realize I was."

"I can't change your mind, can I?" he whispered.

"You could. That's exactly why I can't let you," I answered.

He wrapped his arms around me and pulled me into his chest where I stayed until I finished shedding every last tear for Perry Gillman and the hurt of this last year. When I was done, I pulled away, wiped my face, and walked to the door. I opened it up planning to let him leave. Instead, we stood together in the entranceway and lingered, knowing we might never be this intimate again.

Before he turned to leave, I stood up on my tiptoes and leaned into him. With my heart and voice breaking, I sang his favorite Gershwin lyric into his ear. *"The way you changed my life…"*

A small, knowing smile crept across his face before he kissed me on the forehead, turned, and walked away.

Chapter Twenty-Seven

After Cartier came, took full inventory, and reclaimed about six million dollars' worth of jewels, I finally was able to go back to my hotel for the night. Gideon was up waiting for me when I walked in.

"I thought for sure you'd be long asleep," I said.

He sipped on his nightcap. "I wanted to make sure you got back okay."

I hung my dress in the wardrobe and set my other bags on the floor beside the bed.

"Since you're up, can we talk for a second?" I asked.

Gideon set his drink down on the nightstand. "That doesn't sound good."

I took a breath. "Perry came to see me at The Goring."

"That was gutsy of him. Didn't he consider you might not be alone? What did he want?"

"To talk. About us."

Gideon stood up and paced the length of the room. "Does he want you back?"

"He wanted to explain himself. Give me some long overdue answers."

He stopped in his tracks. "And now that you have them?"

"Nothing's changed." I patted the spot beside me on the bed and Gideon sat back down. "I chose you. I *choose* you."

"You should know I'm falling more in love with you by the day." He pushed a piece of hair behind my ear. "So, if you're looking for an out please take it now. I don't think my heart could take it otherwise."

I leaned over and nuzzled into his chest. "I told you that chapter of my life is over."

"But you still haven't told me what you want this next chapter to look like? You won't come to Badgley Hall, will you?"

I sat up. "I can't, Gid."

"I know," he said softly.

He laid down on the bed and held the blanket open so I'd crawl inside. I inched in and snuggled up against him. A few seconds later he was sleeping soundly, but I was still wide awake. I tossed and turned until finally, sheer physical exhaustion got the better of me and I fell into a deep sleep. I stayed that way until the morning when Gideon shook me awake to tell me my phone had been ringing and buzzing for the better part of the last half hour.

I rolled over and looked at the clock.

"I'm sure it's just the American press reporting on Victoria's looks from last night," I mumbled into the pillow.

Gideon sat more upright. "You have a bunch of missed calls from your mother and your friend Alicia though."

I slowly sat up and kicked the blanket off my legs then reached my arm out for the phone. Gideon passed it to me.

"My mother called me twelve times," I said, standing up. "Oh God, do you think something happened to my father?"

I immediately dialed her back.

"Mom, what's wrong?" I asked as soon as she picked up.

"Georgica. Finally. Thank goodness. Where are you?"

"I'm just waking up. What's wrong? Is it Dad?"

"You haven't turned on the news or seen anything yet?"

"I told you I was just waking up. Can you please just tell me what's going on?"

"Your face is everywhere. Yours and Perry's."

"What do you mean?" I tossed the remote at Gideon. "Quick, turn on the TV."

"What channel?" He asked.

"BBC? CNN?"

He turned on the TV and flipped around until he landed on a British news station. A picture of me and Perry standing in the doorway of a hotel room at The Goring was in freeze-frame.

I dropped the phone. Gideon scooped it up and said, "Mrs. Goldstein, we'll have to call you right back."

I grabbed the remote and turned the volume up. We caught the tail end of the report.

"Sources have confirmed that Perry Gillman and designer of the Duchess of Sussex's wedding gown, Georgica Goldstein, have been concealing a past relationship and possibly even an engagement."

I looked to Gideon. "What sources? Oh my God."

I opened up *The Guardian* on my phone. The first thing I saw were two pictures that'd been secretly snapped last night. One was of Perry coming into my hotel room and the second was me whispering into his ear in the doorway as he left. My hands were trembling so badly, I handed the phone over to Gideon so he could read the accompanying article.

"Are you sure you want to hear this?" he asked.

I tried speaking, but no words came out so instead, I violently shook my head up and down.

Gideon scrolled down a bit and started reading out loud.

"Although fireworks celebrating the marriage of Prince Alexander and Victoria Ellicott could be seen all along the Thames last evening, the real fireworks were taking place at The Goring hotel where Perry Gillman was spotted sharing a very intimate moment with Georgica Goldstein. An article published early last year in the Milbank Monitor links Gillman and Goldstein, who met four years ago while working as counselors at a summer camp in Pennsylvania.

Gillman and Goldstein were allegedly engaged for several months before breaking it off about a year and a half ago at the same time Gillman got involved with Annabelle Ellicott. Neither Gillman nor

Goldstein disclosed their sordid past to the Ellicott sisters, both of whom have reportedly become close friends with Ms. Goldstein. Recent reports have claimed there has been a strain on the relationship between Perry and Annabelle. Could Georgica Goldstein be the reason?

To further complicate matters, Goldstein is the G behind G. Malone, the designer of Victoria Ellicott's wedding dress and several more of her winning looks. She's also reportedly been dating Viscount Satterley, a close family friend of the Ellicotts.'

Well, that's just bad journalism," Gideon said. "Shouldn't it at least say, 'she's also reportedly been dating the wildly handsome and unbelievably charming Viscount Satterley.'"

I rubbed my hand back and forth over my forehead. "Just finish reading."

He pulled the phone back up to his face. "*At this time, no one in the Ellicott camp could be reached for further comment on this story.*"

I sat down on the bed and put my head between my hands. "I'm done for. Nobody's going to believe nothing happened between us. Victoria must be devastated and God, what Annabelle must think of me. Can I see my phone again?"

Gideon reluctantly handed it to me and I scrolled until I found the text I knew would be waiting for me from Gemma.

"*Thank you for your help. We are in receipt of Victoria's final pieces. After today, your services are no longer needed. I will be in touch with Jordana to settle the account.*"

I scrolled a bit further and saw several messages from Alicia, my mother, my father, and then just one single solitary text from Jamie in all caps. Four words.

GIGI, WHAT THE FUCK.

The only person missing from my hit list was Perry

I slapped my forehead. "I have to call Jamie."

There was a knock on the door.

Gideon peeked through the door's peephole. "It's Jordana," he said, opening it for her.

Jordana charged passed him and came tearing into the room. She tossed her laptop on the bed. "The lobby's swarming with press. I didn't think I'd even be able to get back up to my own room, let alone yours. Christ, Gigi, what were you thinking?"

"None of it's true. None of it."

"*None of it's true?* Did you not conceal your past relationship with Perry from Victoria and Annabelle for months and months? Sure, maybe nothing happened between the two of you last night, but you're not completely innocent." She started frantically pacing around the room. "I have no idea what this is gonna mean for all the potential investors or going public. Nobody wants to get in bed with a scandal. Have you seen the *Daily Mirror* yet?"

I squeezed my eyes closed and squeaked out, "No, why?"

"They superimposed a large Scarlet A over your picture on the cover. This is no joke, Gigi. Victoria might be the people's princess, but Annabelle's the country's sweetheart and you just got caught whispering sweet nothings to her boyfriend. Not to mention the fact you've been photographed all over town with the Ellicott sisters for months. The whole world knows you're friends well...*were* friends. Do you understand the optics on this? You didn't just betray the Queen, you betrayed your friends."

I sat down and laid my head in my hands. "What should I do?

"Honestly, for the first time since I started with G. Malone, I don't have the answer. Have you spoken to Jamie?"

"No. Not yet."

"Well, you should. And soon. That, I do know. G. Malone is half his. He should hear it from you, not the press." Jordana picked up her laptop from the bed. "I have a call with our PR firm in New York in ten minutes. It's too late to get ahead of this story *obviously*, but maybe we can fan the flames in a different direction."

Tears sprang to my eyes and I all but crumpled onto the ground. "I'm so sorry, Jord. I really never meant for any of this to happen."

Jordana's face softened as she dropped her arms to her sides. She walked over and put her arms around my shoulders.

"I'm sorry, too. I sometimes forget I was your friend long before I became Global Director of Brand Events at G. Malone."

Gideon interrupted us to say he was going out to get some coffee. He must have wanted to give me and Jordana a moment to talk privately.

After he left, Jordana took a seat on the bed. "What really happened with Perry?"

I sat down beside her. "He came by last night to talk and said all the things I've been waiting a year to hear from him."

"And you got caught up in the moment? He's Perry Gillman. Of course you would. Makes complete sense."

I turned to her. "That's the thing…I didn't."

"Really, Gigi? Nothing happened?"

I was reminded of the time at Chinooka when Perry helped me back to his cabin after a night of too much drinking at Rosie's. When I snuck back into my own bunk in the morning, Jordana had been up waiting for me and the juicy details about the night I spent with Perry Gillman. She was pretty surprised to learn nothing happened between us. Her reaction was the same now.

"Nothing like what they're claiming. Still, I know how it must look. And then there's the article from the *Milbank Monitor* where Gordy gushes about our past love affair. It's not his fault. It's my fault for not being honest when I had the chance."

Jordana looked down at her phone. "It's the PR firm calling. Let me take this. I'll get back to you with our game plan. Until then, try not to leave this room and don't say anything to the press."

About a half-hour later, Gideon returned holding two coffees and a copy of every British and American newspaper he could get his hands on.

"I think every media outlet that was outside Westminster Abbey yesterday has repositioned themselves outside this hotel." He handed me a cup and a stack of newspapers.

I tore open *The Guardian* and closely examined the blown-up pictures of me whispering into Perry's ear last night. Gideon came up behind me.

I turned to him. "Doesn't look great for the two of us, does it?"

"No, I suppose it doesn't," he answered.

"Things played out with me and Perry just the way I told you. This image is just a moment in time—it's not the whole picture."

"I know," he said in a tone that made it hard to believe he really did.

"Gid…" I placed my hand on his forearm.

"My parents are expecting us for brunch. We should start getting ready."

"I can't go. Jordana told me not to leave the hotel until the PR team develops a game plan and response."

He slipped on his blazer. "I see."

Gideon was shutting down. Even though I'd been honest with him about the events of last night, these photos painted a very convincing alternative version of what might have happened. The look in his eyes told me he wasn't sure what to believe.

"Maybe I can meet you after I hear from Jordana?"

Gideon raised his eyebrows.

"What? Should I really stay in hiding? Are they calling for my head on a platter?" I said, jokingly.

"Not quite, but you've successfully managed to offend the entire royal family."

I looked up and searched his eyes. "And what about you? What do you think of me?"

"I think you should probably listen to Jordana and stay here until things die down." He bent to grab his coat and cap from the chair. "I'll see you later."

After he left, I walked to the window and took a peek outside. Paparazzi and reporters were lined up all across the street hoping to catch a glimpse of the most wanton woman in England. I didn't need to take a tour of the Tower of London—here I was in my very own modern-day version of it. I swore I could even hear the angry mobs below chanting "off with her head."

I flipped through the rest of newspapers Gideon had brought back. Most of the articles seemed focused on the close friendship I'd developed with Victoria and Annabelle and my betrayal in failing to disclose my past relationship with Perry. *Perry*. I wondered if any press was hanging around outside of Perry's house or at the theater. I thought about picking up the phone to call him but knew there was one person I needed to reach out to first. I dialed Jamie's number.

"He can't speak to you now," Thom said after picking up on the third ring.

"Please Thom, just let me talk to him for one minute and explain."

"He's with the twins and can't talk," he said sternly.

"I get that he's probably furious with me. But, if you'll just let me talk to him and explain myself I know he'll understand."

"Gigi, don't make me be the one to say this to you."

I gripped the phone in my hand. "Just say it. Whatever message you've been asked to deliver. Just do it."

"All his work from this last year was just erased with a single headline and a moment of carelessness. Did you stop to think about how your actions would affect him or G. Malone?"

"Thom, he's my best friend. Please," I begged.

"I'm sorry, but I have to go."

Sometime later, Jordana called to tell me the PR firm was working on some ways to rebut the story. The decision Perry and I had made not to disclose our past relationship was what people seemed most upset about and that was the one fact that couldn't be refuted or undone. The people of Great Britain had spoken, and I was firmly on their shit list. Jordana advised me to keep a low profile and maybe even spend a few days at Badgley Hall to get out of the limelight 'til things died down a bit more. She rattled off a few final instructions and told me she'd be by later to check on me before heading to the airport for her flight home. After that, she promptly hung up. I tossed the phone onto the bed and crawled in after it. I pulled the covers over my head and stayed there for several hours until I was awakened by a loud banging at the door.

Chapter Twenty-Eight

"**G**eorgie," said a bellowing voice from outside the hotel room door. "Georgie, open up."

"Dad?" I replied, slowly inching out from under the comforter.

"Yes, let me in," he shouted.

I sat up and rubbed my eyes. I had no idea what time it was or how long I'd been asleep. Maybe I was still asleep? Why was my father in London?

"Am I still dreaming?" I called out to him.

"I just flew seven hours to be here. Can you please open up the door?"

I got off the bed and undid the deadbolt to let him in. He pushed his way into the room and tossed his small bag on the floor beside the wardrobe.

"What are you doing here?" I asked.

He opened his arms wide to me. "I got on the first available flight this morning. I thought you might need me."

I rushed into his arms and rested my head on his shoulder like I used to when I was a little girl. He caressed my hair and kissed me sweetly on the head before stepping back.

"How are you, Georgie?"

"I went to bed on top of the world and woke up in a nightmare. I'm on the cover of every paper. I'm the laughingstock of London. The woman who seduced Perry Gillman away from Annabelle Ellicott."

"You know what I always say. Today's headlines are tomorrow's fish wrap."

I looked up at him. "You only ever use that line with your clients who are in the most trouble."

He laughed and took hold of my hands. "You're not in trouble, Georgie, you're just the focus of some unwanted attention. It'll blow over. Things like this always do."

"Don't your clients pay like a billion dollars an hour for your sage counsel? You don't have any other advice to pass on?"

"Be patient, it'll come to me," he said, looking around the room. "Where's your friend, Gideon? What's he up to?"

"He left hours ago to have brunch with his parents, the Earl and Countess of Harronsby." I raised my eyebrows. "What do you think the chances are that he'll be returning to my den of iniquity anytime soon?"

He laughed. "First things first then, let's get you out of this hotel. You're holed up in here like some sort of political prisoner."

I moved the curtain away from the window. "There's still a ton of press outside. How can I get out of here without being seen?"

"You can't, but who cares. I'll have a car waiting for us and we'll get in it. They'll snap a few pictures and that'll be that. The important question is where we can find decent Chinese food in this city?"

Back when I was a dramatic, headstrong teenager, I'd found my father's pragmatic nature nothing short of infuriating. I never felt like he quite understood me or my rollercoaster of emotions. Now, I was beyond grateful for his calm nature and steady resolve. It was comforting and reassuring in a way nothing else had been since I awoke to this storm.

"Go take a shower. Maybe change out of that Camp Chinooka T-shirt unless you really want to feed the gossip mill. Let's go seek out the best eggrolls London has to offer," he said.

"There's a place called Y Ting in Soho. The hot and sour soup is decent, but the fried rice excellent. Gideon discovered it when he was trying to find a place to best Wo Hop," I said with a longing smile.

My father put his arm around me. "He'll come back around, Georgie, just give him some time to digest all this."

I changed clothes and dug around my tote for my largest pair of sunglasses. It was early evening but it seemed the right accessory for my current situation. My father called for a car. When the driver texted to let us know he was downstairs, we headed down to the lobby to meet it.

As the elevator doors opened, my father took hold of my hand and we walked quickly through the lobby. As soon as we stepped foot outside, we were met by a barrage of flashes and people shouting my name. My father ushered me into the car and we sped off toward the restaurant. I looked back to see if we were being followed, but the driver managed to dodge all the trailing paparazzi. We fortunately managed to make it all the way to Y Ting without being followed.

The hostess offered us a table in front, but my father slipped her £20 and asked if we could be seated at the table in the far back corner of the restaurant. I could only imagine what kind of date she assumed we were on. She pocketed the money and led us to the darkest corner of the place, well concealed by several large potted plants and a massive fish tank that divided the space.

"I think you're okay to take off your sunglasses in here," Dad said.

I looked around and then pushed the sunglasses onto the top of my head. The waitress came over to take our drink orders. My father ordered a gin martini and asked me what I wanted. I started to order a vodka gimlet but changed my mind and asked her to bring me out a bottle of sparkling water instead. A clear head seemed the safer route.

I skimmed down the list of specials. "I'm thinking two hot and sour soups and a Moo Goo Gai Pan."

"We should try something completely new."

"Yeah? What are you thinking?"

He perused the menu and then said, "What about sizzling oysters and the prawns in a sweet hot sauce?"

"Wow, Dad, really stepping outside your comfort zone."

He closed the menus and called the waitress back over. We placed our order and handed them over to her.

"How long are you in town for?" I asked.

"I'm going to stop over in the London office tomorrow for a bit and then catch the evening flight out."

"You really came just to check on me?"

He smiled and unfolded his napkin on his lap. A short time later, the waitress brought out our dishes. My father served me two heaping spoonfuls from each dish and then served himself the same. He poured us each a cup of tea and lifted it up to make a toast.

"To my daughter who created a wedding gown for the ages. I could not be more proud of you."

My eyes brimmed with tears. Yesterday's headlines—all the praise and fanfare over Victoria's wedding dress—*had* become today's fish wrap. And today's headlines referring to me as a "cheater" and "the other woman" were all anyone could talk about. In all the frenzy, even I'd forgotten about yesterday's triumph. I was touched to know my father hadn't.

We spent the next two hours eating and catching up on the wedding, Jamie and Thom's twins, and Gideon. Finally and inevitably, the conversation turned to Perry.

"You don't have to tell me, but if things are really over between you two, why was he in your room last night?"

"He thinks he made a mistake letting me go."

"Well, anyone could've told him that."

"He said everything I've been waiting over a year to hear, only he said it a year too late."

My father leaned back in his chair. "Is it ever really too late to try to repair things with the love of your life? Look, Georgie, I know you think I liked Perry because we share a common interest in jazz, MacLellan Whiskey, and The War of the Roses. But, there was only one common interest that ever really mattered to me."

I put down my chopsticks. "Yeah? What's that?"

"You. Are you sure you don't want to give him a second chance?"

"I'm with Gideon. He's a really good guy. Better than I probably deserve—and after today I'm not sure he wants anything to do with me."

My father reached over, placing one hand over my own. He used the other to motion for the waitress. "Let me grab the check and we'll head back to the hotel. Things will look better in the morning. They always do."

He took my hand and we walked out of the restaurant where our black car was waiting for us. My father asked the driver to take us back to The Savoy.

"Do you mind if we drive around for a bit? I'm not ready to face the firing squad just yet."

He nodded and asked the driver to take us on the more scenic route through town. My father opened up his arms and motioned for me crawl in. I leaned into his broad chest and stared out the window as building after building whizzed by. A few minutes later, I could feel his phone vibrating through his pants pocket.

I sat up. "Dad, you're ringing."

He reached in and pulled out the phone. "It's your mother."

I could only hear his side of the conversation but could easily guess what she was saying on the other end. Just as he was reassuring my mother for the fourth time that I wasn't suicidal, we passed St Paul's Cathedral.

I leaned forward and asked the driver if he could stop the car.

"Hold on Kate, let me talk to Georgie for one second." My father took the phone away from his ear. "What's wrong? Why did you stop the car?"

"I think I'm gonna go inside the church for a few minutes."

"It's late. It must be closed?"

I remembered what Gideon had told me on our first date. "Churches never really close. I'll grab a taxi back to the hotel when I'm done."

"No, you take the car. I'll leave it for you and I'll get the taxi."

I reached over and gave him a kiss on the cheek. "Thanks, Dad. I'll be back soon.

"Take as long as you need."

I tiptoed into the church. The evening service had just ended and there were a few worshipers and straggling tourists left in the pews. Immediately, a sense of calm and composure washed over me. I wasn't a particularly religious person but could see why people sought sanctuary in churches. The troubles of the world remain outside the large iron doors and inside the only person you have to face is yourself.

I sat down as a boys' choir shuffled in for their evening rehearsal. I closed my eyes to listen to the beautiful hymns and anthems, getting lost in lyrics about mistakes and redemption—love and forgiveness. So much so, that sometime later, I realized most of the worshipers had gone and I was one of the only people left in the chapel.

I found a guard and asked him if the Whispering Gallery was still open to visitors. He looked at his watch and told me it would be closing in about 45 minutes, so I'd better hurry up if I wanted to visit.

I rushed over to the entrance and bounded up the 259 steps to the top, barely stopping to catch my breath. When I got up the landing, I walked to the railing that peered over the main chapel. I leaned in and listened to a guide explaining the acoustics of the room to the last group of tourists still in the gallery.

"Whisper along the curving wall and—provided there isn't too much background noise—someone positioned anywhere along that same wall should be able to hear you."

The tourists took off in different directions to try it. Maybe they'd have more luck than Gideon and I had our first time here?

I checked my watch. The gallery would be closing in just a few minutes. I turned around to pick up my bag from where I'd set it down and there—like an apparition—was Gideon standing right in front of me.

"How'd you know where to find me?" I asked as he approached.

"I went back to the hotel to talk to you. Your father told me you were at St. Paul's."

I swung my bag over my shoulder. "I needed a quiet place to think."

"When I didn't see you in the chapel, I thought maybe I'd missed you."

I shook my head. "I figured I'd take one more trip up here. Who knows when I'll be back in town next?"

"What do you mean?"

"The royal wedding's done. I think it's probably best if I lay low for a bit. Maybe I'll travel? Find a small town in Italy or Spain where I can become anonymous for a few months while things die down."

"Where does that leave us?"

I took a few steps toward him. "Look, I understand if this is too much for you. You come from a conservative family. Your parents are friendly with the Ellicotts. We have so many things stacked against us. Distance. Gossip. I'm not even sure you really believe nothing happened between Perry and me and I wouldn't blame you for assuming the worst." I stroked the side of his face. "Let's just part ways here and know it was wonderful while it lasted but that nothing this good lasts forever."

"I do believe you." He lifted my bag back off my shoulder and placed it back on the ground. "I'll admit those pictures were tough to swallow. But you told me last night that nothing happened, so I know nothing happened."

"What about the rest of it? This story isn't going to die down anytime soon. Perry's more famous than ever. Last night, Victoria became the future Queen of England. The whole world thinks I betrayed her and her sister."

"Gossip's gossip. People will talk until there's something else more interesting to talk about. We can wait it out."

"And the distance?"

Gideon took my hands into his. "My offer still stands. Don't go Italy or Spain. Come to Badgley Hall. Lay low there. Figure out your next move. Be with me, Gigi. I promise I'll keep the world away. With my bare hands if I have to."

I closed my eyes and thought of the deep hedge maze at Badgley Hall. I pictured myself entering it, outrunning all the paparazzi and photographers who chased close behind. Gideon's steady confident voice coaxing me to the other side while they remained lost in the maze, bumping up against the walls and each other.

When I opened my eyes, I found Gideon's sweet and generous face. He meant every word and I loved him all the more for it. He was not only willing to weather the storm, no matter how long it raged on, but to give me shelter from it. He was dependable and honorable. He was a man who kept his promises.

"If I can't convince you, maybe this will. Go stand over on that side of the wall." He pointed to one end of the gallery.

I raised my eyebrows. "What are you up to?"

"Just do it. I'm gonna go stand over there," he said, pointing to the other end of the room.

I reluctantly took my spot at the far side of the room while he jogged over to the opposite wall. He motioned for me to lean my head in and close my eyes. I tilted my head forward and firmly squeezed my eyes shut.

Moments later, I heard his whisper as it bounced off the gallery wall. I shook my head in disbelief. I couldn't possibly have heard that right? I opened my eyes and looked over at Gideon. Our gaze locked and he began walking toward me.

He approached, kissed me softly, and got down on one knee. He reached into his pocket and pulled out a beautiful antique diamond and platinum ring.

"Will you?" he asked.

"Marry you?"

"I've had this ring in my pocket for weeks now trying to figure out the right way and time to do this. But here we are. Fate has led us back to the same place we spent our first date and I couldn't imagine a more perfect moment. So, I ask you, Georgica Reid Goldstein. Will you do me the honor of becoming my wife?"

I threw my arms around him and then asked him to go back to the other side of the room. Before I could give the question a second thought, I closed my eyes, faced the wall, and whispered… "Yes."

The series continues with *Love You S'more*,
Book Three in the Campfire Series!

Having successfully designed the wedding gown of the century,
Gigi Goldstein is on top of the world – that is until it all suddenly comes crashing down around her. When the paparazzi
captures her and Perry Gillman in a compromising moment the
night of the royal wedding, she finds herself entangled in a scandal of global proportion. Convinced her carelessness has ruined
every relationship in her life, she's surprised and moved by her
boyfriend, Gideon's, sudden proposal of marriage and accepts it
without a second thought.

Four months later, Gigi's living at Badgley Hall contemplating an
entirely new kind of life, while guilt, regret, and obligation keep
calling her back to her old one. Will Gigi stay in South Gloucestershire, marry Gideon, and become the Countess of Harronsby?

**Or, will unfinished opportunities and an old flame bring her
back across the pond to confront her past and reclaim her
future?**

Looking for a new series with a heavy dose of adventure and a bit more *steam*? Check out **The Key West Escape Series** by Tricia Leedom starting with Rum Runner.

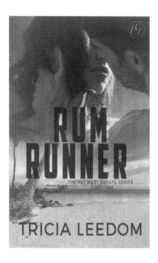

English socialite Sophie Davies-Stone has been longing to meet her father since she was a little girl. When he sends her a mysterious medallion and asks her to forward it to him in Miami, she can't help herself from doing something totally un-Sophie-like. Rather than mailing it as instructed, Sophie hops on a flight to Florida.

But the family reunion never happens. Instead, Sophie is attacked and almost kidnapped by her father's enemies. Her savior is Jimmy Panama, a cocky and annoyingly handsome former Navy SEAL. Sophie isn't the only one who's annoyed. After years of trying to find a way to pay back his CO, Jimmy never thought his debt would get him mixed up with his commander's uptight, British daughter. He just wants to put her on the next flight home and get back to his low-stress life in Key West, but fate has other plans.

As Sophie and Jimmy embark on a heart-pounding adventure through Key West and the Caribbean, Sophie finds herself falling for the snarky American. Still, her head says Jimmy is all wrong for her, and the more she finds out about him – and her father – the more uncertain she is about who she can trust.

One thing is clear. Sophie is in way over her head, and her greatest adventure might be her last.

Acknowledgments

Thank you to the incredible team at Firefly Hill Press for their continued encouragement and belief in the Campfire Series. To my editor, Danielle Modafferi, for her advice, candor, perspective, and friendship.

Thank you to my amazing husband, who takes on way more than his share so I have time to write. You are the archetype for every leading man I write. If it weren't for your unwavering belief and support, none of this would be possible. Finally, thank you to my beautiful Hadley Alexandra, my crowning achievement.

Review Request

Dear Reader,

Reviews are like currency to any author – actually, even better! As they help to get our books noticed by even more readers, we would be so grateful if you would take a moment to review this book on Amazon, Goodreads, iBooks - wherever - and feel free to share it on social media!

We're not asking for any special favors – honest reviews would be perfect. They also don't need to be long or in-depth, just a few of your thoughts would be so helpful.

Thank you greatly from the bottom of our hearts. For your time, for your support, and for being a part of our reading community. We couldn't do it without you – nor would we want to!

~ Our Firefly Hill Press Family

Beth Merlin, a native New Yorker, loves anything Broadway, romantic comedies, and a good maxi dress. After earning her JD from New York Law School, she heard a voice calling her back to fiction writing, like it had during her undergrad study. Amidst her days in The George Washington University's School of Media and Public Affairs, where Beth majored in Political Communications, she found herself wandering into Creative Writing classes, and ended up earning a minor in the field. After 10 long years laboring over her first manuscript, her debut novel, *One S'more Summer*, released May 2017. International bestselling author Kristin Harmel called it "a fast paced, enjoyable read."

In researching and preparing for the storyline of *S'more to Lose*, she also discovered her passion for British history and aristocracy. She is thrilled to have been able to travel to London on and off over the past year (metaphorically speaking!) through her research and writing of this manuscript and she can't wait to see where her next books will take her. When Beth isn't working on the Campfire Series, she's spending time with her husband, daughter, and Cavipoo, Sophie.

Find Beth on Twitter @bethmerlin80, Instagram @bethfmerlin, and at www.fireflyhillpress.com

And keep up to date on all of Beth's future releases, book bargains, sneak peeks, giveaways, special offers, & so much more by subscribing to our newsletter!

Made in the USA
Middletown, DE
22 July 2018